PALADERO

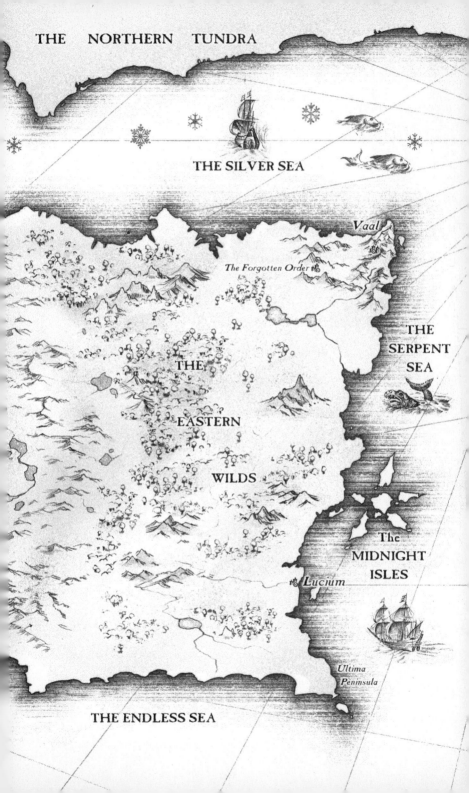

Books in the Paladero series:

PALADERO

THE CHAMPIONS OF THE BLADE

STEVEN LOCHRAN

Hardie Grant

EGMONT

Paladero:
The Champions of the Blade
published in 2020 by
Hardie Grant Egmont
Ground Floor, Building 1, 658 Church Street
Richmond, Victoria 3121, Australia
www.hardiegrantegmont.com

A catalogue record for this
book is available from the
National Library of Australia

Cover design by Julia Donkersley
Cover and map illustrations by Jeremy Love

Printed in Australia by Griffin Press, part of Ovato, an Accredited
ISO AS/NZS 14001 Environmental Management System printer.

1 3 5 7 9 10 8 6 4 2

MIX
Paper from
responsible sources
FSC® C009448

The paper this book is printed on is certified against the
Forest Stewardship Council® Standards. Griffin Press holds
FSC chain of custody certification SGS-COC-005088.
FSC promotes environmentally responsible, socially beneficial
and economically viable management of the world's forests.

From beyond silver seas, from out of blue skies, from the ruins of a lost life, there will come a galamor, *with right hand marked by fate and carrying a* vaartan rhazh. *Only the* galamor *will stand when all else fall, and rise when all else kneel. Only the* galamor *can bring light to the oncoming darkness, and draw hope from a dying dream. Only the* galamor, *and the* galamor *alone.*

– *Excerpt from* The Rakashi Revelations, *as translated by Isra Sarif*

—

CHAPTER ONE

An Unrecognisable Face

'Nothing is impossible.'

THE words jolted Joss from his sleep. Staring at the bare ceiling above him, he wondered for a moment where he was and if the chaos he'd escaped had all just been some cruel nightmare. Then he remembered. And his heart curled up on itself. He wanted to do the same; to cocoon himself in his blankets and escape the world. But he knew the world wouldn't let him go so easily. There was no running from what was coming for him. From what was coming for them all.

Joss wrapped the blanket around his shoulders, stood up and looked around. The ceiling soared so high that it looked more like a distant coverage of smooth white clouds. A lantern hung in the vast space with no visible means of support, producing a dull hum and a warm glow. The window was as impressive as the room itself – frosted glass spanned the entire wall and shifted from opaque to clear with a single wave of Joss's hand. He winced as the morning light rushed inside, the sun rising between the canyon of skyscrapers.

Airships and zeppelins cluttered the city skyline. Below that, rocket cars rode the green beams of electromagnetic speedways. The lustrous vehicles zipped past illumigrams the size of fortress towers, which advertised clothes and cosmetics and Billy Brontosaur's Big Burgers. But the pixel billboards may as well have been invisible to the crowds of pedestrians, who were all busy navigating the floating bridges and suspended walkways that looped around the highest storeys of copper-and-chrome skyscrapers, down towards the platforms for highwire trolley cars and high-speed transport tubes.

This was Illustra. The capital city of the Kingdom of Ai. And it made Joss's eyes water, his ears ring and his head throb. He wanted to retreat to the green fields and blue skies of Round Shield Ranch – his home. But that was impossible now. He settled for making the window opaque, blocking out the visual assault, just as the doorbell chimed.

'Yes?' he called, watching the door cycle open. A sleek silver mechanoid hovered in the hallway.

'Prentice Sarif?' the mek chirped. 'Your presence is requested in the audience hall. The summit is underway.'

Joss rubbed the sleep from his eyes. 'I'll be right there.'

The mek bleeped affirmatively, then sealed the door shut. Trailing a path across the plush snowfield of the carpet, Joss took his clothes from a walk-in wardrobe that was larger than his old sleeping cell back at Round Shield Ranch. He pulled on his trousers, tunic, boots and leather riding jacket. He buckled on his sword belt and settled the Champion's Blade into its customary spot against his left thigh, along with his training sword and humming knife, then looked himself over in the mirror. He barely recognised the face staring back at him. Perhaps he looked older; perhaps he just looked haunted. Either way, he had changed from the boy he'd been a year ago. He had changed even in the past few days. As for who it was that stood in his place, it was too early to tell.

He fished out the thunderbolt pendant that sat against his chest, cool and comforting. Squeezing it for luck, Joss tucked it back into place and then walked from the room, his head aching with memories of the moment his world had come crashing down upon him.

CHAPTER TWO

A WORLD AWAY

Several days earlier …

CRIMSON flames blazed all around Joss. They roared hungrily through the fortress grounds of Round Shield Ranch, consuming his home, while his mentor Sur Verity lay lifeless upon the scorched earth. At the heart of all this destruction stood the dark figure responsible, his stone mask cracked open to reveal the treacherous face beneath.

Lord Malkus's lips twisted around his metal teeth as he snarled, 'What's the matter, boy? You look like you've seen a spectre.'

Joss tried to focus, tried to clear his mind. He wondered where his Bladebound brethren were – Hero and Drake, Edgar and Zeke. They had all been with him only moments ago on their midnight exodus from Blade's Edge Acres, but he had lost them in the ambush that had taken the life of his mount, Tempest. The pterosaur's body, still bleeding, lay not far from Sur Verity's.

Now he was alone in the world. Alone but for the man who stood before him; the leader of his order, the man who had inspired him to become a paladero.

The man who had betrayed them all.

'This whole time,' Joss said, struggling to find the words as he stared Lord Malkus down. 'The Court of Thralls. The Shadow God. The murders, the black magic sacrifices. Everything. You've been behind it this whole time.'

Malkus didn't shrink from the accusation. If anything, he looked strangely proud. 'Correct.'

Joss's brow creased, his head whirling. 'How could you?'

'Easily,' Malkus replied, stalking forward. 'And it all started the day we met.'

'What?'

'When Daheed fell. When the great black tear ripped open the sky and consumed the entire island in one ravenous gulp. I watched with my Bladebound brethren from the shore, and one question repeated itself to me over and over again: *what if it's all a lie?*'

Joss's eyes narrowed as he tried to make sense of Malkus's words.

'The story is told to us from the day we're born – that we live in a beautiful dream conjured by a wise and benevolent deity. *The Sleeping King*,' Malkus sneered. 'A monarch who will provide us with our every wish if we just bow and scrape and *believe* enough. That's the fairytale. The truth is far darker.'

'What truth is that?' asked Joss.

'That life is the perfect trap.' Malkus paused long enough for his words to sink in. 'We're ensnared from birth, unable to move too far above our station or escape the expectations placed upon us, all the while dreaming of a better life that will never come. Surely you've been the victim of it enough times now to see? Or maybe you're still too young. Too naive. After all, you haven't seen all that I have seen. The inequity, the injustice. The rich growing fat while the poor starve in the streets, clinging to false promises.'

Joss grimaced. 'Better to cast the whole world into darkness, then?'

'The universe was born in darkness,' said Malkus, the crimson flames reflected in his metallic teeth. 'From darkness it will be born again.'

'And what do you think will happen to the poor in that darkness?' Joss demanded.

'Many will find their merciful end. Their suffering will be over, their fate no longer excruciatingly uncertain. But some will be willing to rise up and embrace the darkness. And the Court of Thralls will stand with them. Let the darkness claim the weak, the blind, the dumb beasts who refuse to listen. Once that final night has fallen, we can dream a better world for ourselves than the Sleeping King ever could. A world without lies. A world without fear.'

'A world of monsters,' Joss replied.

Malkus stared at him, unflinching. 'A world made for the strong. By the strong.'

'You really believe this?' Joss observed a moment's hesitation in Malkus.

'I have to,' he said. Was his voice cracking or was Joss imagining it? 'Daheed was just a test of His Highness's strength. The first gash he carved in the wall between worlds. He's been marshalling his strength ever since. There will be no defying him. There's only one way this can end, Josiah. Better to make peace with that now.'

'*Coward!*' Joss exclaimed, the word slipping free as soon as the realisation hit him. 'You're a coward! You saw the death and destruction that this creature, whatever it is, brings with it. And instead of standing against it you swore your allegiance and sold your soul. There's nothing honourable about that, no matter how much you try to convince yourself otherwise. You're just a monster's spineless minion. My mother was wrong to put her trust in you.'

Malkus's mouth was set hard. His grip on his blade was as solid as hammered steel. It was clear there would be no more debate. There would only be an end to their exchange, one way or the other. Joss braced himself for the inevitable ...

There was a burst of blinding light. An eruption of noise.

'*Get away from him!*' Drake shouted over the *Fat Lot*

7

of Good's engines. Joss could barely discern the sound of Hero's zamaraqs carving the air to hit their target with what should have been lethal precision. But Malkus barely lost a step as he deflected each strike with his twisted blade.

'Joss – come on!' Edgar called out, wrestling him onto the airship's deck.

'We can't leave Sur Verity!' Joss shouted. He pulled desperately against Edgar's grip.

'She's already gone!' Edgar implored him. Then he shouted to the wheelhouse, '*Zadkille!* I have him!'

The *Fat Lot of Good* rushed upward in a vertical jump, almost crashing into the belly of the dragon gliding directly above them. Zeke managed to pivot quickly enough to avoid a collision, then leaned on the accelerator.

Joss watched from over the balcony as Round Shield Ranch burned to the ground. The lord's tower, the barracks, the granaries and hatcheries, even the circular fortress walls that gave the order its name – all of it was ablaze. And there was Malkus, staring at them from the eye of the firestorm as they sped away.

Still at Joss's side, Edgar looked stricken.

'How can this be happening?' his friend and fellow Round Shield Ranch prentice asked in a small voice. Joss wished he had an answer, or at least some words of comfort. But he was just as lost, just as devastated. Was he destined to lose every place he'd ever called home?

'You said Sur Verity … you said she was gone?' Joss asked. The question felt as if it were being posed by somebody else – someone far away.

'Thrall's followers – or Malkus's, I suppose,' Edgar corrected himself while shaking his head and struggling to swallow. 'They were dressed in the same cloaks and masks they had at Blade's Edge Acres. A handful of them pulled her body from the field just before we got to you. I lost sight of them through the flames. I'm so sorry, Joss. If we could have done anything to stop them we would have.'

Again Joss had no reply. Drake and Hero materialised beside him to offer their support – just as he and the others had done for Hero back at Blade's Edge Acres, when her home had been destroyed and they had fled here for safety. But Drake and Hero's words were like muffled whispers to Joss, lost as he was to his own sense of shock and sorrow. *Another dead mentor*, he kept thinking. *Another lost home. And Lord Malkus to blame for it all.*

The *Fat Lot of Good* tore into the night. When Round Shield Ranch was little more than a distant bonfire, Zeke throttled back the engine and set the ship on a holding pattern.

'We're clear … at least for now.'

'Alright,' said Drake. 'So where to from here?'

Zeke squeezed out from behind the control panel long enough to join the conversation. 'Wherever it is we have to decide quickly and it has to be close,' he said. 'We're so low on spark that we're getting by on the power of prayer at this point.'

'Could we get to Tower Town?' asked Edgar.

'We could get to the next road sign telling us how far away Tower Town is,' Zeke replied.

Somehow, through the smoke and cinders still filling his head, Joss managed to grasp a thought. 'Illustra. We should go to Illustra.'

'Why Illustra?' asked Drake.

'I met Regent Greel at the Tournament. When I won the Champion's Blade,' Joss said, thinking back to his surprise victory and the unexpected role that the Kingdom of Ai's elected leader had played in ensuring it. 'He took a shine to me, from what I could tell. He needs to hear what's happening. He needs to rally the kingdom's forces for what's to come.'

'You think he can be trusted?' asked Hero.

'I don't know,' Joss replied. 'But it's the only option I can see now.'

'I hate to say it,' Zeke said, 'but given that we can't get to Tower Town, there's no way we can get as far as Illustra. It may as well be a world away.'

A gloomy silence fell as the prentices pondered the problem.

'The serpentrain!' said Edgar. 'If we can get to one of the stations in the Backbone Ranges, we can ride the serpentrain all the way to the capital.'

'Can we make it that far?' Hero asked Zeke, who sucked his teeth as he thought it through.

'If I switch off all non-essential systems, fly low and get a good wind – *maybe.*'

'I'll take maybe,' said Joss. 'If you can set a course.'

Zeke slipped back behind the controls and got to work, decreasing their altitude so much that they hovered only a dozen feet above the road to the Backbone Ranges. Sitting out on the deck, Joss watched the night shift into day. Birdsong filled the dawn air.

What kind of day is it going to be? he wondered. Surely nothing could be as horrific as the night he'd just survived. Spotting a road sign leading to the serpentrain, he had the vague hope that there might yet be a way out of all this madness.

Until the deck rumbled beneath him and the engines fell silent, and the whole ship shuddered as it began to fall.

'We're out of power!' Zeke shouted. *'Everybody – brace for impact!'*

CHAPTER THREE

A CARAVAN OF HEARTBREAK

JOSS wrapped his arms around the nearest railing as the *Fat Lot of Good* crashed headlong into an empty field. The earth exploded upon impact and showered the prentices with stones and dirt, the ship carving a deep gouge in the grass until it finally skidded to a stop.

'Next time we crash …' Zeke's voice emanated from the wheelhouse. 'Remind me to buckle my harness first.'

'I can't tell you how much it worries me that you said "next time",' groaned Joss, while everyone else coughed up dirt.

'The animals!' Hero cried as she pulled herself up and stumbled towards the hull. Joss, Drake and Edgar were quick to join her, throwing open the stowage doors to find their mounts staring up at them in confusion; they were shaken but otherwise fine. Azof chittered away in Joss's ear while Zeke examined the *Fat Lot* for structural damage.

'No harm done,' he said. 'But it won't budge without a recharge.'

'We can ride the rest of the way from here,' Joss said, rubbing Azof's muzzle to calm the raptor down.

'And leave my ship?' Zeke exclaimed. When he saw how his friends reacted, he changed his tone. 'And leave my ship.'

They quickly packed what they needed and loaded it onto the backs of their mounts, still uncertain as to whether Malkus had sent his forces after them. But as they were saddling up, they heard the approach of distant riders.

'Sounds too big to be a raiding party,' said Drake. The prentices all looked down the road with dread, preparing to bolt the moment the enemy emerged – only to see a caravan being pulled by a pack of sauropods.

The three tall creatures moved with an elegance that contradicted their size, their long necks swaying with every step. They were towing carts and wagons, and a team of drivers rode high upon each beast's shoulders. The largest of the creatures swept towards Joss and his brethren, slowing to a stop right beside the *Fat Lot of Good*.

'Ahoy down there!' the driver called out, doffing his peaked cap. 'Need a lift?'

The prentices all looked at each other, confused.

'Are you going anywhere near the serpentrain station?' Joss replied.

'Ha! Yer in luck, lad! We've been offering rides to folks

looking to escape those fires at Round Shield Ranch. We're bound for Upsndowns, where most everyone is planning to catch that very same service.'

'Great!' said Zeke, flooded with relief. 'Do you have a way of loading our ship onto one of your flatbeds?'

'Certainly do. But between the animals and the airwagon, it's gunna cost you a comely crown or three.'

Zeke frowned. 'I thought you said you'd been offering rides to people escaping the fires?'

'We have – but we ain't been doing it for free!' the driver scoffed.

Zeke straightened his collar. 'Let me handle this,' he said to everyone, and started negotiating. As Joss waited, he glanced along the line of faces packed into the wagons. They weren't paladeros, or prentices, or fieldservs. They were the shopkeepers, blacksmiths, schoolmasters and labourers who lived in the villages surrounding Round Shield Ranch, just as the driver had said; the people of Thunder Realm, their fellow *thunderfolk* as they were known. They stared off into the distance as they grappled with the hell they'd just escaped, mourning all they'd been forced to leave behind.

He knew the feeling.

'Joss?' he heard someone call out from further down the caravan. 'Is that you?'

Among the villagers' blank stares, Joss discerned one familiar face. 'Eliza!' he exclaimed, quickly closing the distance between them. 'What are you doing here?'

She was sitting in one of the open carts, her eyes bloodshot, her face streaked with ash. 'Sur Verity told me to take as many fieldservs and prentices as I could find and get all the livestock to safety,' she said, struggling to keep herself together. 'But we were ambushed and split up. I don't know how to say it but … but the people who attacked us could have only been our own. From Round Shield Ranch. They were dressed in black cloaks with their faces hidden, following orders from some monster in a stone mask.'

'Malkus,' Joss told her, spitting the name out as if it were a curse. 'It was Lord Malkus who betrayed us.'

'… What?' Eliza gasped. 'That – that can't be true.'

'I promise you, it's true. I saw him giving orders to his followers, saw his mask break open.' He hesitated, but knew he had to say it: 'Saw him kill Sur Verity.'

Eliza lurched back, shook her head, squeezed her eyes shut. Joss watched the pain rolling through her and stayed by her side. Then she asked him a dozen questions, and he told her the full story, stopping only when they were joined by the others.

'It's cost me just about everything I had left, but we've got a ride,' said Zeke. 'They even provided serpentrain tickets.'

'You're sure those are authentic?' asked Hero, scanning the slips of paper with a critical eye.

'I'll be committing justifiable manslaughter if they're not,' Zeke groused.

'Eliza?' Edgar said, surprised at her presence. 'What are you doing here?'

Eliza choked at the prospect of having to relay the whole story again.

'She's joining us,' Joss told him.

The caravan crew loaded the *Fat Lot of Good* onto the spare flatbed. Joss and the others led their mounts back onto the ship, which they were using as an improvised carriage. Eliza lent a hand, and once the animals were settled she remained in the hull. Edgar sat with her, gently talking through their mutual ordeals.

Joss decided to leave them be and sat up on the deck. The sauropods were oblivious to the caravan of heartbreak they were pulling, calling to each other in a warbling chorus. Joss couldn't lose himself in their atonal symphony or the serene scenery, however. He knew it was all just a distraction from the sinister truth. Monsters were waiting for them just over the horizon. And he and his brethren were running out of time to stop them.

CHAPTER FOUR

—

A DREAM GIVEN FORM

'PLEASE *hold for Secretary Lovegood,*' said the blank face emanating from the illumivox. Chamber music filled the line, barely audible over the muffled roar from the Upsndowns station hall behind him. Joss wondered how much time was left on the machine before his money ran out.

'This is Secretary Lovegood,' a voice floated down the line. It was joined a moment later by a face that coalesced in a rush of particles within the illumivox's projector. 'I understand I'm speaking to Josiah Sarif? The Blade Keeper from Round Shield Ranch in Thunder Realm?'

'That's right, sir.'

Joss recognised the man as Regent Greel's aide from the Tournament, the one who'd worn a tailored suit with a top hat the size of six chamber pots stacked atop each other.

'Glad to hear from you, lad,' said the secretary, to Joss's surprise. 'I know you asked to speak to His Excellency, but I'm afraid Regent Greel is otherwise indisposed. Reports are flooding in from across the kingdom of –'

'Dragons? Masked men in hoods?' Joss said. 'Portals tearing the sky open?'

'Precisely.' Lovegood's nose twitched. 'You were present at two of the locations from what I understand?' Before Joss could respond, the secretary continued, 'Josiah, we're convening a summit with all the kingdom's armed forces to plan our response to this unfolding crisis. If you truly have witnessed all that you described to my assistant, Regent Greel would very much like to speak with you and your brethren. You're at the serpentrain station now?'

'Yes, sir.'

'Good. We'll send an emissary to collect you when you arrive in Illustra and bring you to the Ivory Palace. We'll have lodgings arranged. I look forward to your company, as does His Excellency.'

The transmission cut off, leaving Joss staring at a blank screen. Dazed, he stepped from behind the illumivox's privacy screen and got his bearings. A churning mass of people was flowing through the station. He saw his friends on the platform for the serpentrain, having already dropped the *Fat Lot of Good* and their mounts at the service gates.

'Did you get through?' asked Drake as he approached them.

'We've been summoned to the Ivory Palace,' Joss said

with a nod, which gradually slowed to a slant of the head and a furrowed brow. 'I think.'

As he relayed his conversation with Secretary Lovegood, more and more people filed onto the platform, and soon a whistle sounded from down the line.

'There it is!' Edgar shouted. The serpentrain arrived in a flash of polished steel and a whisper of spinning wheels. The engine was fashioned to resemble its namesake – a chrome snake's head with the conductor's windows serving for eyes. It pulled carriages made of silvery plates, which glided to a stop beside the platform. A shiver ran through the scaled carapace as it expelled a build-up of steam.

All his life, Joss had dreamed of riding the serpentrain. Now here he was, ready to board, yet robbed of the chance to enjoy the experience. As far as injustices went it was admittedly small, and certainly the least of his worries. But it stuck in his gums all the same.

———

Joss sat in the livestock carriage with Azof, brushing the raptor's feathers. The serpentrain moved so quietly that the rasp of the brush was louder than the noise of the engine. Once, he might have basked in all the comforts that the serpentrain had to offer; its velvet seats that folded out into plush cots, its generous food trolley, its dining car replete with crystal chandeliers and overflowing buffets. But now, after all he'd been through, he found such decadence sour in comparison to a good, honest day in the saddle. For a while he'd stewed on the inequality of all this excess; then he focused instead on the landscape as it rushed past.

The first major landmark they had come to was Dragon's Tail, where they paused within the subterranean station to take on another influx of passengers. Nobody disembarked, with people muttering about the threat of further attacks. That paranoia only intensified as they passed through the magma-dripping mountain tunnels that ran beneath Freecloud, Skyend and Blade's Edge Acres, and headed to Covora.

The underground tunnel opened out to a night sky spiked with stars. The Rogue City – as it was commonly called – was lodged within the jugular of Black Harbour, where it loitered ominously outside the serpentrain's windows. This was where Hero had been born and spent most of her childhood, though all she shared of her feelings on the matter was a well-worn adage of Ai: 'Nowhere else haunts you like home.' And with that she turned to Drake for a game of castes.

The train passed Crescent Cove so fast that it was little more than a blur on the way to Hammerton, where brick behemoths of buildings clogged the horizon. Many of them were stamped with the Sunforge Industries emblem; all of them were skewered with chimneys that expelled a thick smog, which stained the sky a lurid shade of green.

As their journey neared its end, Joss found himself increasingly preoccupied with dark thoughts of not only the road ahead but the flaming wreckage that lay behind.

He felt cooped up, restless, and unable to maintain the semblance of a brave face. Excusing himself from his brethren – who were discussing their own apprehensions about their upcoming audience with Regent Greel – Joss paced the train's aisles. Before long he had ended up in the livestock carriage, tending to Azof and sharing his woes with him.

'I wish I had your life,' Joss said as he fed the raptor freeze-dried mice. 'Nothing to worry about but what you're going to eat and how long you'll get to nap. Sounds pretty good to me ...'

Joss stopped, suddenly struck by the memory of holding back the blood pouring from Tempest's fatal wound. He could see the red-feathered pterosaur as if it was right there before him, panicked eyes pleading silently for his help. And then the image shifted, and it was Sur Verity lying there with the light from her one good eye fading to darkness.

He shook his head. Expelled a breath.

'But what do I know?' he said, feeding Azof another mouse. 'Maybe one day you're riding high with the sun on your back. And the next day some dumb kid with delusions of grandeur is getting you killed.'

He stopped again, frozen. And then it all caved in on him: the bad faith of the people he had admired most, the end of a way of life he had treasured above all else, the injustice and the grief and the utter disenchantment, and he roared and kicked the wooden pail beside him so hard it cracked in half. Hands balled into fists, he panted and shook, his eyes prickling with tears until he felt a muzzle pressing against his cheek and heard Azof whickering with concern. He took a moment to collect himself, then stroked the raptor's snout.

'… Good boy,' he murmured.

'Joss?' a small voice asked from the opposite end of the carriage. 'Are you there?'

Eliza had been crying so much that she looked drained, her freckled face even paler than usual, her raptor's mane of blond hair particularly disheveled. Joss turned away quickly, rubbing his eyes and kicking aside the broken pail.

'Just tending to the animals,' he said, clearing his throat. 'Thought I could use some quiet before we're thrown into all the noise of the capital.'

'Every time it's quiet I think about her,' Eliza replied. 'And the sacrifice she made.'

He didn't have to ask to know she was talking about Sur Verity.

'She was a brave woman,' he said.

'The bravest I've ever known.' Eliza rubbed at her running nose. 'I wouldn't be a prentice if it weren't for her. No other paladero would have taken me on. Not with Wildsmith as my family name.'

'Your uncle – he's one of the Nameless, isn't he?' he asked. There was a time when the prospect of being stripped of his paladero title, expelled from his order and found to be Nameless would have filled Joss with dread.

Now he was less sure.

Still, it would have been difficult living with the stigma of having your own flesh and blood in that position. So difficult that Eliza had trouble nodding as she replied, 'Not just one of the Nameless; he's their consul. He'd say that would make him their spokesperson, but really he's their leader – and notorious enough to keep any self-respecting paladero from so much as even talking to me. Not Sur Verity, though. She knew what people would say when she took me as her prentice. And she didn't care. "The greater shame would be in letting a talent like yours go to waste," she told me.' Eliza paused. 'I want Malkus to burn for what he did to her,' she said through bared teeth. 'For what he did to all of us.'

Joss saw the fire in her eyes, felt the heat of it radiating from her heart. He recognised it as the same flame that threatened to engulf him. And yet a part of him resented the idea that Sur Verity could possibly mean the same to Eliza as she'd meant to him. It was the part that had made him search out the solitude of the livestock carriage, the part that simmered with resentment and frustration and bitterness. But how could he say any of that to Eliza? So he said the only thing he could say.

'You and me both.'

Knowing that he couldn't continue hiding out, Joss gave Azof one last treat, said goodbye to Hero's sabretooth tiger, Callie, and Drake's tundra bear, Pietro, and walked back to the sleeping carriage with Eliza.

Drake and Hero sat side-by-side on one of the fold-out cots while Zeke occupied an armchair in the corner, all of them watching the miniature illuminator fixed to the wall. The Kingdom Crier news service was being projected in a shimmering beam.

'Where's Edgar?' Joss asked.

'*Shh!*' Hero hissed. 'They're talking about the attacks.'

Joss and Eliza quickly clambered around the others to watch.

'*Hear ye, hear ye!*' the snowy-bearded presenter exclaimed, as he began every report.

'*Chaos across the Kingdom!*' declared the crier, spiking Joss's attention. '*Portals of an unknown nature not seen since the Destruction of Daheed forming all across the country! Many portals open for only a moment before closing again, leaving destruction in their wake! Numerous paladero orders are the worst affected, with Blade's Edge Acres and Round Shield Ranch both burned to the ground!*'

The prentices shared a tense look as the transmission continued.

'*Mysterious creatures and shadowy figures spotted at each location! If you reside near any of these sites, the Ivory Palace recommends to evacuate now! Emergency summit to be convened in the capital! More updates as events unfold!*'

'Is that it?' asked Eliza as the crier moved on to his next report, expressing Joss's thoughts exactly.

'At least we know the word's out,' Drake replied. 'Everyone's aware of the threat we face.'

'Are you sure about that?' Joss said. 'All I heard was talk of portals and mysterious creatures and shadowy figures. There are a lot of blanks between those things – where are all the other portals located?'

'Joss is right. They know enough to know that they don't know enough,' Hero said.

Zeke winced. 'Can you say that again slower so that it makes my head hurt less?'

Edgar burst into the carriage. 'Everybody, quick! You have to see this!' he shouted, and bounded off towards the dining compartment. Joss fretted over what could have provoked such urgency as he and the others gave chase. Had a portal opened above the train? Was Malkus's dragon horde descending?

In the dining compartment, passengers crowded around the windows. Joss found a spot among the throng.

And there it was, shining in the distance: a divine metropolis that seemed to have floated down from on high to be embraced by a coastline of sapphires and diamonds. It was a dream given form, polished, pristine and perfect, comprised of silver spires and glassy towers, of roadways and skycraft that circled about like spun sugar. Even under the weight of his brooding, Joss couldn't help but marvel at the sight.

'Ladies and gentleman, we're now approaching our last stop on the line,' the conductor announced over the serpentrain's speakers. 'Illustra City.'

CHAPTER FIVE

A BAD OMEN

JOSS tried to keep calm in the face of the madness. Everywhere he turned there were buildings and vehicles and people and colour and noise. There was so much to take in, from the steel-and-glass Central Serpentrain Terminus to the towers that soared so high they blocked out the sun, all of them tattooed in shining illumigram advertisements. The din was so great that Joss decided he'd rather face a stampede of stegosaurs than stay here any longer than was absolutely necessary.

He wondered how Thunder Realm and this sleek silver city could exist in the same world, let alone in the same kingdom. What was even more astounding was how naturally its citizens accepted the preposterous sophistication in which they lived. When the rocket car he and his brethren had been awaiting finally arrived, he was grateful for the respite its cabin offered.

'Your animals and vehicles will be transported separately to the palace. A mechanoid of a similar model will meet you there. Farewell,' said the floating mek who'd greeted them at the platform, mustering them into the vehicle and sealing them inside. Glancing into the driver's seat, Joss was surprised to see that it was empty.

'Good day,' a voice intoned all around them, revealing that they weren't seated inside a car but a far more elaborate conveyance mechanoid. 'Please enjoy your ride.'

The mek set off, and Joss tapped his hand rapidly on the hilt of the Champion's Blade as he watched the scenery whizzing past.

'How …?' Drake marvelled aloud. 'How does all this exist? Just … *how?*'

'I always knew there was more in Illustra than what we had in Thunder Realm. But I never knew it was this much more,' said Edgar, his face pressed hard against the glass. It seemed all of Joss's brethren were as stunned by the city as he was – with one exception.

'Crazy, isn't it?' Zeke said flatly. 'Every time I come here I'm floored by it all.'

The conveyance mek zipped around a steepled courthouse, slipped between a pair of castle towers, glided along a carriage ramp and finally pulled up outside a building Joss had never imagined he'd see in person, let alone step foot inside.

Built midway up Illustra's densely forested Coronation

Peak, the Ivory Palace was a wonder in smooth white marble. It had none of the heavy defences of a Thunder Realm fortress. Instead everything was light and airy, with the palace like a flower in a flourishing garden. The only neighbouring building was the Supreme Chamber – the residence of the Attendant Absolute, the Sleeping King's chief emissary on earth – which sat at a slightly higher elevation to remind everyone where the real seat of power lay.

Joss and the others climbed out of the conveyance mek and were greeted by a mechanoid identical to the one from the Central Terminus, as promised.

'Josiah Sarif and company,' the mek said as it scanned their faces. 'You have been provided with accommodation in the guest annex at the far end of the grounds, by the southwest gate. If you could please come this way.'

'Get the feeling you're on a conveyor belt?' Zeke muttered in Joss's ear, earning him the first real chuckle Joss had been able to muster since the fall of Blade's Edge Acres. They followed the mek past finely dressed dignitaries and shouting reporters, up the palace's carpeted steps and into the domed foyer.

As soon as they entered, the shadow of a bad omen fell over Joss and his brethren. It hung from the ceiling as if it were little more than a museum piece or an art installation. A cluster of officials huddled beneath it, making notes and theorising with breathless fervour. Joss felt a damp sense of shock, shot through with the sting of loss. They had travelled all the way to the kingdom's capital and fought through all their fears and apprehensions, only to be confronted with this gruesome sight.

The corpse of the Mighty Bhashvirak.

The great megalodon's eyes were the same bottomless black that Joss remembered from the Northern Tundra, but now they stared blankly at the surrounding walls. His flesh had grown dry, rippled with sickly veins that stemmed from a gaping wound on his side. He looked bloated, broken and spent; even the lifechamber attached to his back was a cracked and desolate ruin.

'Heartbreaking – isn't it?' Joss heard a familiar voice and spun around.

'Qorza!' he gasped, and grabbed her in a hug which she swiftly returned. 'What are you doing here?'

'It was my sad duty to escort our friend here,' she said, tilting her head upward. She was dressed as if she'd just stepped off her ship, her oilskin coat flecked with mud and her little round glasses speckled with dried saltwater.

'What happened to him?' asked Drake, still staring at the giant shark with open disbelief.

Qorza shrugged. 'We found him floating off the coast of the Northern Tundra. Just one of many such corpses that have been filling the seas of late. But this has been the biggest by far. My theory is that one of those portals that have been menacing the mainland has ripped open beneath the waves and now something far more monstrous than this fine creature prowls the Silver Sea's depths.'

'So Captain Gyver sent you to raise the alarm?' Hero asked as they slowly circled beneath the great shark.

'She did. Though all I've seemed to raise is the idle curiosity of these folk here.' Qorza gestured to the throng of observers. 'They were the ones who organised this … *display.*' Disgust dripped from Qorza's voice. With little else to say on the matter, she pressed on. 'Is it true what I've been hearing? About Round Shield Ranch?'

The leather of Joss's coat crinkled as he shifted inside it. 'That depends on how much you've heard.'

As they crossed the foyer, Joss explained the circumstances that brought him and his brethren to the palace. Qorza listened intently, gasping with shock at certain points and shaking her head at others. When he'd finished, her face tightened with grim concern.

'I'm sorry for your loss,' she told him, before turning to the others. 'For all your losses.'

'Thank you,' Hero said quietly. Eliza and Edgar echoed her. Joss had been so lost in his own sorrow that he hadn't thought much about how everyone else was processing theirs. And though he wanted to be sensitive to everything they were feeling, there was something that had been plaguing him ever since his illumivox transmission with Qorza was cut short, all the way back in Blade's Edge Acres.

Hoping he wouldn't scour too many scales, he said, 'Qorza, do you mind if we have a quick word? In private?'

'… Of course,' Qorza said, looking as confused as Joss's brethren. Joss gently drew Qorza beneath one of the foyer's sweeping archways.

'The last time we spoke, we were talking about the Rakashi Revelations,' he whispered.

'Yes, you seemed convinced they had some personal significance, beyond your mother having translated them.'

'Partly translated them,' he reminded her. 'You said you'd been sharing them with some academics?'

'I have, though it hasn't yielded much. Not so far, at least. Why?'

'It's just …' How could he say it? 'My faith – in the world, in people, in everything – it's been …'

'Damaged,' Qorza said.

He nodded. 'It'd be good to know if there's still something for me to believe in.'

'I don't know how wise it is to place your faith in ancient prophecies,' she said, and placed a consolatory hand on his shoulder. 'I'd say you're better off entrusting it to your friends.' She nodded to the others, who were waiting patiently for them.

'Josiah Sarif,' their mechanoid escort cut in as it hovered to his side. 'Continued discourse will egregiously affect the allocated schedule. Please defer for now and resume at another point, if so desired.'

'I think that's the politest way it has of telling me to shut up and get moving,' he said. Qorza laughed.

'Go. I'll see you tomorrow.'

He returned to the others and they fell into line behind the mek.

'What was that all about?' Zeke asked. The others all leaned in, equally curious.

'Nothing. Just some old family business,' Joss replied as they followed the floating mek through the inner recesses of the Ivory Palace, leaving behind the cold and lonely shadow of the Mighty Bhashvirak and the dire warning it posed.

———

'Nothing is impossible,' Malkus's voice boomed from the darkness, driving Joss from his sleep. He couldn't escape the memory – not even in his dreams. He climbed from his bed with his blanket wrapped around him, then started getting ready for the day once the mechanoid had come to summon him.

Looking in the mirror, Joss inspected the bruises he'd taken at both Blade's Edge Acres and Round Shield Ranch. He gingerly touched one and immediately regretted it. His eyes moved to the silvery ghost of a mark he'd been left with from being struck by a wisp on the deck of Qorza's ship, the *Behemoth*. The supernatural whispers it had brought with it had grown quiet, but the scar remained. So too did the faded cut on his right palm, which Sur Verity had given him at his binding ceremony. The cut that he was sure the Rakashi Revelations had referred to as his 'right hand marked by fate'; the sign that he was the prophesied champion dubbed the *galamor*.

Joss sighed. Maybe Qorza was right. Maybe he shouldn't

place his faith in such empty promises. He threw on his clothes, met the floating mechanoid and followed it out to the Ivory Palace grounds.

'Where are the others?' he asked.

'Your companions have been provided with their own escorts,' the mek told him. Joss looked out across the emerald parklands of the palace's estate, which rolled all the way down the mountainside to Sovereign Bay. An armada of ships was anchored in the harbour, the largest of which was a colossal steel-and-glass hulk with a purple lightning bolt 'Z' on its bow.

Zeke's family must be here, Joss thought. He wondered how Zeke would take the news.

After a hike that Joss could have sworn left even the mechanoid feeling winded, they came to the palace's audience hall. Dozens of illuminator consoles were set up throughout the cavernous room, with a team of officials standing by each one. They appeared to be reviewing footage taken from across the Kingdom of Ai, where black holes had torn open the sky.

Joss spotted a technician and an army official going through recordings of Round Shield Ranch. He almost crashed into a nearby monitoring station as he strained to see details of the footage. All he could make out were the scorched fortress walls of his home, the black interdimensional tear hovering above it.

'Mind your step, please,' the mek told him as it weaved through the mass of equipment and people.

'What is all this?' Joss asked, trying to take in all the frenetic activity around him. He'd imagined the summit to be a much smaller affair, isolated to Regent Greel and Secretary Lovegood and perhaps a handful of other dignitaries. 'This isn't the summit – is it?'

'Indeed it is. The first of such scale to ever be mounted,' the mek replied. 'The war room proved to be of inadequate size so the audience hall has been commandeered for the purpose.'

Joss regarded the floating automaton. 'You're unusually chatty for a mechanoid,' he said. He had learned over the years that meks rarely gave more than clipped and painfully literal answers.

'You have been granted provisional clearance as a member of the summit and are to be provided with whatever information you request.'

'Really?' Joss said with surprise. 'Just how bad a situation are we in, if that's the case?'

'That information is above your level of clearance.'

'Typical,' Joss grumbled. 'So what *is* my level of clearance?'

'Josiah Sarif: Blade Keeper. Special envoy for Regent Greel and the Ivory Palace. Key witness to multiple contact incidents,' the mek recited with dry detachment.

Joss frowned. 'Key witness? Multiple contact incidents?'

'You will be expected to supply the summit with details of everything experienced at Blade's Edge Acres and Round Shield Ranch, as well as any relevant information connected to the Destruction of Daheed. Based on the testimony you provide, Regent Greel and his cabinet will decide what course of action to take,' the mek replied. Joss lost a step. Now, for the first time, he understood just how high the stakes were for him in coming here: through the power of his words alone, he would have to win over a crowd of pompous politicians, dispassionate soldiers and cynical cityfolk – all with the fate of civilisation hanging in the balance.

As far from home as he'd already felt, now he knew just how lost in the world he had truly become.

CHAPTER SIX

AN IMMEDIATE AND THOROUGH RESPONSE

WHERE once the regent may have sat in his gilded ceremonial chair, there was now a large crystal table. An illuminator encased within the tabletop cast a ghostly illumigram of the whole kingdom, compiling information from the monitoring stations around the room to offer a live feed of the unfolding crisis.

Round Shield Ranch was represented on the map in miniature as a burned-out ruin with a swirling vortex hanging above it. An entire horde of winged dragons was nesting throughout the fortress grounds and patrolling its skies in strict formation, with tiny masked figures tending to the creatures as if they were prized mounts.

It was the same for Blade's Edge Acres, where Joss and his brethren had first escaped the Shadow God and his Court of Thralls. Gone were the rookeries full of pterosaurs and pens packed with sabretooths. In their place was a menagerie of monsters being groomed and readied for battle.

Why hadn't the beasts and their masters journeyed beyond these sites? Joss didn't know whether to be grateful for that small mercy or worried about the onslaught they were undoubtedly planning. He wasn't alone in that dilemma, with the largest group of officials clustered around the regent's crystal table, muttering worriedly.

'Joss!' Drake called out from the opposite end of the table. Hero was with him, as were Edgar and Eliza.

'Crowded,' Joss noted after edging his way through the throng.

'Very!' said Edgar. 'How are you going to be with talking in front of all these people?'

Joss tried to swallow and only managed to clench his throat.

'I'll be fine,' he croaked. 'Where's Zeke?'

'Good question. We haven't seen fang nor feather of him since yesterday,' Hero replied.

A brassy, rapid-fire shout of trumpets filled the air. Secretary Lovegood stood at the far end of the room, a phalanx of armed guards filing in behind him.

'Gentlefolk,' Lovegood said, sweeping his hat off his head. 'Please be upstanding for His Excellency the Regent Augustus Greel.'

The trumpets sounded again as the regent entered the room with the same rubber-legged mania that

Joss remembered from the first time they'd met at the Tournament. The small, silver-haired man made a point of grabbing the wrist of everyone he passed and greeting them by name. The crowd seemed paralysed, unsure of how to receive the country's leader in the midst of a crisis. But if Greel detected any unease, he didn't let it rattle him. Instead he leapt to his spot at the centre of the illuminator table with his typical showman's zeal.

'My fellow citizens!' he declared. 'A great calamity has been visited upon our land. In the face of this unfolding crisis, each of you has heeded the call and rallied to your kingdom's aid, for which you have our profound gratitude. Now we must take that bravery and dedication and turn it towards its true purpose; the safeguarding of our lands and people. General Swift – could you apprise us of the current situation?'

'Of course, Your Excellency,' replied a man to Joss's right, his face composed of straight lines and hard edges. He wore mechanised power armour enamelled in blue and gold, with a white cloak flowing from a pair of broad epaulettes. Despite how little he knew of life outside Thunder Realm, Joss recognised him as Horatio Swift, the Sentinel of Illustra City.

'Originally, the incursion was isolated mostly to Thunder Realm,' General Swift said as he pointed at the glowing map. 'Additional rifts – or portals, or vortexes, depending on your preferred terminology – appeared in the northern Backbone Ranges. Now, every passing day a new rift forms, with another horde of dragons spewing from it. Their attacks have been limited to raiding nearby towns and villages, though how long that will remain the case is anyone's guess.

'The Royal Army is doing all it can to contain the threat, but its numbers are stretched thin. Reinforcements are required. We've reached out to the Counties in an attempt to co-ordinate a response with Count Barus.' Swift now gestured to the southwest corner of the map where the Counties were clustered right beneath Thunder Realm, the capital city of Nobleseat glistening like a pin tip. 'But so far we've been met with silence. Likewise, wardens in regional cities and settlements around the kingdom have failed to respond, including Dragon's Toe and the Thunder Realm market towns. We put this down to atmospheric interference from the rifts, though that's not to discount the possibility of sabotage.

'A number of the remaining paladero orders have offered their help, though given the part they played in all of this it's hard to distinguish friend from foe. The Grandmaster Council, in their role as the authoritative body of Thunder Realm and its paladero ranks, has put forward Tower Town as a rallying point for the paladeros' forces and the Royal Army, should we be able to bring them all together. From there we can launch a combined attack against the enemy invaders and, with His Majesty's good grace, overwhelm them.'

'And that's what today's summit seeks to accomplish,'

said Regent Greel, who was still bobbing up and down. Joss grew alarmed as the Regent continued, 'We have a group of survivors with us today, witnesses to the destruction that has visited the heart of our land. And their leader is no less than the Blade Keeper himself, Josiah Sarif. Sur Josiah can personally attest to the scale of the threat we face. Sur Josiah, what say you?'

All eyes turned to Joss. He wondered if he looked as mortified as he felt.

'Begging your pardon, Your Excellency,' he said, somehow finding his voice. 'But I'm not a paladero. Not yet. And I'm no leader. These are my Bladebound brethren. We're just prentices ... paladeros in training.'

'*Children!*' snapped a member of the crowd, who was dressed in all the finery of a nobleman. His lips gathered spit and his cheeks purpled as he went on, 'Delinquents and daydreamers, I tell you! It's an insult to ask that we simply accept the word of this pup and his mute companions. Let the thunderfolk play whatever games they've concocted with their cheap props and shadow puppets. And when they're done with their theatrics, we can charge them with the treason they've so obviously committed!'

Through the thick fog of words that had been blown his way, Joss discerned the man's meaning.

He thinks it's all a hoax, he realised, stunned. *And he thinks we're the ones behind it!*

'I should haul him out for zamaraq practice,' Hero muttered. Drake touched her lightly on the wrist.

'Again, sir. We're prentices,' Joss said, trying to choose his words carefully even as the thunderstorm brewing inside him threatened to rumble loose. 'Prentices who've witnessed the nightmare that's coming for us all. A nightmare that doesn't discriminate. It will consume rich and poor alike. You say the thunderfolk are to blame for this? Well … I'll be honest with you. Yes, our people played a part in its summoning. Not all of them. But enough. And their betrayal hurts more than you will ever know. I can tell you this, though – it may have begun with the thunderfolk, but it won't end with them. This isn't just a threat to all our survival. This is a threat to our very souls.'

Joss realised the room had grown silent. Everyone was looking at him with grave concern.

'The lad speaks truth, Baronet Dunkworth,' said General Swift, addressing the nobleman. 'This is only going to get worse. For every wave of refugees that escapes the raids, there are just as many people who choose to stay behind. Judging by our scouts' reports, they are adding their support to the invaders' efforts, as if they were all under some kind of spell.'

'Spell,' Dunkworth spat. 'Treachery, more like. Plain and simple.'

'Be that as it may,' General Swift replied, his voice growing tight. 'The enemy is amassing forces. Which compels us to do the same.'

Again the hall descended into silence, which His Excellency was all too comfortable to break. 'Never let it be said that Regent Greel is not a man of his people,' he crowed. 'You may agree with Baronet Dunkworth that this a hoax – a diversionary tactic to mask a rebellion of paladero orders. If you believe this is so, I will instruct the Royal Army to hold their position and await further orders. But if you believe – as General Swift and young Josiah Sarif would have it – that this threat requires an immediate and thorough response, then we will commit our full military might to the matter. Moreover, we will appoint a special envoy to travel the country and rally the kingdom's forces. So – what say you all?'

Joss tensed, as did his brethren. Was this truly how the world's fate would be decided? By the privileged and influential people of the Ivory Palace? And had he done anywhere near enough to sway them to his side?

The crowd erupted. Joss couldn't distinguish what they were all saying at first, but through the wall of noise he realised the overwhelming majority were demanding that His Excellency rally the kingdom's forces. Smiling, Regent Greel held up his hands in a call for silence.

'Then it's settled. General Swift – dispatch as many reinforcements as necessary to hold the containment lines around the existing portals. Whatever resources you require you shall have. As for the special envoy, we'll require speedy and reliable transport. Lord Xavier, I see your flagship anchored out in the harbour. I understand you've volunteered its use in this effort?'

The crowd parted, revealing a figure in well-oiled

black riding leathers and polished purple plate armour adorned with the Zadkille Station emblem. He had a thick hay bale of blond hair, a bristly silver beard and a scowl branded across his face. He was flanked by a pair of young companions, similarly dressed in the black-and-purple vestments of Zadkille Station. Joss recognised the first as Lord Xavier Zadkille's son, Luther, from the time that he and Joss had both run the Gauntlet. The second was Zeke, groomed and tailored so meticulously he looked like he'd never left his family's order. He fixed Joss with a skittish, guilty glance, then quickly looked away.

'It would be our deepest honour to offer the use of the *Zenith* to the cause,' Lord Xavier told the Regent with the barest of bows. 'As well as our services in leading its mission.'

General Swift seemed surprised by Lord Xavier's bold proposal. Regent Greel, however, clapped his hands as if he were a child who'd just been told he'd be getting his own pet hatchling.

'*Tremendous!*' His Excellency cooed. 'Then I hereby declare this mission has the palace's full approval. Your objective: call upon those forces who have yet to affirm their oaths to their kingdom, starting with the Counties and continuing through to Thunder Realm and anywhere else that may be of aid. Tower Town will be the rallying point in our impending battle – ensure their presence there upon the Regentsday a fortnight from now. This mission will be codenamed Operation Herald. Or perhaps

Operation Daysaver? What say you, Lovegood? Herald or Daysaver?'

'The preliminary documents all have it as Operation Herald, Your Excellency.'

'Then Operation Herald it is! And Sur Joss?'

Joss glanced at his brethren, who all looked just as confused as he did. Straightening his back and clearing his throat, he said, 'Yes, Your Excellency?'

'You and your brethren should prepare for the journey ahead. All the world is counting on you.'

CHAPTER SEVEN

A NIGHT ON THE TOWN

JOSS opened the door to the Ivory Palace's rooftop and walked out into its green sanctuary. Despite night having fallen, the city was still heaving and whirling like a stirred-up snowglobe, with thousands of rocket cars and airships glittering in the darkness. Following a path through the garden beds, Joss was reminded of Tower Town, of Daheed, of Blade's Edge Acres, and all the solitary rooftops where he had sought refuge to reflect and deliberate. None of them had been as lush as this, and none so sorely needed.

He was still struggling all these hours later with what to make of the summit. He hadn't expected Regent Greel to call him into service; to be drawn back out to the battlefield, having only just escaped it. The news had landed on him like a whack in the head from the business end of a stegosaur's thagomizer.

He vaguely remembered mumbling something about not feeling well and then fleeing back to his quarters. What good could it do to put himself at risk again, particularly after everything he'd already suffered? And would those he was fighting for even deserve the sacrifice he would be making for them?

Without clear answers, he'd eventually decided a change of scenery might help, which had led him here. But he wasn't alone. 'Feeling any better?' he heard Drake ask. Rounding a holly hedge, Joss found Drake and Hero sitting particularly close together on a park bench with a view of the city skyline. They wriggled to either side as Joss sat down between them.

'I'll let you know when I've worked that out,' he said. 'How about you two?'

Drake and Hero glanced at each other over Joss's head.

'Let's say you're not the only one still trying to work it all out,' Drake replied, taking a swig from a sarsaparilla bottle before passing it to Hero.

'It's not every day you find yourself conscripted into the royal diplomatic corps,' she grumbled before throwing the bottle back. Joss watched her closely, trying to peel back her layers of invisible armour and work out exactly what she was feeling. The scrutiny was enough to make her ask, 'What?'

'How do you do it?' he said. 'How do you keep going?'

She considered the question for so long that Joss thought she might not answer.

'I honestly don't know,' she said at last. 'I just deal with one problem at a time. And the biggest problem has to be dealt with the soonest. Right now we have a mission to accomplish. I'll worry about the rest later.'

Drake made a small noise of concern.

'What?' said Hero again.

'It's nothing, it's just ...' he waved his hand, then lowered it. 'I remember when I was growing up, before I'd become a prentice at Starlight Fields. Before I'd worked up the nerve to tell my family that my name was really Ganymede and not the one they'd given me. My way of dealing with the pain of all that was to distract myself with the problems of the day. But that meant that my biggest problem was always hovering there, eating at me, unspoken and unchallenged.'

'You don't think Joss and I are up to the challenge?' Hero said, her anger rising quickly.

Drake raised both his hands, yielding. 'That's not what I'm saying. You two are the strongest people I know. Whatever life throws at you both, I know you can handle it. But sometimes I worry you're too strong. That you'll shoulder too much, that you'll both keep charging forward without ever giving yourselves the chance to stop. To face what's really threatening you and find a way to make peace with it.'

'Make peace with it?' Joss said, scoffing. 'I can't make peace with what's threatening me. But I don't know if I can make war with it, either.'

'What do you mean?' asked Drake.

The answer to his question was what Joss had been running from ever since crimson fires had burned his home to the ground and turned everything he'd once believed in to ash.

'When I confronted Malkus,' Joss tentatively began, 'he said something. He said a lot of things, actually. All of them painful to hear. But there was one thing that really cut me, deep down, right to the core.'

'And that was?' Hero asked.

'He said that life's the perfect trap. That we're told a fairytale of what the world is, when the truth is much darker. And the thing is … I don't think he was wrong.'

'You don't?' Drake said.

'Not entirely,' Joss replied. 'I remember the Orphan House, when I'd first arrived and was young and scared and heartbroken. I remember the Attendants from the High Chamber would preach to us, telling us all we needed was to accept the Sleeping King's plan for us; that with prayer and good works our path would be illuminated. So I'd lie in my bed praying to anyone who would listen to bring my mother back, bring my father back, bring back my home and my friends and family and everything I had lost. Nobody ever answered. I was alone in the dark, talking to myself.'

'How does that make Malkus right?' asked Hero. Joss knew how much her faith meant to her, but he couldn't let that keep him from speaking his mind.

'Prayers go unanswered. Evils go unpunished. The world is a cruel place.' He held his breath a moment, trying to rein in his emotion. 'So why bother fighting for it?'

Drake and Hero gawped as if he'd just admitted to being another Thrall. Drake attempted to reply, uttering a series of stuttered false starts as he wrestled with Joss's argument. In the midst of his struggle, there was a rustle from behind the bushes and a flustered pink face popped out.

'What're you all doing up here?' said Edgar, blinking.

'We could ask the same of you,' Hero replied.

'Looking for you,' he told them. 'There's a late-night session playing at a nearby illumie theatre. Eliza and I were thinking of going and we wondered if you all might like to join us. Maybe get your minds off everything that's been going on? Could be fun to have a night on the town.'

Joss, Drake and Hero turned to each other. The air around them still felt unsettled, thick with words unsaid. But there would be time enough for all that later, Joss decided.

'Why the muck not?' he said to Edgar and the others while Illustra shone beneath them.

———

Everywhere Joss looked, he saw scads of rich people. People who'd never seen a shadow of real darkness in all their blessed little lives. He saw them dining at outdoor brasseries, sipping from steaming cups inside gilded tea rooms, hauling handfuls of shopping bags to their chauffeured rocket cars, indulging in lizard-drawn carriage rides. He saw them laughing and chitchatting and luxuriating in all the peace and comfort that their privilege afforded them.

All while the world burned.

He wanted to grab them by their fancy lapels and shake them until their elaborate boutonnieres flew off, shouting in their faces about the peril they were in. But he knew his warnings would fall on deaf ears, dismissed as the ravings of an overexcited child or a peasant envious of their wealth. So he stuffed his hands in his pockets and kept his head down as he walked along the promenade towards the theatre with his brethren.

Drake and Hero led the group side-by-side, as always. Zeke was nowhere to be found, most likely living the high life aboard his father's ship. The idea only rankled Joss further – Zeke had shown real growth beyond the entitled little lordling he'd been when they'd first met and now he seemed to be regressing. Edgar, meanwhile, chatted with Eliza for the longest time until eventually drifting off to the side to steal glimpses at Joss, who was a few steps behind everyone else. Increasing his pace, Joss fell into step beside his friend.

'Nice night,' Joss said.

'You're right about that,' Edgar replied.

'Something on your mind?'

Edgar looked caught off-guard, but answered all the same. 'Drake mentioned something as we were leaving the palace,' he said. 'Something about you seeming like you were …'

'Like I was what?'

'Struggling,' Edgar said, then quickly looked away. 'Or not. I don't know.'

Joss frowned. He knew his friends were concerned for him but that didn't help his mood. 'Sur Blaek and Lord Malkus betrayed us. Round Shield Ranch has been destroyed. The whole world is falling into calamity. And I got both Tempest and Sur Verity killed. How am I supposed to be, Edgar?'

'You didn't get them killed, Joss,' Edgar said. 'Lord Malkus and the Court of Thralls did that.'

'Same difference,' Joss shrugged. He was on the verge of telling his friend everything he'd already said to Drake and Hero when Edgar interrupted him.

'No,' he said. 'Tempest made a choice. Sur Verity made a choice. They chose to fight for what mattered to them.'

'Tempest was an animal, Edgar. He had no choice.'

'Yes he did. He could have followed his instincts and saved himself. But he made his choice to protect your life, even though it cost him his own. I don't mean to browbeat you about it, but it's a disservice to his memory to say he didn't know what he was doing or that he had no choice. Same for Sur Verity. It's our responsibility to honour their sacrifice. To make sure it wasn't in vain.'

Joss stared at Edgar the same way he'd stared at Hero – with such intensity he almost forced Edgar back a step.

'What?' Edgar asked.

'I don't think I've ever heard you talk like that before.'

'I'm sorry. Like I said, the last thing I want to do is kick you when you're already down. Words just seem to pop out of me sometimes,' Edgar said, blushing.

'Wise words,' Joss told him. 'And worth remembering.'

They rounded the promenade and came at last to the Monarch Theatre, where they lined up to buy their tickets. The barrel-vaulted ceiling curved high over their heads, inlaid with twisting golden vines. Joss felt like a trespasser as he crossed the opulent space into the theatre.

The stage was filled with an illuminator twice the size of the Regent's crystal projection table. As the houselights dimmed, the illuminator fired up and a diorama of sparkling light unfolded like a pop-up book, casting a scene of two fieldservs traipsing into a stockyard.

'What a foul mood Sur Render is in today, I'll tell you what! It's like a bronto bounded up and bit 'im on the bizkit, boy howdee!'

The audience chortled. Joss glanced around, confused by how such a broad display of Thunder Realm life could be considered so amusing. That confusion deepened as the illumie continued, introducing the paladero Sur Render, who was as buffoonish as his fieldservs and pompous as well. The trio got caught up in a series of increasingly insufferable pratfalls, the pain of their muddle-headed misadventures coming to an end when the illuminator wound down and the lights came up, signalling intermission.

'Thank His Majesty for small mercies,' Hero exhaled.

'Am I the only one who desperately wants to leave?' asked Drake.

'Not by a long shot,' Joss replied. They pushed their way back onto the promenade where they soon formed a circle.

'That's the most mind-numbing muck it's ever been my displeasure to witness,' Eliza said, scowling.

'Is that really how they think life is in Thunder Realm?' Edgar asked, stunned. 'Do they really think we're that … that …?'

'Witless?' Drake offered.

'It's so insulting!' Joss said, his dismay quickly turning to anger. 'Regent Greel wants us to risk our lives for these people but all they do is look down their noses at us and make jokes at our expense and keep us in our place. I have half a mind to tell him to stick his Operation Herald where the sun doesn't – *Oof!*'

Joss grunted loudly as someone in the crowd smacked into him so hard and fast it left him winded. They didn't stop to apologise, just ducked into the surrounding mass of people instead.

'*You cretin!*' he shouted. 'You absolute muck-eating clump of –!'

And that's when he noticed how much lighter his swordbelt was.

'Joss?' Edgar asked. 'Are you alright?'

'The Champion's Blade!' he gasped. 'That thief stole it!'

—

CHAPTER EIGHT

A CULPRIT & HIS ACCOMPLICE

SPRINTING after the thief, Joss's mind raced faster than his feet could carry him. Was this the work of the Court of Thralls? Had they managed to infiltrate the city? Track him down? Steal his sword from his side? And if they'd gone to all that effort, did that mean the Rakashi Revelations might be true?

He could see the culprit running with an accomplice through the crowded promenade. Whoever they might have been, they were as fast as they were small, slipping through the packed walkways of Illustra with the ease of a knife fitting its sheath.

'*Joss!*' he could hear Edgar and the others shouting. '*Joss! Wait!*'

But slowing down would mean losing sight of the thieves. He sidestepped tourists and vendors, all while keeping his gaze locked on the two cloaked figures scurrying through the crush of people. Joss had nearly reached his quarry when an autowagon screeched towards him, blaring its horn. He had to time his leap perfectly, clambering across its hood and dropping to the ground on the other side.

'*You muck-trotting miscreant! Watch where you're wandering!*' the driver yelled, still hurling curses as Joss set off again, pursuing the thieves into an outdoor market. The cloaked figures had begun overturning fruit carts and wine barrels in a desperate attempt to shake him loose. Joss launched himself onto a windowsill and leapt across the obstacles in his path.

'*Fresh eggs! Fresh meat!*' a vendor was barking. His shouts took a foul-tempered turn as the thieves pulled his cages to the ground and smashed them open, scattering microraptors in a dozen different directions. Between the loose thunder lizards and the vendors scrambling to grab them, Joss's path was totally blocked. He could only watch and fume as the thieves sprinted through the entranceway of a nearby shopping arcade.

Joss refused to be defeated. Scaling the nearest market stall, he climbed onto its roof and navigated the treacherous path across it, the thin sheet of corrugated iron bending and banging with every step as he kept running, right to the next stall, and then the next.

Finally he landed on the other side. '*Out of the way!*' he shouted at the shoppers milling outside the arcade, then remembered his manners and added, 'Thank you!' Sprinting on, he passed glass-fronted confectionary stores, boutique ateliers and specialist wine merchants basking in the warm glow of crystalline chandeliers. But no sign of the thieves.

Joss scanned his surroundings: missing tiles, cracked glass, tarnished gold. While the east bank was still affluent by Thunder Realm standards, Joss felt a creeping sense of being on the rougher side of town.

His gaze fell upon a discrete side door – a slice of light shone out as it swung shut. Bursting through, Joss found himself in a chokingly thin alleyway. At the far end were a pair of running figures.

'*Stop!*' he yelled, earning a bewildered glance from the shorter of the two. There was something familiar about the small face that gaped at him before it vanished from sight, leaving Joss no choice but to push ahead. The brickwork was closing in around him, but if he could manoeuvre his way through the Gauntlet he was certain he could do the same here. Holding his breath, he edged forward as fast as he could, at last tumbling free and emerging into a laneway.

The sound of barking hit him in the ear like a crossbow bolt. He rolled aside and caught sight of a massive direwolf chained up just a few feet away. Other than the immense beast, the lane was empty. Joss scanned for an exit: a nearby fence was missing a couple of posts. Seeing nowhere else to go, he crawled through it. And there, he found the thieves.

Joss seized his chance and dove for them, grabbing the smaller one by the ankle.

'Let go of me!' the thief cried as his companion skittered away.

'Who are you?' Joss demanded, rising to his feet to get a better grip on the culprit. 'What do you want with the Champion's Blade?'

'I don't have your poxy blade,' snarled the thief. Joss pulled the thief's hood back and was struck by a stinging familiarity.

'I know you,' he said. 'You're that pickpocket who led us to the catacombs in Dragon's Tail while we were on the Way.'

'On the way? On the way where?' the young thief demanded, looking as confused as he did irate.

'*The Way!* The quest they send you on to prove you're ready to be a paladero,' Joss said, then sighed with exasperation as the boy only stared at him blankly. 'It doesn't matter. What are you doing here?'

'I could ask you the same thing,' the thief replied, taking advantage of Joss's relaxed grip to wrench himself free. 'And the name is Crimson.'

'Crimson,' Joss said. He glared down at the boy the way Sur Verity had whenever he'd run afoul of her. 'Why did you steal my sword?'

'Supply and demand. There's a good price for swords right now. Everyone's running scared, desperate for whatever weapon they can get their hands on. Fancy sword like that would fetch a good cache of coin. Or it could just be handy in a pinch. Either way it was there for the taking, so we took it.'

'Give it back.'

'Like I told you, I ain't got it.' Crimson held out his empty hands.

Joss narrowed his eyes. 'Your friend then. Where's he?'

Crimson scowled right back, twisting his mouth around. Then he nodded at the dilapidated warehouse that overshadowed them. 'He'll be through there.'

Joss looked up at the building's rusted steel and dark stonework. 'Is this your headquarters or something?'

'Headquarters?'

'You and the other …' Joss struggled for a polite word. 'You and your friends.'

Crimson expelled a single, dry laugh. 'Hardly,' he said. 'Come on. I'll show you.'

Crimson guided Joss through the piles of rubble that littered the yard. The entrance to the warehouse was little more than a hole that been torn in its side like a spear wound. Inside was cold and dark. It took Joss's eyes a moment to adjust, while all around he could hear the sound of breathing and muttered words. Crimson's cohorts must be massing around him, he thought, ready to attack. But as his vision cleared, he saw that couldn't be further from the truth.

'Who are all these people?' he gasped, looking around at the crowds huddled throughout the warehouse. Many of them were families, with mothers nursing babies as small children played among barrels of burning timber and grandparents watched on with blank stares. They were so tightly packed into the space that they were practically living on top of each other, with dirty old blankets spread out to serve as makeshift beds.

'The survivors,' Crimson said. 'When the towns around Dragon's Tail were raided by those mucky monsters, we thought the best thing to do was pack up and head for safety. And we weren't the only ones.'

'Isn't there somewhere safer for you all to go?' Joss asked as he watched a little girl making a tower from the loose bricks that littered the warehouse. She was dressed in rags, her feet bare and her face covered in dust.

'Everywhere else is full,' Crimson told him. 'And besides, we barely had homes where we lived. So who's gonna take us in here?'

Joss's heart felt like it was swirling down a drain as he surveyed the squalid surroundings and the people who were trying to make the most of them. All this time he had been so consumed by his own hurt and anger that he had lost sight of the true victims of this conflict. Here they were in their masses; trembling in the dark, waiting and hoping, finding only ashes and shadows.

The little girl's tower toppled over.

While Joss watched her rebuild it, Crimson excused himself to track down the missing sword. He returned a moment later with his remorseful-looking accomplice, who was brandishing the Champion's Blade.

'Crimson sez this is yours,' he said, offering the weapon back to Joss. 'Sorry. He said we shouldn't steal from them who've done us a good turn. Said you was decent to him back in Dragon's Tail.'

'And that you paid well,' Crimson said with a firm nod. 'Gotta have a code after all.'

Joss looked at the boy, who had the same eerie familiarity as Crimson. He didn't look much younger than Joss himself, with scrawny shoulders and a hollow face. Joss was almost tempted to tell him to keep the sword; to sell it and spend the money on food for everyone here. But he needed it far too much to give it away.

'Thank you,' Joss said, accepting the blade. 'What's your name?'

The boy looked at Crimson, who appeared to be the one in charge.

'His name is Cloud,' Crimson said. The answer came with such decisiveness that it sounded like it had been made up on the spot. Joss decided not to challenge it.

'Cloud. Crimson,' he said, settling the Champion's Blade back into place. 'How would you both like a job?'

———

Joss found his brethren still searching for him in the arcade. The walk back from the warehouse had been challenging, not only because he'd had to evade the direwolf again, but because of all he was leaving behind. As he considered the faces he'd seen in the warehouse, he couldn't help but think of Daheed. If anyone else from his homeland had survived they would have gathered somewhere similar, hunkered in the dark and hoping for mercy. If only there was someone to offer it.

'Joss!' Drake called out, alerting the others. Together they ran over to him with concern carved into their faces.

'Did you find them? Did you find the thieves?' Edgar panted.

'I found more than that,' Joss said. 'I found something worth fighting for.'

—

CHAPTER NINE

A RUSTLING OF A CROW'S WINGS

T HE *Zenith* put all other ships to shame. Sleek yet solid, it didn't look like a machine made of disparate parts assembled on some factory line. Instead, it looked sculpted and tailored and hand-polished; a bespoke artwork in onyx and amethyst, raised from its original berth in Sovereign Harbour on powerful thrusters to dock on the fiftieth floor of Illustra's Central Terminus.

Joss admired and reviled the machine in equal measure. He thought again of the people he'd seen sheltering in the warehouse. Surely there would be enough cabins on the *Zenith* to accommodate them, if the space hadn't been taken up with however many hundreds of crewmembers awaiting launch orders. He comforted himself with the knowledge that he and his brethren were answering the call of duty, protecting those who were unable to protect themselves.

Edgar whistled in admiration from his place sitting between Joss and Eliza, all three staring through the window of the tram speeding them towards the *Zenith*.

'What a sight,' he said wistfully. 'Looks like a Holy Messenger whispering in the Sleeping King's ear.'

'Or something more infernal,' Hero groused, clearly unimpressed with such an obscene display of wealth. Drake, meanwhile, pressed forward to absorb as much of the view as he could.

'Zadkille said he'd meet us there?' he asked, never looking away. He was practically vibrating with the anticipation of getting to see such a marvellous contraption up close.

'That's right,' Joss replied. Zeke had left a brief note scribbled out on Zadkille Station letterhead which gave a time and place to meet before setting out on their mission but, frustratingly, nothing else.

The tram rumbled into the subterranean labyrinth of the terminus's tunnels. Following the crowd, Joss and the others ascended the station's lavish soapstone stairwell, passed through the palatial main hall and into a spacious conveyance pod, which shot them to the fiftieth floor within the span of a choked gasp. The pod doors opened and a pair of wardens jumped to attention, with a walkway of glass and light running towards the *Zenith* just behind them.

'Papers, please,' the taller of the two said, while his colleague gripped his weapon and scrutinised the youths before him. Edgar was quick to offer up the documentation that had been provided by the Ivory Palace officials. The warden flipped through it all with an air of suspicion before finally relenting and handing the papers back.

No sooner had they cleared the checkpoint than Joss noticed a pair of familiar figures standing at the bottom of the ramp leading up into the *Zenith*'s hull.

'… You have to understand,' Zeke's father was telling his son, his back turned to Joss and the others and his voice carrying down the length of the glass corridor. 'This is a chance that neither of us is likely to see again. I shouldn't need to tell you that the Zadkille name has suffered unprecedented disgrace as a result of all your failings. If I ever have any hope of securing a seat on the Grandmaster Council, this mission must be seen as an unqualified success.'

'Yes, father,' was all Zeke said in response. He looked small in comparison to the armoured figure looming over him, though he seemed to grow ever so slightly taller as he raised his head and asked, 'Though isn't the kingdom's safety what matters most in all this?'

'It's exactly that kind of smart response I don't want to hear. So let me be plain about it; I won't brook any humiliation from you. Not again. And I won't have you costing me what is rightfully mine. You have a duty to repair the damage you've done to the family name. Not to mention setting an example for this rabble of new recruits we've had to take aboard. So stiffen that lip and ride straight, or suffer the consequences. Is that understood?'

The extra inch of height that Zeke had claimed for himself shrunk away.

'Yes, sir.'

'Good,' Lord Xavier replied, marching up the ramp. 'I'll see you on deck.'

Zeke stood alone while the others watched on, stunned by what they had witnessed. All this time Joss had dismissed Zeke's existence as one of mostly untroubled privilege, even if it were tainted at times by a bullying brother or two. The truth seemed far more complicated.

'Should we … should we give him a moment?' asked Drake, just as Zeke caught sight of them all. He slid on a smile like he was lowering a helmet's faceplate into position.

'*Joss!*' he called out with a wave, striding towards them.

'Hi, Zeke,' Joss said. 'Everything alright?'

'Oh, that? That wasn't anything. That was just …' Zeke searched for the words, then cleared his throat as they failed to materialise. 'I'm sorry for having not been around more. It's been hectic since we arrived, particularly with Luther having set off for home.'

'Who's Luther?' Edgar asked.

'Zeke's brother,' replied Joss, quickly returning his attention to Zeke. 'I thought he'd be joining us.' Not that he was all that let down by the news. Based on his encounter with Luther at the Tournament, Joss couldn't think of anyone worse to have along with them. Other than Lord Xavier, it would seem.

'Father sent him home to lead Zadkille Station's defences along with the rest of my brothers. I pity any dragon horde that troubles those four thunderheads,' Zeke said, issuing a dry laugh before adding more brightly, 'I've made sure you've all been provided with the best quarters. We may be on a life-or-death mission but there's no reason we can't do it in comfort.'

'About that,' Joss said as they hiked up the passenger ramp. 'I've invited along a few other people. I hope you don't mind.'

'You have?' asked Zeke. 'Who?'

There was a crash by the conveyance pod, followed by angry shouting. Everyone turned to stare.

'Them.' Joss pointed to Crimson and Cloud, who were being detained by the wardens.

'*Getchyerhandsoffme!*' yelled Crimson, squirming out of the taller warden's grasp.

'You can't just sneak in here and stow away while we're on watch!'

'We weren't sneaking, you boot-polisher! We were invited.'

'And I'm Regent Greel in an entirely convincing disguise,' the warden said. 'Now move along quietly or I'll have no choice but to take you down to the cells and promptly forget all about you.'

'Excuse me, sir, but he's right,' Joss said, stepping forward. 'I'm the one who invited them. We're in need of deckhands and these two fit the bill.'

'They do?' both the wardens and Zeke said simultaneously. Joss shot Zeke a look and he fell silent. The taller warden stared at the group with his mouth open. But then a second conveyance pod arrived, breaking the warden from his stupor.

'Hello,' said the figure stepping from the pod. 'I believe I'm expected.'

'Qorza!' Joss called, pushing past the wardens to hug her. 'You came!'

'Of course,' Qorza replied with a grin, her bronze spectacles flashing brightly. She was dressed as if she were about to take the deck of a seafaring vessel, with her well-worn oilskin coat and knee-high plesiosaurskin boots. A red kerchief was tied around her neck, and over her shoulder was a satchel laden with the equipment of her craft.

'Don't tell me,' Zeke said. 'Another deckhand.'

'Hardly,' replied Joss, sharing a laugh with Qorza. 'This is the ship's ethereon.'

'Ethereon?' Zeke said, confused. 'But we've already got a physician. Two of them. And a communications officer, a navigator, and even a High Attendant. No offense to your friend, but we hardly need an ethereon.'

'We're travelling into hostile territory surrounded by supernatural beasts and the sorcerers who've summoned them … and you don't think we need an ethereon?' Joss scoffed. 'Trust me, Qorza is the most essential crewmember we could hope to have aboard. You'll be counting your blessed crowns to have her.'

'And the deckhands?'

'Think of that as a community service,' Joss told him with a shrug.

Zeke sighed. 'Fine,' he said. 'I'll smooth it over with my father. But you owe me.'

'Deal,' Joss replied. The wardens glowered as Crimson and Cloud strode past them, Crimson sticking his tongue out as they went.

'This way, everyone,' Zeke said as he led the group down the corridor. 'Try not to wander off; I make no promises of being able to find you again if you get lost.'

The group ascended the steel ramp and stepped onto the airship, where they encountered a warren of long, black corridors illuminated by tracks of violet light. Traversing the shadowy maze, they came to a staircase of razor-thin black steps that seemed to float before them.

One by one, they climbed upwards. Joss struggled not to overthink his footing on every step and lose his balance. With great relief he reached the top and entered an expansive deck lined with soaring, purple-tinted windows. A latticework of walkways circled around a bank of glowing illuminators and control panels, each with a crewmember monitoring the readouts.

At the apex of all this advanced engineering was a single, gantry-like platform. The vessel's master and commander stood there, his resplendent set of armour shining under the spotlights and looking as immaculately maintained as the ship that bore his family's emblem. The confrontation he'd had only moments ago with his youngest son looked to have been brushed aside like so much dust from his shoulder.

'I see we have additional crewmembers,' Lord Xavier intoned, dispensing with formal introductions. He stared down at them through the pulsing lights of the illumigram map of Ai that separated them.

'I can explain,' Zeke ventured forward, though his father waved him off.

'That can wait. All hands are present and accounted for; now that the Blade Keeper and his companions have joined us we can get underway. Ensign?'

One of the dozen faces sitting in the glow of the control array looked up. 'Yes, my lord?'

'Weigh anchor, raise thrusters to speed and set course for Nobleseat.'

'Yes, my lord.'

The crew shouted commands and confirmations as klaxons cried out a warning of imminent departure. Joss and the others were forced to shuffle out of the way and watch as the ship detached from its dock and pulled away into the air with a booming metallic *thunk*.

Illustra buzzed beneath them, as frenetic as ever and still indifferent to the threat it faced. Joss wished he could be as oblivious as the cityfolk, but he knew far too much for that. As he watched the metropolis shrink into the distance, he turned his mind to the the voyage ahead and to all those already lost along the way.

He recalled the advice Sur Verity had given him when he'd first set off from Tower Town. *You'll all need to work together if you're to have any chance of success.* He wondered what advice she might bestow if she were here now. But she was gone. Just like his mother and his father, just like Tempest, and just like the rest of the world if he and his friends failed in their mission. Sighing, he turned away from the speck Illustra had become and receded into the shadows of the ship's corridors.

———

She could see only darkness. Hear only the echo of dripping water. Feel only the cold that enveloped her, and the feverish heat that was burning from her shoulder down the length of her arm. Her hands were shackled behind her back, but she was alive. She could work out the rest.

She exhaled, long and steady. Held her breath. Listened. The echo bounced off curved stone. Sitting with her back to the rocky wall, she touched the ground, then ran the heels of her boots along it. Compacted earth, she concluded. Though she'd been fighting unconsciousness from the wound she'd taken, she didn't feel as if she'd been moved very far following her duel with her treacherous lord. There had been no long journey in either a saddle or a wagon, at least not that she could recall. That meant that she was most likely being held in the old crypts beneath Round Shield Ranch. Or whatever was left of it.

Taking another breath, she pulled against her shackles.

Her body felt stiff. The bandage around her left arm was loose and odorous; her wound had been tended to without care.

'You're very fortunate, you know.'

He wasn't there. And then he was. A gloomy light clung to him as he slid from the shadows, barely visible against the blackness. The mask that Sarif had cleaved in two had been restored to hide his face. But she would recognise this traitor no matter what he cowered behind.

'Fortunate?' she scoffed. 'Fortunate indeed. I may have to buy a jackpot ticket with all the fortune I have to spare.'

'If my blade had been an inch to the side, you'd be dead now.'

'If you wanted me dead then I would be. That's not fortune. That's design.' She drew herself up as high as she could muster, leading with her chin. 'What do you want, Malkus?'

He observed her with the detached curiosity of a hunter tracking maimed prey. 'You have a fever.'

'An infected wound will do that.'

'I am ...' he said. There was a lengthy pause. '... Similarly afflicted.'

He took a tentative step forward and his cloak bristled, shedding a clutch of feathers that were as long and sharp as daggers. She eyed them closely, then looked to see him rubbing the wrist of his right hand through his glove, a small gesture that betrayed his otherwise inscrutable appearance.

'Occasionally the fever breaks. And I see myself, garbed as I am. Saying the things I'm saying. Doing the things I'm doing. And a cold sweat pours over me.'

She watched him with muted suspicion. What game was he playing? Whatever it was, she wouldn't give him the satisfaction of joining in. *Better to let him lead where he may and seize whatever opportunity comes from it*, she thought.

'I told Sarif that darkness breeds life. And it's true. From destruction there must inevitably come rejuvenation. Like new growth after a wildfire. Brilliant green saplings in a field of ash, reaching through the smoke towards the light. I believe that. I do.' He tilted his head in contemplation. 'At least … I think I do.'

'Malkus.' She ventured to shuffle forward, wincing as her shackles tugged at her enflamed flesh. 'You don't sound well.'

'I'm not,' he said. He let go of his wrist to scrape a fingertip along the stony jawline of his mask. 'And I haven't been for some time.'

'I can help. All you have to do …' she shuffled forward again. Her chains snarled like gaolers giving orders, keeping her firmly in place. '… Is release me.'

Malkus turned the full weight of his gaze upon her. 'I'll have someone tend to your wound.' He moved back towards the darkness.

'There's nobody left who's qualified for that,' she called out, making him pause. 'You killed them all.'

His cloak and hood blocked him from her view with

the totality of a fortress wall. 'Our numbers grow daily. If we don't yet have the help we require then we will soon enough,' he told her. 'The darkness will keep you company in the meantime.'

The rustling of wings announced his departure. She waited, poised for his sudden return or even a surprise attack. When neither came, she slumped down and rested her hot flesh against the cold stone wall.

With only the distant dripping of water to break the silence of the surrounding void, Sur Verity removed the two long black feathers she had palmed from Malkus's cloak, pressed them to the lock on her shackles, and set to work.

—

CHAPTER TEN

A MAN-MADE MOUNTAIN

BEFORE taking Joss and the others to their rooms, Zeke gave them a guided tour of the vast ship, leading them from the bridge down a network of staircases to what he called the observation deck. With its padded armchairs, blackwood tables and discreet drinks station, the stately room could easily have been mistaken for an aristocrat's salon. Zeke had described the *Zenith* as a livestock freighter, but Joss was beginning to realise it was far more of a pleasure vessel. It even had an open-air balcony, which Zeke ushered them onto.

'Always a good place to retreat if you need to clear your head with a breath of unrecycled oxygen,' Zeke told the group. From there he showed them the way to the galley and adjoining mess hall. A bank of roasting cabinets lined the galley wall, each one glowing with a charred entelodont carcass rotating inside, while the table opposite overflowed with bowls of thunderfruit and lizardberries. Joss heard Edgar's stomach snarl at the sight.

'Dinner's served at sundown and the prize cuts go fast, so don't be tardy,' Zeke told them as they descended into the ship's bowels, where the group's mounts were stabled.

'Hi, boy,' Joss said to Azof as the raptor bounded over to him. 'Are they treating you well?'

Azof clacked his tongue and snuffled at Joss's ear as Joss cast a close eye over the fleet of mechanoids and the single fieldserv in charge of running the livestock pens. There were even more hands over in the hangar, which Joss could see through the adjoining blast doors. Jet-cycles, hoverwagons and other vehicles were being tended to by a mob of technicians and their meks, with the *Fat Lot of Good* holding chief position.

'We can load the mounts into the *Fat Lot*'s hold in under a minute if we need to make landfall and there's no anchorage for the *Zenith*,' Zeke noted proudly.

The remaining tour became a whirlwind trip through the laundry facilities, the library and the illumie theatre. That left only the quarterdeck, where Zeke led them all to their rooms. Joss's was the last door at the end of the hall, giving him and Zeke the chance to talk alone.

'Here's your pass to get into your room and around the ship,' Zeke told him as he handed him a black disc. 'Grab some grub and then make sure to get some rest. We should be in Nobleseat by early morning.'

'Thanks, Zeke.'

'No trouble.' Zeke beamed at him. 'Despite everything we're up against, it's good that we're able to face it together.'

Zeke turned to leave, but Joss stopped him. 'You know – all this?' Joss waved his hand at the opulent surroundings. 'Growing up with all of this would have messed with my head, too.'

Zeke looked at him questioningly. 'It's not how most people live, I know.'

'It would probably mess me up even more if I ever decided to leave it all behind,' added Joss.

Zeke's confusion seemed to grow deeper. 'Get some rest,' he said, and ventured up the hallway and out of sight.

———

Bright green pastures surged and dipped like rolling seas, divided by rows of trees so thick they could be mistaken for rampart walls. Farmhouses and barns were scattered among a seemingly endless array of orchards, pastures and wheat fields. Small villages clustered where roads merged.

Joss watched the unfolding landscape of the southern Counties from the elevated vantage point of the *Zenith*'s bridge, where Zeke had invited him and the others to see the final approach to Nobleseat. Lord Xavier was positioned at his command post as if he'd never left. He paid them scant attention as he barked commands at his crew, all while the woods outside the window grew thicker. A single road cut through the dense foliage, curling towards a walled city that sat on the horizon like a man-made mountain.

'Nobleseat, this is the *Zenith* of Zadkille Station,' the ship's communications officer said into his microphone. 'Requesting access to your airspace for approach to Noble House.'

There was a long pause filled only with static, during which Joss gave Zeke a questioning look.

'Just a formality,' Zeke explained. 'They shouldn't be too much longer.'

The static continued, until at last a voice faded in from the ether. '*Negative*, Zenith. *All outside aircraft have been prohibited from entry, per Count Barus's orders.*'

Confusion snaked its way through the flight deck, with Lord Xavier frowning the hardest.

'Please repeat, Nobleseat?'

'*Permission denied,*' the voice on the line fired back. '*If you wish to visit Noble House, you must do so on foot.*'

———

Zeke hadn't lied when he'd bragged about how efficiently the mounts could be mustered onto the *Fat Lot of Good.* Under Lord Xavier's strict supervision the animals had all been loaded in a matter of seconds, with his lordship having permitted Joss and the rest of the prentices to be included in the envoy to Noble House: the official residence of Count Barus.

'Perhaps you and your friends will have the same luck convincing the count as you did Regent Greel,' Xavier said as the *Zenith* crew prepared his jet-cycle for deployment. It was the largest machine of its kind Joss had ever seen: a muscular monster of galvanised steel and glistening pistons assembled around a leather-clad bucket seat from which Lord Xavier could operate the controls. It growled like a sabretooth as it hovered into the *Fat Lot*'s cargo hold.

'*Ezekiel!*' Lord Xavier shouted from within. 'Get this contraption of yours moving or get out of the damned way.'

Zeke grimaced at his lordship's caustic tone.

'Excuse me,' he said to Joss and the others, scurrying off. Joss watched him with a growing sense of concern, though he kept his thoughts to himself as he boarded the ship and found his spot in the hull.

With his father's rebuke still ringing, Zeke worked quickly to get the *Fat Lot* started. A quick relay with the *Zenith*'s flight crew and the hangar bay doors slid open, sucking all the air out of the hull in a riotous whirlwind and allowing the ship's departure.

The voyage to the ground was relatively painless, though between Lord Xavier, Zeke, Joss, Drake, Hero, Edgar, Eliza, the *Zenith* crewmembers who'd accompanied them and all of their mounts, there was very little room. Joss kept his arms tucked in close and his breath held tight as they made their descent one lurching foot at a time, the wind hammering the hull as they went.

'Thank His Merciful Majesty!' Edgar exclaimed as they finally touched down. His face had taken on a distinctly green tinge during the short journey, which lingered as they saddled up and began the ride into Nobleseat.

Joss had been struck by the Counties' verdant beauty from above, and it was all the more beatific on the ground. Diamonds of light skimmed the surface of the crushed sandstone road, cast by the sunshine filtering through the trees. The air was as crisp as chilled cider. In the distance, Joss could see strawberry fields that seemed to go on forever, surrounded by blueberry hills and crystal waters.

But for all this abundant beauty, the valleys and farms were eerily quiet. There were no labourers in the fields, no other travellers journeying down the highway. Looking for a way to fill the silence, Joss drew Azof up alongside Zeke, who was staring off across the strawberry patches.

'That was a little intense with your father back there,' Joss said, startling him from his daze. 'Are you alright?'

'Oh – that?' Zeke replied. He slid a rubbery, lopsided grin onto his face. 'That was nothing. The words of his song cut deeper than the edge of his sword. Really. Don't worry about it. But thanks for asking.'

Within the hour they were at the city gates. A large drum tower built of stone and flint served as the main entrance, with the leafy green flag of the Counties flying at the centre of its parapet. Joss noted the absence of the Kingdom of Ai's flag. He also noted several regiments of city wardens.

At least, Joss assumed they were wardens. The figures who lined the city gates weren't dressed as would be expected, with uniforms of boiled leather in place of plate armour and chainmail. Their faces were obscured with scarves that had been pulled up high and hoods that had been drawn low, and they were wrapped up in cloaks of green, brown and grey. They kept a close hold of their shortswords and longbows as they watched the party approach.

'I see that the Counties remain even bigger traditionalists than the most backward paladero orders,' Lord Xavier observed from the safety of his saddle, failing to notice the additional figures that lurked in the surrounding greenery. Joss watched the moving shapes with growing concern. He was about to say something when the portcullis cranked up and the city gates opened, and a rider on a white-feathered physornis cantered out.

His cloak was a rich shade of emerald, pinned at the collar with a pewter badge depicting an arrow piercing a cleaved apple. He had the bristly muzzle of a traveller who'd not seen the whetted edge of a razor in over a fortnight, and a tangle of salt-and-cinnamon curls that had been pulled into the shape of a bread roll atop his head.

'Good day and welcome,' he said with a nod, leather-gloved hands loosely holding his bird's reins. 'I'm Lieutenant Tyne of His Grace's Ranjer Corps. You're the crew of the *Zenith*, I presume? Welcome to Nobleseat. We've been expecting you.'

CHAPTER ELEVEN

—

A CREATURE OF
CHILLING INTENT

'I'M Lord Xavier of Zadkille Station,' his lordship declared to Lieutenant Tyne, his jet-cycle purring. 'Sent on behalf of His Excellency the Regent Augustus Greel to charge Count Barus in the defence of his kingdom; a duty of the utmost urgency, and not to be hindered by outlandish airspace restrictions or excessive formalities.'

Joss almost fell out of his saddle. He looked at Zeke for confirmation of what he'd just heard, and received a shrug in response.

'I see,' Lieutenant Tyne soberly replied, giving nothing away. 'If you'll all kindly follow me …'

The lieutenant turned his mount and led the visiting party through the looming gates.

The city inside was a humble collection of old stone, organised into curving cobbled streets. Jewellers, apothecaries, haberdasheries and a modest High Chamber sat jugular to jowl with hotels, taverns and greengrocers; the guests, customers and even shopkeepers were all spilling out onto sidewalks crowded with tents and wagons. Clearly the farmers who'd vacated their lands had set up camp within the city walls, with many of them bartering their produce in place of rent. Cottages were mashed in around the narrow storefronts, which ran along an incline that grew steeper with every step. The crowds petered out the higher Joss and the others climbed.

'Patience, boy. We're almost there,' Joss told Azof as he offered the raptor a comforting pat. He'd expected that their strange convoy might draw curious glances from the locals, but they all looked far too preoccupied to pay them any mind.

Gradually the cottages gave way to a host of stately terrace homes, each one taller and more elegant than the last, until finally the party came to what could only be Noble House. Garbed almost entirely in ivy, all that could be seen of the grand old building beneath the greenery was the many windows that gleamed from between the leaves like brass buttons on a finely tailored coat. The house sat several stories high behind a spiked iron fence that rivalled the city gates in size, patrolled by twice as many ranjers as there'd been upon the ramparts.

Lieutenant Tyne's presence meant they were waved through the gates, prompting a host of footmen to tend to the guests. Joss handed Azof's reins to a butler as everyone dismounted, while Lord Xavier sized up the manor with no small hint of disdain.

Oak doors as foreboding as a drawbridge made a groaning protest as they opened, revealing a hallway of polished limestone, with green-and-gold tapestries blanketing flocked green wallpaper and a lush green rug that beckoned the visitors inward. Ranjers lined the walls and looked down from the upper floors of the atrium entrance. In the surrounding woodlands their forces had been practically invisible. In all this sizeable splendour they looked as conspicuous as a feathered thunder lizard in full intimidation display.

'His Grace is practising his archery,' Lieutenant Tyne explained as he led them to the acres of coiffed turf and spurting fountains that served as the house's gardens.

A man resembling a stack of apple crates draped in crushed green velvet was standing in the centre of the lawn firing golden arrows at a moving target. Every arrow he loosed was met by his roving bullseye, which was being wielded by a footman who seemed to have a wealth of experience in making sure the archer met his mark.

Another regiment of ranjers was assembled along the walkways of the garden wall and up onto the manor rooftop, where a host of stone Messenger statues gazed vacantly at the horizon. The regiment kept a close eye on the count, while Joss and his fellow visitors gathered behind him.

'You stand in the presence of Count Barus the 13th,'

Lieutenant Tyne proclaimed. 'Keeper and Protector of His Majesty's Counties, Patron and Provider to all of the Kingdom of Ai's hungry masses, Guardian of the Great Green.'

Joss exchanged a sceptical look with Drake and Hero at the laundry list of ostentatious titles, while the lieutenant spun towards his master and dropped to one knee.

'Your Grace,' he said. 'May I present Lord Xavier of Zadkille Station and the crew of the *Zenith*, sent on behalf of Regent Greel.'

The count did not acknowledge the lieutenant's presence in the slightest. He was far too preoccupied with sighting his target, lining up his shot, and letting his arrow fly. It strayed so far from the mark that Joss was sure it would hit the footman in the ear, but with whiplash speed the target was raised just in time to make for a perfect shot.

'*Ha!*' the count exclaimed to himself, wiggling in satisfaction. Handing off his longbow to the closest servant, he replaced it with a cartridge-loaded, pump action crossbow. A drop of sweat rolled down the forehead of the footman holding the target.

Count Barus cast a momentary glance at the group assembled behind him.

'From Thunder Realm, are you?' he asked, loosing a volley of crossbow bolts that landed with a staccato thrum. The footman exhaled.

'Yes, Your Grace,' said Lord Xavier. 'For the most part.'

'Our ranjer corps has been having a blasted time

protecting our borders from the beasts your lot unleashed.'

'That's precisely why we're here,' Lord Xavier replied. 'A summit was held in Illustra. We've been tasked with rallying all our forces at Tower Town. From there we'll be mounting an offensive against the surrounding enemy camps. The Ivory Palace has attempted to inform you of this but there seems to have been signal interference blocking the transmission.'

At last, Count Barus turned his full gaze on the visiting party. His eyes were as green as pond scum and just as cold. 'We received those communiques.'

Lord Xavier stared at him, aghast. 'And you ignored them?'

'We've been far too occupied safeguarding our territory to busy ourselves with needless chatter,' said the count as he levelled his crossbow at the target and took another shot. The jewels he was wearing twinkled in the sun's last rays. Joss could only assume the precious stones came from the mines that spotted the Counties' coastline: only the secondary source of the region's considerable wealth. 'If the Counties fall, the Kingdom starves. You thunderfolk have never appreciated the fact that people can't survive on lizard meat alone. Not that there'll be much of that to go around with Thunder Realm at the centre of all this strife. Best that we secure our fields and farmlands while they still stand.'

Lord Xavier's scowl grew acutely arched. 'I see many of your forces standing here. In fact, I've seen more of them in this garden than I did anywhere else throughout the Counties.'

Count Barus lowered his weapon. 'They're ranjers,' he said, his face twisting in an unctuous smile of triumph. 'It's their job not to be seen.'

Joss felt something tighten inside him, like a trigger being pulled. 'Then they've been doing a cussing good job at it,' he snapped. 'All while the kingdom burns.'

Barus rocked back on his heel. 'And who is this insolent sprout?' he demanded.

Lieutenant Tyne opened his mouth to give an answer he couldn't possibly supply. Joss decided to save him the trouble. 'I'm Josiah Sarif. Blade Keeper and Prentice to Sur Verity Wolfsbane, who gave her life fighting to protect the kingdom from the darkness that's coming for all of us. And when it finally arrives here, as it will, it'll take more than a golden arrow or a treasure trove of gemstones to keep it at bay.'

Count Barus narrowed his eyes. Then with an angry flourish he spun around and shot the last of his crossbow bolts at the target. The footman let out a whimper as his shoulder was grazed.

'Stay still, Worthington!' the count barked at him while reloading his weapon. 'You're not made of tissue paper, you won't tear!'

Count Barus scrunched his eyes shut, sucked in a lungful of air, then turned his attention back to Lord Xavier. 'It really is a shame you've travelled all this way,

Zadkille,' he said, while the heat that had fired Joss up inside now chilled to something more sickly. 'With our forces stretched so thin, we shan't be joining your little rally at Tower Town. Give my fond regards to my cousin, should you see him.'

'Your cousin?' Hero repeated, expressing the surprise running through the rest of the party.

'Mayor Bovis. Distant relation. Thrice removed, if I remember my family tree correctly. But he's a cousin nonetheless.' Count Barus kept his eyes locked firmly on Lord Xavier. 'You'll find there's very few people throughout this kingdom with whom I'm not well acquainted. And you'd do best to remember that before you ever again consider bursting into my lands and my home to have your novices accuse me of dereliction of duty. Do I make myself clear, Lord Xavier?'

'Transparent,' Lord Xavier replied, shaking with the effort of containing himself. 'Your Grace.'

'Lieutenant Tyne will show you out,' the count concluded. The *whump* of his crossbow bolts trailed the group as they returned to the house.

'So … that could have gone better,' said Eliza.

'He didn't fill any of us with crossbow bolts. I'm calling that a win,' Zeke replied.

'I shouldn't have said anything,' Joss fretted as they weaved their way through the manor. 'I should have kept my mouth shut.'

'Indeed,' Lord Xavier said, his tone far less irate than

Joss would have expected. 'Not that I believe it would have made any difference.'

Joss blinked. 'My lord?'

'Barus has a reputation for being petty and vain. Not to mention cowardly. This was always going to be a fool's errand,' he explained. 'Though with all that's at stake, we had to try.'

Joss mulled over this revelation all the way to the front door, feeling both confounded and oddly comforted by it.

'Farewell,' Lieutenant Tyne said. 'May His Majesty keep you.'

Outside, the weather had taken a dramatic turn. The clouds had blackened with such intensity that the day could be mistaken for night, while the wind bayed like a ravenous beast.

'Something's wrong,' Drake observed, searching the air as if it might provide answers.

'Very wrong,' Hero replied. She pointed at the ripple of clouds directly above them that was swirling faster and faster into a roiling vortex. Joss barely had time to recognise the ominous sign before a creature of chilling intent was spat from the rift. It spun for a moment like a missile launched from a catapult, then splayed its wings wide. It stared at Nobleseat with scorching red eyes as the townspeople below screamed in terror.

The dragon inhaled a long and crackling breath, held it, then rained fire down on everyone and everything below.

CHAPTER TWELVE

A TERRIBLE PURPOSE

'ZENITH, open fire! I repeat: open fire!' Lord Xavier shouted into his comm-link. 'Bring that kingforsaken beast to bear!'

Joss watched as the airship turned to starboard. The dragon failed to notice as it focused its fury on the township. The hotel, the haberdashery, even the High Chamber all fell under the creature's flames, lighting up as if they were made of kindling. Beside him, Azof trilled in panic while Joss's brethren bunched together.

'We have to do something,' Drake said, unslinging his family's Icefire spear from over his shoulder.

'I'm open to suggestions,' Hero replied.

'We are doing something,' said Zeke, pointing to the *Zenith*. 'Look!'

The ship had repositioned itself, ready for attack, with

more than a dozen cannons jutting from the hatches on its starboard side and all of them pointed at the dragon. They fired, lighting up the sky even more brightly than the monster's flames. But the dragon was too fast, wheeling out of the line of fire. Rather than hitting their target, the cannons instead hammered the town. Whole buildings were torn apart in violent explosions.

'*No!*' Lord Xavier shouted into his comm-link. 'Cease fire! *Cease fire!*'

The *Zenith*'s cannons fell silent. The cries from the town rose. The dragon, satisfied with the destruction, soared back up towards the portal and out of the ship's firing range.

'What shall we do, my lord?' asked the *Zenith* crewmember at Lord Xavier's side.

'Barus has his ranjers to protect him should the dragon attack again. Our duty is to the people. Let's move.'

The *Zenith* crew fell in line behind their lord, riding for the town their ship had fired upon. Joss kept a close eye on the dragon, which circled around as if to dive again. Certain it was about to make its move, he grabbed Zeke's arm to keep him from following his father.

'We need to stop that thing,' he said as Drake, Hero, Edgar and Eliza crowded in around them. 'Your father's underestimating just how much of a threat that dragon poses – you know he is.'

Joss thought Zeke might bristle at his words, but instead he simply nodded. 'What do you suggest?' he asked.

Joss looked at the rest of his brethren. 'Edgar, you and Eliza should go help Lord Xavier and the ranjers put out those fires and rescue anyone trapped in the destruction. Hero, Ganymede, Zeke and I are going to – we're –'

'We're what?' asked Drake.

Joss took a steadying breath. 'We're going to fight a dragon.'

The dragon roared and dove down, flying with terrible purpose towards Noble House. With one stroke of its wings it hurtled straight past the high iron fence and into the manor grounds.

'It's going for Barus,' Joss said. 'We have to stop it!'

'Do we?' asked Zeke. 'Better Barus than the not-horribly-unpleasant townsfolk, surely?'

'If we let it kill Barus then we can kiss away ever getting help from the Counties,' Hero said.

'Not to mention it being the right thing to do,' added Drake.

'That too,' Hero shrugged.

Together they charged for the manor. The ranjers who'd been guarding the entrance had either taken off to fight the fires or run after the dragon, leaving the gates wide open. Barging through them, Joss and the others followed the sounds of havoc to the back of the house, where the sprawling gardens were burning. Ranjers were scattered everywhere, broken and bleeding, with Lieutenant Tyne unconscious by Barus's side. The count himself was splayed out on the lawn with his crossbow just out of reach, shrieking as the dragon stalked towards him with both nostrils smoking.

'So we've found the dragon,' Zeke said. 'Now what?'

Joss took a quick inventory of their surroundings, trying to pinpoint something – *anything* – that they could turn to their advantage. 'There!' he shouted, pointing to the Messenger statues on the rooftop.

'I don't know if prayer's the answer right now, Joss,' Zeke told him.

'We'll lure the dragon over to the house and drop that centre statue on its head.'

'You really think that will work?' asked Hero.

'We don't have a wealth of other options right now, do we?' Joss said, the semblance of a plan forming in his head. 'Ganymede! Hero! You two circle around and get Barus to safety. Zeke and I will take care of the dragon.'

'Wait, what?' said Zeke, stunned.

'Good luck,' Drake told them both, brandishing his spear as he turned to Hero. 'Follow me.'

'No. You follow me,' she said, before slipping away into the bushes. Drake shrugged, then joined her.

'If you head up to the roof I'll lure the dragon over,' Joss told Zeke, who shot him a no-nonsense look.

'You mean you'll be bait.'

'If that's what it takes.'

'No,' Zeke told him. 'You go to the roof. I'll lure the dragon.'

'Zeke, we don't have time to argue about this. You're

stronger than me, you should go knock the statue down.'

'You're right – we don't have time to argue about this. So you better start running for the roof because I've got a dragon to lure. Now go!'

Zeke pushed Joss to get him moving, and Joss raced for the stairwell inside the manor. He vaulted up the steps three at a time, climbing higher and higher around the curving bannister, his breath coming in ragged bursts as he heaved through the doorway onto the rooftop.

'Hey! Ugly! *Over here!*' Zeke shouted from below. 'Yes, *you* – I'm talking to you! The overgrown lizard-bird with bad breath and an even worse skin condition! Why are you bothering with that lump of old gristle when you could have something fresh and juicy!'

Joss crouched low and scurried over to the edge of the building to steal a glimpse of the dragon. The beast was just as intimidating at this height, its flesh like spiked armour and its face like a steel trap. It was staring in angry confusion at Zeke, who was directly beneath the statue's target zone. His shock rifle was in his hands and he was firing wildly into the air, stealing the dragon's attention away from Barus as Drake and Hero crept around the edge of the garden towards the quivering old man.

'Come on, you scaly-faced excuse for an overgrown salamander! Come and get me!'

Knowing he had precious little time to act, Joss put all his strength into pushing the statue. It refused to budge. Cursing, he drew the Champion's Blade and began hacking at the base, all while Zeke kept shouting at the dragon below.

'You dented can of carbonated crud! You pus-filled parasite sucking on a kraken's egg sack! You – you – you absolutely terrifying nightmare that's getting closer by the moment!'

Again, Joss glanced over the edge of the building. The dragon was stalking towards Zeke with burning eyes and a growl on its curled lip, while Drake and Hero snuck up behind it, grabbed the count and led him to safety.

'I tried. I really did try,' Zeke was saying now, the words tumbling out of him like coins from a torn purse. 'But you are huge and you are horrifying and I no longer have anywhere to run, so all I can say is *JOSSSS! NOW, JOSS! NOW! NOW NOW NOW!*'

Joss shoved at the statue. It wobbled. He slammed his shoulder against it. It teetered. The dragon lumbered over to Zeke. Raised itself to its full height. Stared at him with all its ravenous fury.

'*JOSS! NOWWWWW!*'

Joss threw every ounce of his strength against the statue. With a crunch it snapped loose, the Messenger flying down as if it had been expelled from the stars above. It landed right on target with a bone-shattering squelch. There was a tense moment of silence as Joss scrambled to see exactly what had happened.

Zeke was staring in complete bewilderment at the creature, looking as if he'd just shaken hands with death itself. But then he threw up his arms in victory and let out a long and triumphant, '*Wooooohooooo!*'

Joss turned and ran. He rocketed down the stairwell and into the gardens to find the dragon pinned beneath the statue, its wings beating weakly against the ground. He couldn't tell if it was knocked senseless, mortally wounded, or bluffing. With the Champion's Blade still in hand, he edged towards the creature.

'Joss – *don't!*' he heard Zeke call out, just as the dragon surged forward with its mouth wide open, exposing a simmering firepit at the back of its throat. Scrunching his eyes shut and baring his teeth, Joss stabbed the beast with his sword. The Champion's Blade caught the dragon's neck, provoking a sharp and startled cry. Joss pushed forward, driving the blade deeper into the scaly flesh. Ash and brimstone spurted from the creature's wound like an erupting volcano, choking the air with soot.

Coughing through the smoke, Joss struggled to pull his sword free as the dragon thrashed and screeched before him. He had just pried it loose when the beast crashed forward, forcing him to tumble away from its gnashing fangs and scrabbling claws. With sweat stinging his eyes and soot staining his face, Joss watched the dragon bleed a dark plume of smoke and rest its head on the garden's last patch of green grass. He felt a profound stab of guilt watching such an extraordinary creature meet such an untimely end and, as the dragon's scales blackened and it crumbled into ash, Joss wondered if he could have found some other way to stop its rampage.

'Joss, are you hurt?' Zeke huffed as he skidded to a stop at Joss's side. 'That thing almost killed you!'

'Almost killed you too,' Joss noted dimly as he watched the dragon disintegrate, while the portal it had arrived through simultaneously began to shrink. Within moments, both were gone. It almost seemed as if they'd never been there – except for the city left burning to the ground.

'Nobleseat,' Count Barus croaked as Drake and Hero carried him from the cinders of his garden, his face dirtied and distraught. 'Please – you must save it!'

The prentices looked at each other with a shared resolve. Leaving the count at the doorway of his ruined manor, Joss and his brethren ran for the township to offer whatever aid they could.

—

CHAPTER THIRTEEN

A SACRED WEAPON
& A CURSED OBJECT

I T was sunset before the last of the fires was extinguished. The ranjers and the *Zenith* crew worked together, pulling survivors from the wreckage under the supervision of Lord Xavier, with Joss and his brethren helping right up until Lieutenant Tyne approached them. The head wound that had left him unconscious during the dragon attack had been bandaged up, though blood was still weeping through the dressing.

'His Grace would like a word,' he said, sounding far more deferential than he'd initially been. 'With all of you.'

'Understood,' replied Lord Xavier, despite the fact that the lieutenant had addressed Joss. His lordship was quick to join them as Tyne led them up the hill to a small pavilion that had been erected outside the gates of Noble House, overlooking what was left of the town. Count Barus was standing beneath the canopy with his hands folded in front of him, full of solemn dignity.

'You've done a fine deed here today,' he told the prentices as they lined up before him. 'We would not have survived this attack if it weren't for your intervention. Particularly that of your young Blade Keeper. We owe you a great debt.'

'So then you'll send your forces to Tower Town?' asked Lord Xavier, seizing the opportunity so readily that Joss could only admire his boldness.

The count harrumphed, puffed out his chest and stuck out his bottom lip. 'Now that we know for certain that we're in the direct line of attack? I sincerely think not.'

Joss slumped, as did his brethren. All this and it was still for naught.

'But,' Barus continued. 'We could possibly spare a regiment of archers.'

'Archers?' said Lord Xavier.

'I'll have them march for Tower Town once they've finished in the rescue efforts. And in the meantime Lieutenant Tyne will accompany you on your journey to testify on behalf of the Counties of what was witnessed here. Does that sound equitable?' Barus concluded.

'Yes, Your Grace,' Lord Xavier replied. 'And thank you.'

———

'A single regiment of archers!' Lord Xavier raged as they walked back down the hill. 'Barus's generosity knows no bounds beyond his shrivelled pit of a heart.'

'Help is help, though. Isn't it?' asked Zeke. 'Not to mention the fact that Joss slayed a dragon! Now we know they're vulnerable to attack. We can defeat them if ...' Zeke trailed off as he caught a look from his father that would make even a tyrannosaur twitch.

'Get the transport ready,' Lord Xavier told his son. 'I want to take off the moment Lieutenant Tyne drags himself back down from Noble House. The sooner we're away from this fetid compost heap, the better.'

His lordship stomped away, leaving the prentices blinking at each other.

'So glad I said something,' Zeke muttered, seeming to take some comfort in the hand Joss laid on his shoulder as they filed onto the *Fat Lot of Good*.

'I haven't had the chance to say it until now, but what you did really was brave,' Edgar told Joss, Drake and Hero while helping them secure their animals in their pens.

'No braver than what you and Eliza did to help the people caught in the attack,' Drake replied.

'Hardly the same as slaying a dragon,' Eliza said. 'Did it really disintegrate?'

'It did, strangely enough.'

Edgar scrunched his face in confusion. 'Do they usually do that?'

'Can't say I'm a dragon expert,' Joss shrugged. 'But I know someone who might have an idea.'

Once Lieutenant Tyne had joined them and they had returned to the *Zenith*, Joss and his brethren searched out

Qorza. They found her in the labyrinth she had made of her quarters, settled beside a wall of books.

'I watched it all from the observation deck, though I lost sight once the dragon entered the manor grounds,' she told them without looking up from the dusty tome laid across her lap, full of detailed diagrams of dragons. Two more sat before her, opened to chapters on interdimensional portals. 'The boatswain said you'd managed to trap it and that it blew up after being stabbed?'

'More like tumbled apart into ash,' Joss replied.

'Fascinating! Did you collect any samples?'

'Sorry, no. It all scattered to the wind.'

Qorza's face fell. 'Pity. Though an even greater pity that you weren't able to bring the creature back alive.'

Joss felt another slash of guilt cut through him. 'It was the Champion's Blade that made it disintegrate,' he told her, unsheathing it. 'Because it's made of aurum, right?'

'That's a distinct possibility,' she said.

Offering her the sword, Joss watched as she stood, took the weapon over to a small desk in the corner of the room, and adjusted the table lamp to shine off the golden blade. The others bundled in behind her while she carefully ran a thumb along the blade's edge, collecting the specks of dust that had managed to cling there. She dropped the tiny collection into a jar.

'Maybe even quite likely,' she concluded.

Joss's eyes widened. His stomach tightened, his heartbeat hastened. All this time – since the discovery of his mother's journal in the ruins of Daheed – he had been living in uncertainty. Now, here was proof. Here was his destiny. 'So then it is a *vaartan rhazh*,' he breathed.

'A what?' asked Drake.

Joss stiffened. He hadn't meant to say anything about the Rakashi Revelations to the others. Not yet, at least. It had just slipped out. But now that the brontosaur was halfway out of the barn, who was he to try stuffing it back in?

'A *vaartan rhazh*,' he repeated, speaking calmly while feeling anything but. 'A sacred weapon referenced in a prophecy that my mother had been translating just before she … just before the Destruction of Daheed.'

'What kind of prophecy?' Hero asked.

'They're called the Rakashi Revelations,' Joss continued, wondering how much to divulge, how much would make him sound like a madman. 'Qorza's been helping me translate them. They talk about a, well, a promised one, I guess. Someone who's meant to use a sacred weapon at a time of great darkness to save the world. The sacred weapon is called a *vaartan rhazh*, which translates as …'

Drake jumped in where Joss hesitated. 'Champion's Blade.'

Joss blinked. 'How did you know?'

'I tied the threads together,' Drake replied. 'You think the Champion's Blade is a sacred weapon that will save the world?'

'And you're the one who's going to wield it?' asked Hero.

Already Joss could feel his conviction waning. 'I don't know,' he replied. 'Maybe.'

An awkward silence fell as they considered the proposition. Joss shuffled his feet, cleared his throat, tried not stare at everyone to gauge just how arrogant or crazy they thought he was. But, unable to help himself, he looked up at them. Hero was as inscrutable as ever behind her goggles. Drake was tapping his chin in quiet contemplation, while Eliza chewed her cheek and Zeke furrowed his brow. The only one who Joss thought might even halfway believe him was Edgar, who was gazing at him in wide-eyed wonder.

'It's been a long and frankly incredible day,' said Qorza, mercifully breaking the silence. 'What say we continue this conversation in the mess over a heaping of hashed potatoes? And we'll raise a toast to the gallant warriors who won the first victory in the battles to come.'

Everyone allowed themselves a moment of pride to cheer at Qorza's words. As they filed down the corridor, Joss took the chance to pick her brain just a bit more.

'There's something that still worries me,' he said to her in a hushed tone. 'It didn't seem to occur to Count Barus. Not that he let on, at least. But how can it be a coincidence that the Counties came under attack at the exact time that we visited them? And not from a full force but from a single dragon that feels as if it's been submitted as evidence of the threat we're facing?'

'You think it was staged?' asked Drake, giving away the

fact that he'd been eavesdropping. 'By who?'

Entering the mess hall, Joss saw a now calm Lord Xavier at the far end, giving Lieutenant Tyne a tour of the ship. His lordship was going into great detail about the craft's top speed when he noticed Joss and the others approaching.

'Ah – Sarif. I should have added my congratulations to Count Barus's earlier. Commendable effort today.'

'Thank you, my lord.'

'We'll have to convey your exploits to the lord mayor of Dragon's Toe.'

'Dragon's Toe, my lord?'

'Our next stop. Tomorrow. Sunrise. Make sure you get your rest. There may yet be more dragons to slay.' Lord Xavier gave a frosty smile, signifying that he was joking. Lieutenant Tyne chuckled politely.

'Enjoy your meal, everyone,' his lordship concluded, leading Lieutenant Tyne away.

Joss thought again of Lord Malkus and Sur Blaek and their treachery. 'If there's one thing dealing with the Court of Thralls has taught me,' he muttered in answer to Drake's question while the others took their seats, 'it's that their agents can be lurking anywhere.'

———

The feathers from Thrall's coat had splintered and worn away inside the locks of Sur Verity's shackles, and her bonds felt no weaker for the effort. Worse, her infection had spread. Her skin was burning up, her brow dripping with sweat, her head rolling around her shoulders like a boulder let loose in a gorge. Her time was running out, as were her options. The darkness was closing in.

A whisper of movement caught her attention, and with bleary vision she scanned the shadows for its source. Malkus materialised as he had before, though now he looked noticeably different. His hood was drawn over his head but his stone mask was absent, exposing a forbidding face.

He was rubbing his wrist again, this time with bare hands. Without his gloves on, Sur Verity could see that a string of beads was wrapped three times around his wrist, and at its end there dangled a golden pendant in the shape of the sun. Malkus was so fixated on it that he seemed to have stumbled into Sur Verity's confines by mistake. He remained in preoccupied silence for so long that it was left to Sur Verity to speak up.

'I was starting to wonder if your face even remained beneath that grotesque mask, or if it had been wholly consumed.'

Her insult didn't seem to register. Malkus continued to stare at the sun-shaped pendant and fret over the dozens of delicate beads keeping it in place. And then, just as she was giving up any thought that he might actually say something, he spoke.

'I was given this the day the world changed.' Still he stared at the small golden disc, the clicking of the beads becoming their own kind of music. 'It was meant to be for safekeeping, to be passed on when the time was right. That time came and went and yet I kept it for myself. I don't know why. Perhaps as a memento of the last time in my life when I felt whole and clear and uncorrupted. A time without hidden intent or dark purpose.'

He let go of his wrist, folded his hands and almost sighed. 'What a cursed object it is.'

He looked at Sur Verity for the first time, his gaze as threatening as a drawn sword. When he spoke, the introspection that had clouded his voice only a moment ago had gone. 'A sacrifice has been demanded.'

Sur Verity froze. 'Of what kind?'

'The kind that ends in blood and revelation.' He let the warning sit with her, allowing her to silently study it. 'I hope, when the time comes, you can find it in yourself to trust me,' he said. 'Do you understand?'

Sur Verity considered bluffing, but her mind was too fevered. 'Not in the least,' she admitted.

Malkus's feather cloak rippled. 'You will.'

He faded from the room as quietly as he had arrived, the light from his pendant still spotting Sur Verity's eyes as she hunkered in the darkness and waited.

CHAPTER FOURTEEN

A GOOD WAY TO END UP DEAD

THE Chief Warden of Dragon's Toe was not an accommodating man. He met Joss and the rest of Regent Greel's party at the subterranean city's gates with his young steward in tow, and was curt in both his manner and his message.

'We've all heard what happened in Nobleseat. And Nobleseat's further from Round Shield Ranch than we are. No way are we going to open ourselves up to attack by sending even a single member of our forces.'

'Your regent has summoned you. Would you deny him?' Lord Xavier said, matching the Chief Warden's blunt tone.

'Let him summon all he wants. And when the smoke clears we'll see if it's the same regent sitting pretty in Illustra. If there's any palace left standing,' the Chief

Warden grizzled as he turned his back on the group. 'Ormar, with me.'

The redheaded steward stooped in apology then ran after his master. Dragon Toe's taloned gates roared shut the moment the pair passed through them. The handful of wardens left at the gatehouse watched Joss and the others with an indifference bordering on outright hostility.

'We have our answer,' said Lord Xavier, eyeballing the wardens until they had no choice but to avert their gaze. 'Let's go.'

The envoy rode their mounts back down the ridge to the *Fat Lot*, while the *Zenith* held its position circling high overhead. A bleak mood settled over the party members like silt. Joss wondered how anyone could dare defy a direct order from the Regent himself, and then remembered how close he'd come to doing that himself. But at least he had his reasons. He couldn't tell if the attitude they were being met with came from cowardice, self-interest, ignorance, or a destructive combination of all three.

'I know it might not be the time to mention it,' Qorza said, staring at the statues and carvings that littered the path. 'But it's such a shame we weren't allowed in. I've always wanted to visit the great weredragon cities. I've never had the chance before now. But just look at these carvings! They're spectacular! The threshold where the Chief Warden was standing would have easily dated back to Lord Raza the First, and yet every engraved scale was as flawless as the day it was first sculpted. Not to mention these beautiful road markers, and the statue over there of Lord Raza the Tenth!'

Qorza pointed first at the scallop-edged stone lanterns that lined the roadside, and then down the mountain towards a statue of a man with reptilian wings sprouting from his back. The statue was placed on a stone prow built out over a deep ravine, its wings splayed wide and its scaly face turned to the heavens above. It reminded Joss of the statue he'd seen back in Dragon's Tail, the Toe's sister city; he and his brethren had passed through there while on the Way. At the time he had been struck by how a once great civilisation could so thoroughly vanish from the world, much as Daheed had. The longer this mission wore on, however, the better he understood how hard it was to inspire people to save themselves in the face of extinction.

'They've done such an amazing job at preserving all of this!' Qorza said, continuing her history lesson. 'Astonishing, really, that it's survived all these centuries; not only through the elements and the various incursions the Backbone Ranges have faced, but also the weredragons' own civil wars and their eventual exodus. The royal family had a reputation for tearing down whole palaces if as little as a cracked tile displeased them – when they weren't tearing each other apart, that is. It's a miracle that it's all still standing. Really sets a wind in your sail, doesn't it?'

The wonder in Qorza's voice had reached a breathless pitch that earned her a round of blank stares and confused grimaces from all those riding alongside her. She cleared her throat and shrugged.

'But like I said ... now's not the time.'

'No. It isn't,' said Lord Xavier from the head of the party. 'I'd rather you save your enthusiastic expertise for the next official we petition. If we're even permitted to see them.'

'Perhaps we'll have more luck then,' Edgar said. The withering gaze from his lordship was more than enough to silence him, though his words would echo all the way through to Axehead Flats where the fieldservs standing as gatekeepers said they were under strict instructions not to permit entry to anyone. And the wardens at the Eastern Market insisted they couldn't abandon their posts and march to Tower Town no matter who was making the request.

'We're not paladeros, are we? We're just simple thunderfolk what never took any oaths of service,' the market's Chief Warden said, conveniently and steadfastly ignoring the fact that this summons was coming from Regent Greel himself and not the Grandmaster Council.

The only place they encountered no objections was Rampart Run, and that was because it was abandoned. The soil surrounding the fortress was churned up with tracks leading off in a dozen different directions. Presumably the paladeros, their prentices and the fieldservs had all felt they had a better chance in fleeing than in staying to fight.

'Did you stop at Rok's Nest on the way to Nobleseat?' Lieutenant Tyne asked after the party reconvened on the

Zenith. With only a few short days until the rally at Tower Town, desperation had set in enough that everyone was now involved in the discussions of where to go next. 'They may be willing to part with a number of their archers.'

'We bypassed it as we'd assumed their support to be a certainty – foolish as that may seem in the face of all this refusal,' Lord Xavier admitted from the heights of his command platform. 'Though without intending any offence to your lord and master, Lieutenant Tyne, I can't say I have much stomach for haggling over another dozen or so archers.'

Joss swayed on the heels of his boots, opened his mouth, drew breath to speak, thought better of it and stayed where he was. But it was enough to catch his lordship's attention.

'You have something you wish to say, Prentice Sarif?'

Reluctantly, Joss mustered up the nerve to step forward. He already knew how his idea was likely to be received, but what other choice was there? 'All this flying we've been doing, all this petitioning and debate, and there hasn't been any mention of speaking to the people as affected by this crisis as the paladero orders have been,' he said.

The plates of Lord Xavier's armour scraped against each other as he folded his arms. 'And who might that be?'

Joss steeled himself and said it. 'The Nameless.'

The expressions surrounding him ranged from surprise to disgust. The two he chose to focus on belonged to Eliza, whose face was burning red as she watched for what he might do next, and Lord Xavier, who looked as if he'd just been told to seek sanctuary down the back of a tyrannosaur's tonsils.

'You cannot be serious.'

'With all due respect, my lord – why not? The Nameless call Thunder Realm home every bit as much as the paladero orders. Why shouldn't they have the chance to fight for it? And we have their consul's own niece right here with us.'

He pointed to Eliza, her blush deepening to a violent shade at being singled out. The moment he did it he knew it to be a mistake, but still he persisted.

'I'm sure if given the chance, Eliza could convince her uncle to –'

'*Absolutely not!*' Lord Xavier thundered. 'I'd sooner treaty with all the vampire clans of the Midnight Isles than so much as share a mug of mead with those oath-breaking traitors.'

'But –'

'But nothing! You may think you're the solution to every ill plaguing the kingdom, Sarif, but I can assure you that you are not. Now if you'd like to avoid being confined to your quarters for the remainder of this mission, step back where you were and hold your tongue.'

Joss shrank back as the room plummeted into silence. Zeke placed a hand on his shoulder, returning the gesture Joss had extended to him. Eliza, however, looked far less consolatory.

'Why did you do that?' she hissed at him. He opened his mouth to answer and found himself without words.

'Your lordship,' Qorza said, her voice courteous but firm. 'I may be a guest on this vessel but I nevertheless feel it's my responsibility to say there's no need to admonish Josiah so ardently – especially as what he's saying isn't such a farfetched proposition.'

Lord Xavier's thin lips twitched behind his beard. 'You would seriously have me sit down with such rabble?'

'Perhaps. Given the threat we face, we should be willing to consider help from whichever quarter it may be offered. But it's in the east where I think we may find folk who could prove to be useful allies.'

Sighing wearily, Lord Xavier screwed his eyes shut and pinched the bridge of his nose. 'Did you have a suggestion, ethereon? Or am I to guess?' he asked through gritted teeth.

'Indeed I do, my lord,' Qorza said, offering a small but winning smile. 'How much do you know of the Wraithslayer of Lucium?'

———

Lucium was an ancient city that looked every year its age. Skinny streets bisected squat buildings of oppressive black rock, built on a patch of earth between paved marshland and an extinct volcano. Fog wreathed the city day and night, turning roadways into canals and making shadowy towers of all the homes, halls and shopfronts. Light looked to be a precious commodity, shed sparingly by ornate gaslamps that paraded the narrow pathways like a procession of mourners, the surrounding tenements better resembling a graveyard laden with tea candles.

There was a hunger to this place; an insatiable ache that gnawed all the way to the city's bones. It showed in the drawn faces of the citizens as they peered from behind heavy drapes, and in the shuttered market stalls and empty taverns. And it was a hunger that was shared by the beast that prowled the fog, growling faintly with every clacking step it took.

The beast had been hunting for weeks on the outskirts of the city. But now its prey was shut up in their dens, cowering against the night, leaving only the odd stray for the beast to pick off when the opportunity presented itself. Now it was searching for those opportunities within Lucium itself, having grown so bold and so ravenous that it didn't care about the risk.

Through risk came reward. Down by the waterfront stood an unsuspecting victim, gazing across the eddying River Tenebris at the pleasure palaces of Lucium's New Bank, where affluent tourists congregated in the warm glow of all the light that appeared to have been plundered from the older, poorer side of town.

The victim had unwittingly strayed from the safety of its pack. It gave no sign of noticing the creature's noiseless approach until it was too late. And even then it remained perfectly still as the creature reared up, snatching its prey in a blur of claws and fangs. And just as fast, the trap was sprung.

The creature screeched as it whirled, spinning mane over tail as invisible wires hauled it up by the ankles. It writhed and snarled, caught as hopelessly as a plesiosaur in a trawler's net. Its thrashing only grew more violent as an old woman hobbled from the shadows of a nearby underpass with a heavy satchel strapped to her back, grasping a long staff carved from bone.

The woman had chevron stripes of black-and-white hair suspended in a hive on her head by two wooden sticks. Her face was lined with almost as many scars as wrinkles, and her dark attire helped her blend with the shadows in a way that rivalled the monster she had just subdued. Holding her staff aloft, she stole a breath and began to sway. An eerie tune took to the air, weaving up and around the creature. The woman's swaying shifted into a dance. Her movements came to her with the ease of a woman a quarter her age, flowing without strain or hesitation. By the time she was done, the creature had fallen into a hypnotic state as deep as dreamless sleep.

'Quite the specimen you've caught there,' Qorza called from beneath the Bridge of Flames, where she and the rest of the Regent's envoy had been quietly watching her efforts.

'You and your people were hanging back in the shadows so long I was starting to wonder if you were ever going to show your faces.'

'We'd hardly want to get in a wraithslayer's way when she's dealing with a chimera,' Qorza shrugged. 'Good way to end up dead. Or worse.'

The old woman *tsked*. 'Wraithslayer. Such an absurd title.'

'Is it?' asked Joss, genuinely befuddled. He'd only ever heard of wraithslayers through campfire tales, none of which ever suggested them having any ambivalence about their role.

The old woman flapped her hand dismissively. 'What I do is a family tradition. We are exorcists and mystics. Naturalists and trackers. And on the very rare occasions that demand it, yes, we are hunters. But our work is not far removed from that of an ethereon, all be told,' she concluded with a nod to Qorza. 'Though without the respectable title to go with it.'

'Then what title would you prefer?' asked Hero.

Again, the woman waved away the question. 'I just go by Dafne,' she replied. 'Dafne l'Darq.'

'I can see how a name like that would serve in place of a title,' said Zeke, earning a reproachful glare from his father. Shuffling his feet, Zeke pressed his lips shut while Joss edged forward to examine the chimera.

Its head was almost like that of a sabretooth tiger, with stubbier fangs and a mane of bristly black fur. It had large, clawed paws in front and cloven hooves at the rear, with lean limbs leading from a scaled and fleshy body that tapered into a reptilian tail tipped with a venomous barb. Its eyes were half-lidded in its hypnotised state, but Joss was shocked to see how human they were.

Qorza moved closer to Joss, equally curious to examine the creature. 'You could tell I'm an ethereon?' she asked Dafne.

'I know an ethereon when I see one, rare as they may be around these parts. Just as I know you're here to plead the Regent's case for war.'

'How?' Lord Xavier demanded. 'That's classified information.'

Dafne expelled a chuckle so dry it could have been used for kindling. 'A discussion for another time, I think. First we have to haul away this beastie. And yes, before anyone offers, your help would be much appreciated.'

Joss and the others all recoiled at the prospect.

'How hard could it be?' said Zeke. 'Just like bridling an untamed raptor. Right?'

'I wouldn't know. I've never done anything remotely like that,' Drake told him.

'I was part of an expedition to catch a wild sabretooth once,' said Hero. 'It did not end well.'

Joss clenched his fists and did his best to keep his knees from shaking.

'So long as it stays asleep, we should be fine.'

'That's the spirit!' Dafne proclaimed, brandishing a customised muzzle and a set of chains. 'You may find these of use.'

'More helpful than a stick, I suppose …' Zeke muttered under his breath.

'It's a quaverstaff, my lad,' said Dafne. She struck the

end of the bone staff on the cobblestone in front of her, drawing a resonant note from its barrel. 'Not that far removed from your song swords, so I wouldn't get too snide about it. Now – whenever you're ready.'

Dafne rattled the restraints at them. Hesitantly, Joss and his brethren stepped forward to take them. But before any of them even had a chance of putting the muzzle or chains in place, the chimera lurched violently awake. Screeching, it pulled against the cord holding it aloft, ripped itself free and dropped to the ground below. Everyone jumped back as the creature found its footing, bristled its mane and snarled at its captors.

And then it began to charge.

CHAPTER FIFTEEN

—

A FIRM FAREWELL

THE chimera roared as it rushed towards Joss and the others. There was no time to hesitate. With instinctive fluidity, Joss and his brethren drew their humming knives, Lord Xavier unsheathed his song sword and Dafne brandished her quaverstaff. The group began a pacifying song. Joss had no idea if a tune intended to soothe a thunder lizard could work on a chimera, but there were precious few other options as the beast advanced.

With every forward bound, the chimera grew slower. More sluggish. Just as it was within striking distance of Joss and his friends, it swayed, rolled its head towards the sky, and keeled over. Joss breathed a heavy sigh of relief.

'I can't believe that worked,' Qorza said with curiosity.

'We're lucky,' Dafne replied as she holstered her staff. 'It's only a juvenile: too young to breathe fire. Though we'd best be disposing of it now if we want to avoid any further scuffles.'

Together they lugged the chimera's body down an adjoining spillway that had been drained of all water, where a carriage had been left waiting. It was twice the size of a funeral wagon and painted in the same glossy black, which matched the pair of pantheras pulling the vehicle. The great cats remained entirely unperturbed as the chimera was dragged past them to be bundled into the carriage.

'I assume you didn't arrive here on foot,' Dafne said to Qorza and the others once they'd locked the carriage doors. 'I'll wait while you fetch your motley menagerie of mounts and we can ride out to where this specimen originated.'

'We have precious little time for fuss,' groused Lord Xavier, his patience wearing blade-thin.

'As do I,' Dafne replied without any hint of contrition. 'So the sooner you collect your rides the better.'

Despite Lord Xavier's dark demeanour, the group followed Dafne's directions to join her for the journey beyond the city. Riding along in Azof's saddle, Joss was struck by the daunting landscape of the kingdom's eastern reach: its pitilessly rugged patchwork of lochs, bogs and sulphurous geysers, broken up by crumbling roads and clutches of townships, by abandoned plague houses and rambling graveyards.

'Unnerving, isn't it?' Joss said as Dafne's carriage veered from the road and down a winding dirt path, guiding them through a barren pine wood.

'As unnerving as a lost sense of trust, I'd say,' Eliza replied. Joss was about to ask what she meant when a shriek pierced the air.

'*Eeeeeeek!*' It was Edgar, recoiling in his saddle after the bony fingers of a bare tree branch had prodded his neck.

'Are you alright?' Eliza asked.

Edgar waved off the concern with one hand while clutching his chest with the other. 'I'm … I'm fine. Just practising my war cry,' he huffed.

'Save the dramatics if you would,' Dafne told him. 'There really will be trouble if this beastie wakes up any earlier than it should.'

At last they came to a gully overrun with tree roots. Whatever water had worn this channel into the earth had long ago run dry, and in its place something far more malevolent was brewing. The shiver that ran through Joss mirrored that of the black carriage as it jolted to a stop. Dafne leapt out and walked to the edge of the precipice.

'It opened a few weeks ago,' she said, staring down at the vortex that swirled in the gully. 'Too small for much to get through. But the beasts it's produced have set enough of a death toll to keep the locals terrified. I've been plumbing the pits in my efforts to catch every creature and return it from whence it came, not to mention trying to close this accursed thing. Thus far, the solution eludes me.'

'I can help with that,' Qorza offered.

Dafne fixed her with a curious eye. 'For now you can help me with this creature.'

Ensuring the chimera was still unconscious, Dafne opened the carriage doors and directed the group in hauling it out. They carried the beast to the edge of the gully and, on the count of three, tossed it back into the rift. The vortex accepted the burden without protest.

Dafne stared at the churning void, its darkness draining her face of all its colour. 'This is why I can't leave,' she said, gesturing to the tear in the fabric of her home. 'I know you don't come here lightly. I know the threat we face. But a wraithslayer – regardless of how I feel about that name – has a duty to keep their people safe. And I can't shirk that responsibility when they need me most.'

Qorza sank back against the nearest tree while Lord Xavier glowered behind her.

'But I shan't leave you completely empty-handed. If the Count can spare his lieutenant' – she nodded to Lieutenant Tyne, who looked astonished at the extent of her knowledge – 'then I can at least spare you some supplies. If you'll follow me.'

They followed Dafne back to her hut: a globule of rendered clay with a thatched roof of twigs, small and dark and shielded by all manner of talismans.

'Quite the coup, ethereon,' Lord Xavier said as the *Zenith* crew waited outside after Dafne had excused herself. 'We've travelled all the way across the kingdom to fill our stores with magical potions. Perhaps we should abandon Regent Greel's mission altogether in favour of setting up our own shopfront. Or better yet! We can establish a schoolhouse for all these young novices we've accrued. You can tutor them all in the ways of superstition and humbug.'

Qorza offered his lordship a sweet smile with just a hint of citrus. 'You are the definition of dry wit, my lord. Perhaps when the day is won and our fine young warriors have proven their worth we can install them as teachers in this college of yours. We could even name it in your honour, if you'd be happy to pay for its construction.'

Xavier was still fuming when Dafne stepped from her hut brandishing a stuffed satchel.

'Here you are: everything I thought you could use from my own personal stockpile. I've even included a few texts that you may find informative.'

'Thank you, that's very generous,' Qorza replied, struggling under the satchel's weight as she readily accepted it. 'It may be some time before I can get any of this back to you. Unless you'd be willing to meet us at the rally point in Tower Town? We'll be convening there this coming Regentsday.'

Dafne shook her head. 'I'm needed here. We'll find some other chance, no doubt. I hope this material proves useful in the meantime. Good luck, and may the spirits guide you.'

With that, Dafne bid them all a polite but firm farewell. Joss and the others made the journey back to the Lucium skyport in silence, stewing over their latest setback. This continued all the way into the tiny conveyance pod that serviced the skyport's docking tower, where Qorza took the opportunity to examine all that Dafne had gifted her. Among the bottled herbs, dried mushrooms and dehydrated lizard skins she found a heavy tome with an arcane symbol on its cover.

'Would you look at *this*,' she said as she hauled it out.

'What is it?' asked Joss.

'A grimoire,' she replied. Noticing Lord Xavier's and Eliza's blank stares, she added, 'A compendium of magic.'

'Maybe it'll have something on the Rakashi Revelations,' Joss murmured.

'The what?' asked Lieutenant Tyne, surprising Joss with how closely he was listening, just as the conveyance pod slowed to a stop and the doors sprung open. Crimson stared back at them from the *Zenith*'s entry hatch, where he and Cloud were mopping the floors.

'You're back early,' Crimson noted. 'How did it go?'

'Well, we didn't get any reinforcements,' Zeke replied as everyone filed inside. 'But Qorza got a bag full of magic tricks and a big heavy textbook, so –'

'Hey! Watch where you're stepping with those muddy boots!' Crimson said.

'Now the deckhands are making demands,' Lord Xavier grumbled as a crewmember ran towards him, panting.

'My lord,' she said. 'You have to come quickly. We've just received a distress signal.'

'From who?' asked his lordship, snapping to attention.

'Dragon's Toe, my lord,' the crewmember replied. 'They're under attack.'

CHAPTER SIXTEEN

A TASTE OF RAGE

SMOKE gushed from the ruin of Dragon's Toe like blood from a fatal wound. The road leading to the subterranean city was littered with the flaming wreckage of all the vehicles that had attempted to escape, with the bodies of city wardens strewn between them. As Joss surveyed the damage he kept a close watch on Crimson and Cloud. Both boys looked stricken at the destruction, but Joss knew there was more to it than that.

'You're thinking of Dragon's Tail,' he said.

Crimson nodded faintly. 'Most everyone's evacuated, but there are still some left behind. What if they're next?'

Joss wished he could reassure the boy. But if the Court of Thralls was willing to attack the Toe all the way down here in the south, what would stop them from doing the same to its larger, richer sister-city? It felt as if such a strike was inevitable. But then it felt like the whole kingdom was living on borrowed time.

Joss had been left with the two deckhands after everyone had split up to help the rest of the *Zenith*'s crewmembers search for survivors. *If only that warden had listened to us instead of turning us away*, he thought, ruminating on the fate that had befallen this place. *If only anyone would listen.*

'Over here!'

Zeke was calling from a ravine that ran just below the city's tunnel entranceway, past the weredragon road markers that Qorza had so admired. Everyone rushed to find a half-burned body propped against the canyon wall, clinging to life. With a shock, Joss recognised him as the Chief Warden. His breath was a rattling gasp that took all his remaining strength to summon.

'They – they –' he coughed, shaking with effort. 'They came – out of nowhere. We had no time to defend ourselves. Black masks and – and whole hordes of dragons. Tore through our barricades. Slaughtered everyone in sight. Took everything. We got as many people out as we could … Whoever we couldn't get outside we sent further down the tunnels. But … but …'

'But what?' asked Lord Xavier, kneeling beside him. The Chief Warden looked up with watery, bloodshot eyes.

'They took prisoners,' he gasped. 'Chained them up. Marched them away. You have to – you have to save –'

The warden was overtaken with a heaving cough that seemed to shake the life from him, and he slackened into the gravel. His eyes stared blindly at the ironclad sky. Lord Xavier leaned forward and closed them, then looked up at the faces surrounding him. 'We have to find those people.'

Everyone was quick to agree – even Zeke, who once would have been the lone voice to raise an objection. That dubious distinction went instead to Lieutenant Tyne.

'These tracks are a muckslide,' he said, pointing to the countless footprints that had churned up the earth. 'It'll take hours to single out which set belongs to the attackers and their prisoners. By which time they'll have too great a head start for us to catch up.'

'I don't know about that,' Hero replied. She was scrutinising the tracks with a hunter's focus, tilting her head left and right to examine them from every angle. 'They double around on themselves before leading off along the high road. But those appear to be a diversion. You can see where they cut off and then retraced their steps down the slope over there …'

She pointed down the curving mountain road to a spot where Joss could barely make out a smattering of indentations in the dirt. How she could pick out such a detail, he couldn't hope to guess.

'I'd say the more likely path to follow is the single-line march that seems to lead up and around the pass.' Again she pointed, this time over the shoulders of those closest to her. Joss squinted to see a narrow mountain trail.

'You may be right,' Lieutenant Tyne replied, grimacing as he studied the tracks.

'Then there's no time to lose,' said Lord Xavier, straddling his cycle. 'We ride now to free the prisoners.'

'Shouldn't we take the *Zenith*?' Joss asked. 'It would give us an advantage, wouldn't it?'

'That will only alert the enemy to our presence. Better that we take them by surprise while they're still separated from the bulk of their forces.'

'What about the dead?' asked Zeke. 'Someone should stay to bury the dead.'

Joss regarded Zeke with surprise, thinking back on the brash youth he'd been when they'd first met and how far he'd come since then. Zeke's father seemed to take a different view as he pinned his son with a critical eye. 'Frightened of what we might find further down the mountain, are you?'

Zeke jerked as if he'd been stung. Joss and the others shifted their feet, uncomfortable at the unkind accusation. 'That's not it,' Zeke said. 'Wild animals roam freely here. These bodies will be desecrated if we don't do something.'

Lord Xavier stared his son down in quiet assessment. 'Very well. Our two deckhands can stay to bury the dead,' he said, nodding to Crimson and Cloud. 'And you can supervise.'

'I can ride with you. I can fight,' Zeke protested as he marched to his cycle, saddled up and slotted the ignition rod into its terminal.

'You can do as your lord commands,' his father told him. 'Or do you need reminding of the talk we had back in Illustra?'

Zeke stiffened, then sagged into his seat with a self-conscious glance at the group. Joss wanted to offer him some support, but Lord Xavier's presence was too daunting.

'We're wasting light,' his lordship barked. 'Everyone, saddle up!' He kicked his cycle into gear and took to the air, blasting gravel in his wake. The others were fast to follow. But Joss lingered long enough to lead Azof to Zeke.

'That took real heart,' Joss said. 'I'm proud of you.'

Zeke sat staring at his cycle's display. He blinked twice, hard and deliberate, and looked up at Joss with remarkable composure. 'Thanks,' he said. 'I wish that sentiment was more popularly shared.'

Joss struggled to think of a reply, eventually uttering the old saying, 'Not even a king can be universally adored,' then winced at his clumsy words.

Zeke offered a threadbare smile. 'You should go. Those people will need your help.'

'Give those craven mucksuckers a kick in the tenders for us!' Crimson shouted across the ravine.

Joss gave a small salute and checked over his shoulder as he left, stealing a glance at Zeke. He thought back to their time on the Way together, and the stories Zeke had shared of the hardships he faced in his family. Hearing stories had been one thing. Seeing it in person was another.

Talk was sparse as Joss fell into line with Drake, Hero, Edgar and Eliza. Their quarry could have been leagues ahead of them or just around the corner. With no way of knowing, the best way forward was to remain silent.

Lord Xavier led the pack with his cycle set on a low gear, making it whisper-quiet as it hovered over the tracks left in the gravel. They rode on for hours until they came to a point where two extra tracks split off to run high overhead of, and parallel to, the first trail.

Everyone stopped. With great deliberation, Lord Xavier stared at each track. Then he signalled to his crew, using the gestures Joss and his brethren had learned in their skyborne training. Half the crew would take the upper path to the left. The other half would take the upper path to the right.

The wisdom of this strategy struck Joss immediately. Judging by the tracks, most of the enemy had likely taken the lowest path. By seizing the higher ground the *Zenith* crew would have an advantage over their quarry, who would have a limited line of sight and be unable to charge at them. *Like culling a caged carnotaurus,* he thought.

As silently as they had started, the group split in two to pursue their parallel paths. Edgar and Eliza fell in with the group riding to the left, while Joss ventured to the right with Drake, Hero, Lieutenant Tyne and Lord Xavier. The rest of the *Zenith*'s landing party – also split across the two groups – was composed of all the ensigns his lordship had armed and charged with fighting for their kingdom. Joss hoped they would have enough numbers to stand a chance against the Shadow God's forces.

They found them sooner than Joss expected. The Shadow God's troops marched in single file with their prisoners manacled together. They consisted of one small squadron, split between the front of the line and the rear. They wore the same masks they had sported back at Blade's Edge Acres, made of lacquered bloodwood and crudely mimicking Thrall's own disguise. Their armour, however, had seen a steep improvement.

Joss could only assume that all the steel and iron they had plundered in their raids had been fed into their war effort, with newly fashioned black plates worn over padded leather jerkins and tightly linked chainmail. Their weapons ranged from broadswords to crossbows to thundersticks and bolt rifles. The senior officers rode raptors, leaving the foot soldiers to march along with the prisoners.

The townsfolk of Dragon's Toe were bruised and bloodied, weeping as they limped along with their heads lowered, nobody daring to look their captors in the eye. It filled Joss with a rage he could almost taste, bitter and poisonous and ready to be spat in the face of those responsible for this cruelty.

Lord Xavier gestured to everyone to slow their mounts. Joss readied himself for battle. The Champion's Blade was halfway out of its scabbard as Lord Xavier peered over the ridge to get a better look at their quarry. At the same time, a clutch of rocks tumbled loose. They bounced off the helmets of the soldiers at the rear of the procession, who quickly turned around.

'*Enemies sighted!*' the closest of the masked soldiers shouted.

—

CHAPTER SEVENTEEN

A MASKED MENACE

THE rocky mountainside exploded around Joss's ears as the Shadow God's soldiers fired upon them all, a lightning-bolt-burst burning his cheek as it flew past.

'*Charge!*' Lord Xavier shouted, and led the way down the ridge with his jet-cycle blaring. Joss was stunned to see him so quickly give away the high ground, but followed his lordship into the void. The bolt blasts came for them with white-hot fervour. Lord Xavier dodged them all. With his song sword drawn, he crashed into the enemy.

'*The chains! Break the chains!*' he roared at Joss and the others over the noise of clashing blades. Joss quickly rode for the line of prisoners, vaulting from Azof's saddle to carry out his lordship's orders.

'Help! *Help!*' the prisoners screamed, rushing forward and baring their shackles.

The Champion's Blade had little trouble with the shoddy chains. It cleaved each set of manacles with a shower of sparks, releasing the prisoners and allowing them to run for cover.

'Thank you, sur,' said the last of those freed. He looked barely older than Joss himself, with a tangle of red curls, glistening green eyes and a uniform that had been torn in the attack. It took Joss a moment but he recognised the boy as Ormar, the Chief Warden's steward.

'Get yourself to safety,' Joss replied. 'And I'm not a "sur".'

'Truer words were never spoken, you mongrel,' someone snarled behind him as Ormar ran off. Joss spun around, knowing full well who it was confronting him despite the mask he wore.

'Lynch,' he said, sizing up the traitor. 'You've grown.'

The loathsome little prentice's wiry frame had been bulked out with dark iron and black leather. On his chest was the Shadow God's sigil – an upended crown wrought in silver that Joss recognised as the Crest of the Unhallowed. The mask Lynch wore was a monstrous approximation of Thrall's, substituting wood for stone and mock scars for magic runes. The mouth was a snarl of slitted holes, the eyes as wide and watchful as an owl's. He kept it firmly in place as he stared Joss down, his breath a ragged wheeze.

And then he attacked.

His sword hurtled towards Joss's head with frightening speed, and was blocked just in time. The clang of metal was piercing, the shrill tone lingering long after the strike.

'You never shoulda come here,' Lynch said as he rained down blow after blow. 'It's gonna cost you. And I'm gonna take that price right out of your hide.'

'You're pretty mouthy for such an unremarkable foot soldier,' Joss told him. In his peripheral vision he could see Drake, Hero, Edgar and Eliza freeing the last of the prisoners. They were safeguarded by Lord Xavier and the *Zenith* crew, who fended off the enemy with every ounce of strength they had to spare. If Joss could keep Lynch distracted, he knew they just might stand a chance of getting everyone to safety.

'We're not foot soldiers, you fool. We're acolytes,' Lynch said. 'And we're going to tear you apart. From the inside out.'

'Is that supposed to scare me?' Joss said, giving his best impression of an unflappable paladero even as his prentice heart pounded.

'Only if yer smart enough to know it for the truth.'

Joss remembered Lynch's ruthlessness from Blade's Edge Acres, and his service as an acolyte seemed to have honed his savage instincts to a dagger point. He attacked with overwhelming force; all Joss could do was keep his guard up and try desperately not to lose his balance, fending off each strike with less than a second to spare.

But it proved too much. A rock snagged Joss's heel and threw him off his feet. Between heartbeats he was on his back and scrabbling through the dirt, the tip of Lynch's sword hovering inches from his throat.

'When I'm done with you, there'll be so little of your remains left that not even the darkness will take you,' he sneered.

Joss tried to retort but his throat was bone dry. All he could do was gape at Lynch as the masked menace advanced on him, his every move made with murderous intent.

'*Look out below!*' someone shouted from overhead. Joss looked up to see Zeke, Crimson and Cloud beside a massive boulder, high up on the ridge. While Lynch was distracted, Joss kicked him in the midsection, sending him stumbling backwards just as Zeke unloaded his shock rifle on the teetering boulder.

The massive rock came bounding down the mountainside, picking up speed along with a tumble of smaller stones. By the time it was within striking distance of Joss and Lynch it had become an outright avalanche. The two of them had to scramble in opposite directions to avoid the crush of rocks, which poured down between them like a steel gate slamming shut.

Coughing through the dust, Joss squinted up at the wall of rocks that had sealed him off from Lynch and the other remaining acolytes.

'*Hoo!* That went down like a brontosaur with a busted ankle,' Crimson exclaimed as Zeke holstered his rifle and slid down the gravelly incline to land beside Joss.

'You alright?' he asked, offering Joss his hand.

'Better than I would have been if you hadn't shown up,' Joss replied as Zeke helped him to his feet. 'You couldn't have timed that better if you'd tried.'

'The secret of my success is making dumb luck look intentional,' Zeke winked at him.

'Ezekiel!' Lord Xavier thundered from the far end of the ravine. 'I ordered you to stay at Dragon's Toe.'

All the colour drained from Zeke's face as his lordship stomped towards them, flicking his song sword clean of all the filth it had collected in battle.

'You did, but –'

'But nothing,' his father said, slamming his blade back into its scabbard. 'You disobeyed a direct order from your lord commander. If you were any other crewmember you'd be strictly disciplined for such insubordination. But as it is, be thankful we have enemy combatants just behind that pile of rocks ready to swarm us, not to mention a host of civilians to get to safety.'

'All thanks to Zeke,' Joss said, the words boiling up from his insides.

Lord Xavier stared at him with astonishment. 'Excuse me?'

'Joss, leave it.' Zeke placed a hand on Joss's arm, but Joss shook him off.

'No. If it weren't for Zeke and Crimson and Cloud, there'd be no wall there to keep us safe from those enemy combatants. You could at least acknowledge that before baring your fangs.'

Xavier's bewilderment at being reprimanded cooled to something hard and blunt.

'It's increasingly clear where Zeke found the inspiration for his newly acquired sense of defiance,' he said. 'But we'll discuss this later. For now, we fall back and get these civilians to safety. Understood?'

'Yes, my lord,' Joss and Zeke replied, turning their faces away from his lordship to share a look of commiseration. They saddled up and started to ride, guiding the freed prisoners back towards Dragon's Toe where the *Zenith* could more easily collect them.

Joss was sure he could hear the rocks behind them moving, sure he could discern the shouts of Lynch and his cohorts as they tried to scale the boulders blocking their way. He wondered if he and his friends had the strength to fend off another attack. All he could do was ride faster and hope that the wall would hold.

———

Joss stared out from the *Zenith*'s observation deck as the airship docked with the serpentrain station's elevated gantry. With Dragon's Toe a smoking ruin and vulnerable to further attack, it had been decided it was wisest to evacuate the survivors to Illustra via rail. But looking down at the crowds mobbing the Upsndowns station, Joss wondered if it truly was the right decision.

The queues at every entranceway had grown in the time since they'd first visited, and become more unsettled and distressed. Thousands of people were crushed together, all desperate to escape the looming threat. It filled Joss with the dread he imagined came with being corralled into a slaughterhouse.

'Here you are,' Drake said, venturing outside with Hero quickly following him. They did their best to avoid the arcane sigils Qorza had already inscribed in charcoal across the deck in an attempt to ward off any further supernatural forces. 'We've been looking all over for you. Edgar and Eliza have gone to see if they can help transfer the Dragon's Toe survivors. We thought you'd want to come along.'

'What about Zeke?' Joss asked. 'Is he coming too? Or has his father overruled that as well?'

Hero and Drake glanced at each other with uncertainty.

'He did the right thing today, going against what he'd been told to do,' Hero said, to Joss's surprise. 'I don't know if you'd be here right now if not for that.'

'You're right. He did. But I just don't understand the power that Xavier holds over him.' He sighed with exasperation, mystified that someone as self-assured as Zeke could be overrun so easily.

'Family can be like that,' Drake said gently. 'Their expectations are a hard weight to shift.'

Hero nodded, though her head was tilted at an angle that conveyed a differing perspective.

'A weight that can crush you, if you let it. Let's hope today was Zadkille making the first real efforts to climb out from under it.'

Joss considered his brethren's reflections, admitting, if only to himself, that his point of reference was far narrower than either of theirs. He had never had any family expectations to deal with. But he had dealt with the expectations of his superiors at Round Shield Ranch, and it was in thinking of them that he felt a familiar twinge of suspicion.

'It was strange, though – don't you think?' he said distantly. 'That Lord Xavier wouldn't call in the *Zenith* for aerial support? That he ordered us to charge on the enemy once we'd been discovered, rather than hold our ground and attack from above? And how those rocks falling loose gave us away in the first place?'

Drake and Hero turned to each other, then back to Joss.

'You don't trust Xavier?' asked Drake.

Joss cast his gaze downward. Lord Malkus's words echoed in his mind.

Nothing is impossible.

'You found him!' Zeke exclaimed as he popped his head out from the doorway, his golden hair dancing in the wind. Reading their faces, he paused. 'What are you all talking about?'

Hero and Drake turned to Joss, to see if he might share his suspicions.

'Just reflecting on the day,' he said, summoning an air of nonchalance. 'Are you joining us?'

'Father's asked that we escort the survivors to the stationmaster's office. Hopefully they can be processed from there. But before that he's requested our presence on the bridge.'

'Can't keep his lordship waiting, can we?' said Joss, keeping his tone as even as he could manage. Still, the bruised look on Zeke's face made Joss immediately regret the comment as the prentices filed back inside.

'I was just saying how you showed some real grit today – not to mention some fine shooting,' Hero told Zeke as they navigated the inky shadows and patches of purple light that chequered the *Zenith*'s circuitous corridors. 'Couldn't have done better myself.'

Zeke shrugged, offering her a modest smile. 'It helps when your target is huge, immobile and within point-blank range. Maybe I can turn my talent to becoming an expert marksman who specialises in boulders.'

Hero and Drake chuckled and continued ahead while Zeke fell back a step to walk with Joss.

'I appreciate what you did, by the way. Or tried to do,' Zeke told him in a low voice. 'I've seen plenty of people who've tried and failed to stand up to my father. Most often in the mirror.'

There was a frankness with which Zeke spoke that made Joss pause, thinking of how best to respond. Had Zeke overheard their conversation? And if he had, what was worse? To keep harping on the matter or to let it go? He chose for the path in-between.

'I never thought I'd be telling you of all people that you should be more confident.'

'Big difference between confidence and bluster,' Zeke said, his face falling into shadow. The light didn't find it again until they were on the bridge, where Lord Xavier stood at his command station with his hands clasped behind his back.

His lordship waited until everyone had assembled before he began his address, remaining absolutely still as he spoke.

'Time is running out. Our options are dwindling. We have only a few days remaining until we're expected in Tower Town, and I refuse to arrive empty-handed. And as we've witnessed from their raid on Dragon's Toe, the enemy grows bolder and more ruthless by the day.' He fixed his sight on Joss and the others. 'You have a deep streak of defiance that should have been reined in by this point in your training. But that doesn't mean you're wholly lacking any worthwhile notions.'

Joss and the others looked at each other in confusion.

'Does that mean –?' Eliza tried to ask.

Lord Xavier interrupted. 'We'll meet with the Nameless,' he told them. 'And if they have even a scrap of honour left to claim, we will add their forces to our own.'

CHAPTER EIGHTEEN

A PLACE ONLY FIT FOR DYING

ELIZA led the way between the red mesas of Thunder Realm's southwest corner, riding a raptor she'd been lent from the *Zenith*'s pens. Lord Xavier followed directly behind her, his cycle humming as it floated over the fissures of dried earth, while everyone else clustered behind. The landscape was rugged and inhospitable, as parched as an old bone left out in the sun. It felt right that the place was called Gravemarker, Joss thought. It was fit only for dying. All the weathered animal skeletons they passed only reinforced the notion.

Eliza was riding high in her saddle, back stiff and hands tight on the reins. Joss had barely shared a word with her since Lucium. Everything had been so hectic that he hadn't had the chance. Though perhaps there was more to it than that. Each conversation came with the weight of their shared loss. Still, there was time to talk now and more than enough reason to, so he urged Azof on until finally they were riding alongside each other.

'Thank you for doing this,' he said. 'It may make all the difference.'

'True,' she breathed, keeping her eyes on the road. 'Though I wasn't left much choice, was I?'

Joss frowned. 'I'm sorry?'

'I'd have liked the chance to decide on sharing my family's secrets myself,' she said. Only now did she look over at him, and the look hit Joss like a gauntleted fist. 'Rather than having that decision made for me.'

'So that's what you meant back in Lucium? About a lost sense of trust.'

'I'll let you figure that one out for yourself,' she replied, then rode on ahead.

Joss didn't know what to do. Yes, he'd been aware that Eliza might not have volunteered her uncle being one of the Nameless so publicly. And maybe doing that for her had been wrong of him. But surely she could see the situation they were facing? What would Sur Verity have made of trying to keep such matters private when so many lives hung in the balance?

He considered catching back up with Eliza to demand an answer to his question, though he wasn't sure she'd have the same opinion as Sur Verity – even if Eliza may have been the most prodigious prentice that the Sleeping King ever sought to bestow on the world. So he decided to simply do what their mentor would have done, and left Wildsmith to ride on alone with nothing more said between them.

Passing through the shadows cast by the towering rock formations, they came to a narrow gulch with a wooden bridge running beside it. Eliza drew her mount to a stop. Everyone behind her did the same.

'We're here,' she said.

'I don't see anything,' Lord Xavier said, surveying their surroundings.

'Give it a moment.'

A pterosaur call rang out nearby, picked up in the distance by another, and then even further away by a third. Then from behind every rock and boulder there sprang an entire legion of camouflaged paladeros brandishing an armoury of blades, crossbows and bolt guns.

Looking closer, Joss saw that they wore no emblems or insignias or order colours, that the song swords they wielded were crude objects fashioned of iron rather than steel, and he reminded himself that these weren't paladeros they were facing. These were former paladeros who had been stripped of their rank and shunned by Thunder Realm society, now living as little more than mercenaries. Of course they had no insignias. They had little of anything left.

'*Halt!* Who goes there?' demanded the nearest member of the pack, peering at them from behind an overly long thunderstick.

'*Who goes there?*' repeated his barrel-chested companion, his hatchet of a moustache twitching. 'Surely you can't be serious, Archibald! Couldn't you think of anything that might be a whisker more original to say? *Who goes there? You make it sound like we're running a clubhouse for runaway delinquents.*'

'Shush up, Ichabod! I'm in no mood for your fuss and muck today. I might have something more novel to say if I were better practised, but we don't often have anyone foolish enough to wander straight up to our threshold, do we?'

'Gentlemen?' Lord Xavier said, and the two guards snapped to attention. 'May we return to the matter at hand?'

'We may, and that matter has to do with you all stating your business for being here or suffering a swift rebuke for your bother!' said Archibald, the scruffier of the two, to which Lord Xavier simply looked towards Eliza.

As high as she'd already been sitting in her saddle, she somehow grew even taller. 'I'm Eliza Wildsmith of Round Shield Ranch, prentice to the fallen hero Sur Verity Wolfsbane, daughter of Toliver and Anjelica Wildsmith,' she told them. 'And I'm here to see my uncle.'

Archibald and Ichabod gawped at Eliza, gawped at each other, and then lowered their weapons.

'Well … why didn't you say so?'

———

The Nameless flanked them on all sides as they rode along the groaning bridge. Joss did his best to take in his surroundings while not coming across as nosy. The camp was a modest affair. Hidden behind a pair of rusted iron gates, it was composed mostly of huts erected alongside the opposing riverbank, along with tarps spread across a honeycomb of caves.

Joss had expected the hideout of the notorious Nameless to be more impressive somehow – more imposing. His disappointment quickly changed when they came to the end of the gulch.

A shallow watering hole served as a moat to a fortress at the yawning mouth of an immense cavern. Built from the same red sandstone as the surrounding rock face, the fortress was a brutally fashioned mass of arrowslits, bulwarks and wooden hoardings, fronted by a corroded portcullis ornamented with the skulls of a dozen different thunder lizards. The whole edifice had the demeanour of a war-ravaged veteran held together by bandages but still ready for a fight.

The portcullis shrieked open, revealing a towering shadow. A guttural growl preceded a thunderous footstep, followed by another and another, until finally a full-grown tyrannosaur emerged from the gloom. Azof screeched in fright, forcing Joss to wrestle him under control while making the split-second decision to either run or stand his ground. Had they been led into a trap? Had the Nameless joined forces with the Court of Thralls and unleashed this monster as their final gambit?

'I'd stay still if I were you,' warned Ichabod, the moustachioed guard. 'The beast is more likely to chase you if you bolt. Fear gets it all hopped up.'

Joss tried to remain stock-still as the tyrannosaur lumbered forward, exposing not only the armour it was wearing but also the bridle around its enormous head, with reins leading to an elaborate riding rig. Perched high in that saddle was a man as hardened as the fortress from which he'd ridden. His head, neck and shoulders seemed to have been carved from a rock formation, with his clippered black hair a shadow on the mountain's summit. He stared down at the group from beneath an overhanging brow of granite, his grimace accentuated by a clenched jaw and a cleft chin so deep it could have been scored by an axe.

His mount, the king of the thunder lizards, made for a regal and awe-inspiring sight, its feathers a shimmering collage of royal purple and midnight blue. But even more astounding than its plumage was its roar, which it unleashed in a fearsome display as it drew to a stop before the interlopers gathered below. The sound sent what felt like a shoal of electric eels corkscrewing through Joss's innards.

'You'll have to pardon Balthasar's greeting. He hates the stink of hilt-gripping paladeros,' the tyrannosaur's rider called out. 'But then who can blame him?'

'Fine way to welcome your family, Uncle Silas!' Eliza shouted at him from the shore.

'Ellie – is that you?'

The rider swung a leg over his saddle and slid down his mount's armour, landing with both heels in the sediment at the water's edge. His burly arms were striped with tattoos resembling claw marks, left exposed by his modest attire of black leather chestplate, black riding breeches, knee-high boots and a two-handed song sword strapped between his shoulders. Joss got the immediate impression that this was a man who would never stab anybody in the back. He'd simply stab them in the face instead.

'If it ain't my favourite niece, accompanied by my least favourite creed of faithless thunderfolk,' Eliza's uncle growled. Joss couldn't tell if he was bemused by their presence or deeply affronted. 'And the high and mighty Lord Xavier Zadkille, at that! Tell me, to what do we owe this dubious honour?'

Lord Xavier showed no sign of being intimidated by the beast before him – nor the creature that he rode. 'I think you well know, Nameless.'

'Call me Silas. Most everyone does. Though you'll be wanting to strike a more respectful tone when you say it. Balthasar's not been fed for a few hours.' His tone darkened as his tyrannosaur rumbled behind him. 'And he could do with a bite to eat.'

CHAPTER NINETEEN

A SPIRIT OF GOOD WILL

'YOUR kingdom is under assault,' Lord Xavier told Silas Wildsmith of the Nameless while Joss, his brethren and a slathering tyrannosaur looked on. 'We face the greatest threat we've ever known. And you sit here in your cave by your fetid little stream and dare to jest with me. I knew it was pointless to come here. You've only proven it so.'

Silas Wildsmith regarded Lord Xavier with consternation and contempt.

'My kingdom?' he said, stalking forward through the ankle-deep stream. 'A kingdom that turned its back on me, that stripped me of title and position and standing, all on the word of a treacherous lord not worth the meat he'd make at market? A kingdom that did the same to all my brethren here; that calls us Nameless and treats us with nothing but scorn? You mean *that* kingdom?'

'The same kingdom that birthed you and raised you, and serves as home to your kith and kin,' Hero interjected from Callie's saddle. 'Your niece included.'

Silas turned to Eliza. 'Ellie, you led these glorified minstrels to my door?'

Eliza looked stricken, but she pushed her discomfort aside and stood her ground. 'I did, uncle. They thought – and I agreed – that you and your brethren might heed the call to duty, given the dire situation we face.'

'What duty? We were relieved of the oaths we took. Or don't you remember? If you came here looking for a posse of paladeros to saddle up and save the regency, you came to the wrong cussing place.'

'And yet you still observe our customs and attend our binding ceremonies,' Drake said, earning a confused cock of the head from Silas. 'That was you, wasn't it? I remember you from Tower Town. You and a number of your Nameless brethren all made the pilgrimage to come watch four prentices be sent on the Way. Quite the effort for someone so disenchanted.'

'It always helps to keep tabs,' Silas shrugged, refusing to be drawn any further on the subject, while a crowd formed to watch the unfolding quarrel. They were assembled on either side of the riverbank, lined up along the bridge and gazing down from the huts on the opposite shore.

Scanning their faces, Joss was struck by the wide array of people that made up the ranks of the Nameless. Old and young, scarred and fresh-faced, thunderfolk and so-called outrealmers. They had all found a home here in the wastelands of the realm that had rejected them. But one face stood out to him, and it made his blood boil.

'*You!*' Joss pointed at her from across the stream. 'I know you.'

The woman with pale blonde hair and even paler skin looked shocked at being singled out, and gazed around as if Joss might be talking about someone else.

'You're Alabaster Jane!' he continued, dropping from his saddle and walking into the stream to confront her directly. 'Your brother, Midwinter Jack, was the leader of the Red Grin Gang.'

From the uneasy demeanour of the figures surrounding her, Joss quickly surmised their identities. 'And that's the rest of them, isn't it?' he stared at each in turn, their faces obscured behind bandanas, kerchiefs and sandmasks. Several weeks ago their gang had attacked Joss and the others in Freecloud during their mission with Sur Blaek, though now there appeared to be two more members. The remaining pair wore no masks, but they had their cloaks pulled close and their hoods drawn over their heads. Joss recognised them all the same.

'And you two were part of the Grim Rider's gang!' He pointed to the taller of the duo. 'Parsefal,' he said, noting the quiver of arrows slung over the man's shoulder that marked him as the archer of the group. He pointed at the smaller of the two. 'And Kilwart.'

'My name is Kade,' the young man snapped, his cloak billowing open to reveal the copper cables of his hand-mounted bolt throwers: the same ones he had once used to hurl balls of electricity at Joss and his brethren.

'Whatever you want to call yourself, you're an accomplice of the Grim Rider.'

Kade glowered at Joss from beneath his hood as Lord Xavier turned on Silas. 'Is this true, Wildsmith? You're harbouring known felons?'

Silas Wildsmith shrugged. 'The Nameless harbour all sorts, your lordship. We don't discriminate here. We're a fair, open-minded and democratic collective, unlike the paladero orders. Which means I won't speak for one of our number when they can speak for themselves.'

All eyes turned on the pale-haired woman. 'The boy's right,' she admitted. 'I'm the Jane he says I am and this here is my crew.'

'And you stole your way into the ranks of the Nameless to avoid the King's justice,' Joss said, his ire swiftly rising.

'I did no such thing!' Jane exclaimed. 'My brother and I had nine seasons of training as skyborne prentices under our wings when a senior paladero took an overly keen interest in my training and we set him straight on the matter. The lord of the order didn't see it that way, though, and we were tossed out on our training blades. We'd have gone Nameless back then, but we had it in our heads that we wouldn't be accepted. Can't be Nameless when you've never been named as paladeros in the first place, we figured. If only we'd known better. Maybe we wouldn't have made such bad choices and fallen in with the rough crowd that we did.

'It took my brother's death at the hands of that traitor Blaek for me to finally seek shelter here. We made the pilgrimage the night of the Blade's Edge fires, picking up a couple of stragglers along the way who were likewise hoping to make new lives for themselves after falling afoul of that stone-masked monster.' She nodded to Parsefal and Kade, who pushed out their chests.

'You call Thrall a monster despite having tried to kill us just the same as he did,' said Joss, his anger burning through him. 'Why shouldn't we call down the rest of the crew from our airship and have you all arrested?'

'I wouldn't blame you if you did. All I can say is none of us wants to live that life anymore. Not after all we've seen. Losing my brother ... that was like being cleaved in two. It's a wound that won't heal, the kind I don't have the appetite for inflicting on anyone else. Not anymore. And I'm sorry for ever having tried to inflict it on you. Believe me or don't, that's the truth.'

Joss was unsure what riled him the most: the idea that Sur Verity could be dead and gone while a pack of cutthroats could so easily make a new life for themselves, the gauntlet Silas was making them run through, or just the ever-growing frustration of their mission.

Hero stepped forward to address Silas. 'You heard her – your own people here witnessed firsthand the destructive power we're facing. The power that destroyed my order. Whatever our differences in the past, we need your help now. Will you stand with us?'

Silas considered her a moment, his thumbs tucked into the loops of his swordbelt. 'My heart goes out to you, miss. It truly does. But like I said, we're a democratic collective here. It's not my place to give orders,' he told her. 'If you want our help then we'll take a vote and see if we're all willing to offer that help. Before we can do that though, you have to prove you're worth the bother.'

'And what exactly does that entail?' asked Lord Xavier.

'You have the Way. We have the Crucible,' Silas explained, marching from the shallow water onto the shore. 'A trial by combat – a demonstration of the petitioner's merit and mettle. And seeing as we have an Honest-to-His-Majesty Blade Keeper here with us, I think it only right that he acts as your champion in this trial.'

He slapped Joss on the shoulder. Joss blinked. 'Me?' he asked, stunned. Judging by Silas's expression, it was no joke.

'Who do you suggest he challenge?' Lord Xavier demanded, his face growing redder by the moment. 'You, sitting atop your ambling abattoir?'

The tyrannosaur snuffed the air and stomped the water. Silas raised a hand. The beast fell silent. 'The duty would ordinarily fall to me as consul of the Nameless, but that would hardly seem a fair fight, would it?' a smirk crept across Silas's face. 'So in the spirit of goodwill and generosity, I choose another Wildsmith in my place.'

'You don't mean –?' Eliza asked, just as stupefied as Joss.

'I hope you've been practising those fighting moves I showed you, Ellie,' Silas told her. 'You'll need them.'

CHAPTER TWENTY

——

A KILLING STRIKE

JOSS examined the weapon he'd been given as if it were
a curio from an eccentric's collection of exotic wonders.
It was as long as a song sword, but thicker and rounded
and made of iron, with dulled edges coated in a film of
mysterious dark liquid. Just as he reached out to examine
it, someone grabbed him by the wrist.

'I wouldn't touch that if I were you,' said Ichabod, the
Nameless gatekeeper who'd given him the weapon. 'Ain't
you ever seen a cicuta blade before?'

Joss's confused expression was enough of an answer.

'That gloop you were about to poke with your bare
finger is poison,' Silas said. 'Non-lethal, but it packs
one mean sting. Cicuta blades are coated with it so you
don't quickly forget the mistakes you make in training. I
lost count of all the welts I racked up over my time as a

prentice, though I can still feel the bite of them.'

'I haven't seen one of these in years,' Lord Xavier said wistfully. 'They were deemed too severe for use.'

'We might not be paladeros anymore, but we maintain some traditions here regardless,' Silas replied.

Joss and Eliza faced each other in the middle of the stream that ran through the Nameless camp, the patchwork fortress looming over them. They had been led there by Ichabod and Archibald, who were to serve as their seconds in the duel.

'This is lunacy,' Eliza said to her uncle as Archibald furnished her with a weapon. 'You honestly expect me to fight a member of my own party? What makes you think I won't throw the fight to force your hand in joining us?'

Silas expelled the driest of chuckles. 'You mean the same hand that trained you? I'm confident I'll be able to tell if you're holding back in any way. So don't.'

The surrounding spectators withdrew to the water's edge. The last to leave were Zeke, Drake, Hero and Edgar.

'Are you up for this?' Zeke asked Joss.

'Do I have any other choice?' Joss replied.

'Good point,' Zeke admitted, then added, 'and good luck.'

The others echoed Zeke's well wishes, with Edgar adding his own postscript. 'Try not to get hurt. Try not to hurt Eliza while you're at it.'

Joss smiled softly at Edgar's perennial goodwill. 'I promise.'

Edgar splintered away from the others to offer Eliza his support. Joss couldn't fault his friend's generosity, even as he tried to extinguish the flash of jealousy he felt. Once Edgar was done, he and the others took their place with Lord Xavier and the *Zenith* crew, leaving the stream clear of everyone but the two combatants.

There was silence, save for the babbling of water, as Silas climbed a nearby bridge and announced in his loudest voice, 'We don't stand much on ceremony here, so I'll keep this short. We got ourselves a good old-fashioned Crucible; place your bets, pick your spots and show your champion your full-throated support!'

The crowd of Nameless spectators erupted in a frenzy of noise and activity. A dozen members of the crowd shouted out odds, Joss unable to discern the numbers over the din. Money changed hands, tickets were scribbled out and stamped, and then, with the rush of business concluded, the spectators settled into a tense silence to watch.

Silas nodded to Ichabod and Archibald. Joss noticed that the pair of gatekeepers stood with Alabaster Jane and her cohorts to his left. Jane watched with a keen interest that made him wonder if she wished the blades they were holding were real.

'*On my shot!*' Ichabod proclaimed, holding his thunderstick high. He paused before pulling the trigger, the blast of noise bouncing around the gully to signal the start of the duel.

Joss and Eliza snapped into their defensive positions.

They locked eyes and began to circle one another, making the smallest hints towards attacking without ever following through. Just as Joss was starting to doubt if either of them would actually make a move, Eliza lashed out with a speed that startled him and smacked him on the shoulder. The pain from the cicuta blade was flame hot and instantaneous.

'*Ouch!*' Joss hissed.

'Sorry,' Eliza said, and resumed her defensive posture. Joss tried to shake off the pain coursing through him but the poison worked much the same as an actual wound, both numbing and agonising at the same time. He was still trying to deal with the shock of it when Eliza took advantage of his distraction by launching another attack, forcing him to defend himself. Their blades came together in a quick succession of blows that ended with Eliza swiping Joss across the shin.

'*Muck!*' cursed Joss.

'Sorry,' Eliza said again.

Pain was now flaming through the whole left side of Joss's body, and with it came a rolling wave of anger. He could hear the echo of Sur Verity in his head, barking instructions at him that he needed to find his footing and keep his guard up. But what good had all that expertise done her in the end? So he took the fight to his opponent. His blade was a blur as he whirled it from attack to attack, each blow landing with the clang of an iron bell.

'*Joss!*' Eliza exclaimed. 'Calm down!'

'Your uncle said we were meant to take this seriously, didn't he?' he grunted. In the corner of his vision he could see the crowd watching them, could feel their eyes burning into him. 'You've already landed two strikes. And I can't lose this fight.'

'This isn't how Sur Verity would have taught you to fight. It's not what she taught me.'

Joss's eyes narrowed. 'You have no idea what she taught me.'

He swung the cicuta blade at Eliza's head, making her stumble backwards and fall into the stream. She rolled with the motion, churning up the water and splashing Joss with it, quickly finding her footing again.

'Joss – what's going on with you? Sur Verity wouldn't –'

'Don't tell me what Sur Verity would or wouldn't do! Don't tell me what she would want or think or feel!' Joss told her, slashing his sword with every word. 'Five years I was her prentice! *Five years!* And I had to fight for every crumb of her approval! You were her prentice for five minutes and somehow you became her favourite!'

'Are you – are you serious?' Eliza stammered, parrying his attacks and matching them with her own.

Her confusion sparked both uncertainty in him and a deeper, primal anger. 'As serious as I am about winning this ridiculous duel your uncle is putting us through!' he said through gritted teeth.

Eliza blocked blow after blow, until finally her luck ran out and he managed to rap her across the knuckles.

She hissed as her fingers swelled from the toxin. Anger blossomed on her face, red and ripe. 'You've got your head stuck so deep in your own hole you can't see how much you meant to her,' she said, pushing back on Joss. 'I couldn't sharpen a sword or shoe a megaloceros without hearing about how you would have done it, how good a job you would have done, what a long shadow I had to get out from under!'

She slashed at Joss's chest, chopped at his shoulders. He scrambled to evade her, deflecting what attacks he could and jumping away from the ones he couldn't.

'Anyone else might have found that galling,' she went on, growing more heated with every word, every slash. 'It sounds like you sure would have. But I found it inspiring. That you could have fought against all those odds and accomplished all that you did – it taught me you aren't your family; you're not your past. You're only the work you put in and the good you do.'

Joss tried not to let her anger unnerve him, tried not to let her into his head. He had to block her words as surely as he had to block her sword. To allow doubt in would be to admit defeat, right there and then.

'There's only one woman who could say for sure,' Joss said, forcing his way through any hint of hesitation. 'But she's gone. And she's never coming back.' He feinted to the left, moved to the right, saw his opening and took it. The tip of his blade came within a hair of Eliza's throat. He held it there, keeping her from moving.

'Do you yield?' he asked her, gasping.

'I don't know,' she panted in reply. 'Do you?'

She was looking down. He did the same. The tip of her sword was hovering at his belly, poised to make a killing strike just the same as his. Everyone watching stayed absolutely still, absolutely silent. And then Silas raised himself up, held his hands high in the air and declared, '*A tie!*'

The crowd exploded in applause. The reaction only left Joss confused. Did this mean the Nameless would refuse to offer their help in the battle to come? Or had this all just been sport for them? Whatever the answer, there was one thing Joss knew for certain as he and Eliza stared each other down. Any chance of friendship between them was over. Nothing would ever be the same again.

—

CHAPTER TWENTY-ONE

A Cloud of Gloom

'YOU did well, Blade Keeper,' Silas told Joss as he and Eliza walked back to the riverbank. 'Anyone who can hold his own in a fight against a Wildsmith must have some skill. And Eliza? I'm as proud of you as ever.'

'Thank you, Uncle Silas,' Eliza replied with her head bowed.

'Does this mean you'll join us?' Joss asked, barely registering the presence of Archibald and Ichabod as they collected the cicuta blades from the two prentices. All around them the Nameless spectators were either collecting their winnings or forking out their losses. And there were a lot more losers than winners.

'Don't get too far ahead of yourself, lad,' Silas told him. Joss watched as his friends, along with Lord Xavier and the *Zenith* crew, emerged from the crowd, all looking just as curious about the situation as he was. 'This means we'll vote on whether or not we join you, as I explained before. Sure, I've seen how you can swing a sword, but that doesn't mean much. Now – if you'll kindly wait outside the gates, we'll let you know when we've reached a decision.'

'We can't stay?' Lord Xavier exclaimed.

'Painful as it must be to go without our company, we conduct our votes away from the eyes of outsiders.'

'How do we know you'll be honest with the results?'

'You don't trust me, your lordship?' Silas asked with mock offense. When Lord Xavier only glowered in response, Silas raised one hand and put the other on his heart. 'You have my word as consul of the Nameless that we'll be straight and true with you. Will that suffice?'

'I suppose it will have to,' Lord Xavier replied, and turned to leave.

Joss didn't know if it was the pain from his wounds or the guilt over how he'd behaved, but something made him push forward to plead with Eliza's uncle. 'It doesn't have to be this way, you know. This hostility between us,' he said. 'We're facing down the end of the world as we know it. Which gives us the chance we need to start building a better one. We just can't do it alone.'

Silas regarded him with genuine esteem. 'Fine words, lad,' he said. 'We'll see if my brethren agree.'

With no more arguments to be made, Lord Xavier led the *Zenith* crew back down the gulch. Joss didn't look at anyone as he guided Azof along the bridge and out past the gates.

He couldn't stop thinking of everything that Eliza had said, and all the terrible things he'd told her in return. He glanced at her, but she kept her eyes averted. Once they'd drawn rein to wait, Edgar climbed down from his saddle and took to her side to have a whispered conversation.

'How you holding up there?' Zeke asked, sliding in beside Joss as Drake and Hero trailed behind.

'Sore,' Joss replied. 'In more ways than one.'

'You should go talk to her,' Drake said. 'I'm sure you can work it out.'

'I don't know. I was kind of a –' He paused, unsure of how exactly to put it.

'Yes. You were,' said Hero. 'And an apology would go a long way towards correcting that.'

Joss knew she was right. So, screwing up his nerve, he started towards Eliza. He was almost there when Silas reappeared from behind the rusted iron gates, on foot and looking grim.

'Your appeal was voted down. The Nameless will not be lending their aid to your cause,' he wasted no time in telling them. Joss felt as if he were a piece of glass that had been struck with a hammer. All of that effort and animosity for nothing. Judging from the looks on everyone's faces – including the glance he stole of Eliza – he wasn't the only one left defeated by the announcement. This had been their last resort. What could they possibly do now?

'The truth is,' Silas continued, 'despite all my bluster I truly wanted to help. I may no longer belong to a paladero order, but my heart will always belong to Thunder Realm. Fort Ironfang was my home. Now I hear it's counted among the orders that have fallen. I suspect Lord Ivo of being one of the stone-faced traitors responsible. It would certainly explain my expulsion.'

'Then come with us,' Eliza implored him. 'Fight. Claim the justice you were denied.'

'Nothing would bring me greater satisfaction. But I must abide by my peers' decision,' Silas said, shaking his head.

Lord Xavier grunted. 'Thank you for your candour, Wildsmith. I'm sure I'll look back on it with appreciation when the darkness descends on us all,' he said, then turned to the rest of his company. 'Let's go.'

———

Eliza didn't give Joss a second look as they rode back to the ship. The welts Joss had all over his body were a stinging reminder of all that had happened, of every barbed word and pointed insult. He wished he had a salve that could cure every complaint, inside and out. He would have gladly shared it with Eliza, if she might look at him again.

Landing in the *Zenith*'s hangar, they found a pale-faced young ensign awaiting them. 'My lord,' he said, bowing to Lord Xavier. 'We've just received a communique from the Ivory Palace. There was a raid three days ago on Sunforge

Industries in Hammerton. Their entire inventory of experimental weapons was stolen. The palace has requested all ships report in and lend their aid to the search.'

'Yet more tails to chase,' his lordship sighed. 'Hail the palace. I'll take the transmission on the bridge. Better that we offer our help with the search on our own terms, rather than be given marching orders on where to go. Either way I'll require a full briefing.'

Without a word to the rest of them, Lord Xavier marched off. Everyone went their separate ways. The cloud of gloom hanging over them would have to be dispelled some other time.

Joss's quarters were cool and quiet as he pulled off his boots and riding leathers and inspected the wounds from Eliza's cicuta blade. The welts were an angry red, swollen and sore to the touch. He wondered how long it would take them to heal – how long it would take *him* to heal.

Despite how mad he'd been after Malkus's betrayal, despite all the disillusionment and resentment he'd felt in Illustra, he'd still held out hope that all the kingdom's forces would rally together. How could people be this blind? This selfish? This stubborn?

But then hadn't he been all those things, and more?

Maybe if Sur Verity had been with them, she might have won them all over. She certainly would have stood a better chance at it than Lord Xavier with all his disdain and hostility. Better than Joss, too, with his hotheadedness and fevered pleading. He'd always respected Sur Verity, even though he had never been sure if that respect flowed both ways. According to Eliza, it had. It was hard to know what to do with that revelation, especially while feeling so overwhelmingly defeated.

He was buttoning up his shirt again when he heard a knock at the door, and found Edgar pink-faced and puffing on the other side.

'It's Cloud's blessingday tomorrow,' he said.

'Oh – it is?' replied Joss. 'How'd you find that out?'

'Crimson let it slip. So we're going to throw a party to celebrate!'

'Edgar, that's a really friendly gesture but I don't know if now is the best time,' Joss gently told him. 'With everything going on and –'

'But now's exactly the time to do it! Think of how it'll cheer everyone up! Not to mention how it'll help everyone get to know each other better.'

Joss opened his mouth, but didn't utter a single syllable before Edgar cut him off again. 'Just give me an hour and then have everyone come to the observation deck, OK?'

Clearly Edgar would not be put off. 'OK,' Joss said, and Edgar scurried away down the hall.

An hour later, as promised, Joss and the others gathered on the observation deck. Joss was surprised but more than a little relieved that Eliza was absent.

'What's the story here?' Crimson demanded, dressed in his customary red cloak along with the uniform of a *Zenith* deckhand. Cloud was beside him, similarly garbed and looking none the wiser about what was going on. 'Your little friend banged on our door telling us to be here at dusk. What's going on?'

'You'll have to ask him,' Joss replied. 'He's in charge of this whole shindig.'

'Shindig?' Hero blinked through her goggles. 'What shindig –?'

The doors swung open, revealing a lavish soiree. Streamers garlanded the ceiling while a revolving rainbow of lights patterned the walls, and an illumigram of Theophilus Thicket and the Thunderfolk Three crooned in the corner.

A spit-roast cabinet was rotating an entelodont carcass over a charcoal flame, sending mouth-watering aromas through the room. The furniture was pushed up against the walls to create space for a dancefloor, while the bar in the corner was stocked with barrels of sarsaparilla, ginger ale and creaming soda. Standing at the centre of all this splendour was Edgar, his arms outstretched.

'Hello, everybody!' he beamed. 'And welcome to the party!'

CHAPTER TWENTY-TWO

A Scream of Sirens

'I DON'T believe it, Edgar,' Joss said, staring in amazement at the party the young steward had somehow pulled together. 'How did you manage all this?'

'It was pretty easy, really,' Edgar replied as the guests crowded in around them. 'You just ask the right people in the right way and you can get almost anything done.'

Joss blinked at the simplicity of Edgar's wisdom. He was still pondering how to act on it himself when Zeke brushed past on his way to the bar.

'I'll pour the drinks,' he proclaimed, lining up a row of tankards to take everyone's order. When all their cups were filled, Edgar returned to the centre of the dance floor to toast the guest of honour.

'I know we've had a hard time since setting out together. Today being one of the worst. Not that fighting a dragon would rank as one of the easiest days we've had …'

'I'll second that!' Zeke called out, earning a ripple of laughs.

When the room had quieted again, Edgar continued, 'It seems to me that with all the hardship we're facing and with all that's at stake, it's more important than ever to make time for our friends and celebrate the good in life. So here's to two of our newest friends, Crimson and Cloud, and to Cloud in particular – blessed with life by the Sleeping King on this day and blessing the world in return!'

'*Happy blessingday!*' everyone cheered. Cloud looked dumbfounded that the party was in honour of him. Proving slow to respond, he needed another round of applause as encouragement to step away from the safety of Crimson's side and take the floor beside Edgar, wincing through his embarrassment.

'Thank you. All of you. Edgar, especially,' he said, blinking hard. 'Nobody's ever really – I've never – I can't begin to –'

'He looks so familiar, if only I could place him,' Hero muttered as Cloud continued to hem and haw.

'So it's not just me, then?' Joss whispered in reply, squinting at the young deckhand in his latest fruitless effort to work out where he'd seen him before. Cloud, still tongue-tied and getting worse by the moment, found himself mercifully put out of his misery by Crimson cutting in and throwing an arm around his shoulder.

'What my friend here means to say is –' Crimson declared. 'Everybody, *thank you*, and have a wonderful time!'

Everyone cheered again, and the illumigram kicked back in with an up-tempo toe-tapper of a tune.

'May I have this dance?' Hero asked Drake, offering her hand.

'I thought you'd never ask!' Drake laughed, and together they took to the dancefloor. Joss watched from the sidelines with Zeke leaning over his shoulder from behind the bar.

'Of all the ways I imagined today ending, this would have to be the most unlikely,' Zeke said. 'Edgar really is a miracle worker.'

'Yes,' replied Joss as he watched Edgar slipping outside, the glass hatch sliding shut behind him. 'He really is.'

Excusing himself, Joss followed his friend onto the external deck. Edgar was at the far end with his elbows resting on the rail, watching the sky as it went swimming past.

'What are you doing out here?' Joss asked. 'I thought you'd want to enjoy the rewards of all your hard work.'

Edgar jumped, startled by the unexpected voice. But then he turned around to offer Joss a gentle smile. 'Just thought I'd get some fresh air. Throwing everything together left me feeling a little winded,' he replied. 'Besides – it's beautiful out here.'

Joss looked out at the of panoply of stars rising against the rosy purple of twilight. The moon was already full – it felt as if Joss could simply lean forward and run his fingers across it.

'It really is,' he said, taking a place beside Edgar at the rail.

After the longest time, Edgar shifted, tilted his head to the side and asked Joss in a hushed voice, 'You grew up in Makepeace. Didn't you? Before you came to Round Shield Ranch?'

'Mostly,' Joss said, thinking back to the Orphan House. His time there felt like a dim memory, even though it had been his home for several years. Or a kind of home, at least. The truth was that, despite how young he'd been when he'd first arrived there, he had never allowed himself to grow too comfortable within its walls. It was Round Shield Ranch where he'd truly learned to let his guard down. He could never have imagined what that would cost him.

'I grew up in Resilient,' Edgar said, drawing Joss back to the present.

'I passed through that way with Sur Verity once,' he replied. 'On the way to Tower Town. It's beautiful. Made of all the old train carriages that crashed there years ago, right?'

Edgar nodded faintly. 'I just heard through the illumisphere that it's been evacuated.'

'Really?' Joss said, stunned.

'It's expected to fall to the enemy within the hour.'

It took Joss a moment to understand all that Edgar was telling him. Still grappling with the ramifications, he asked, 'Have you heard from your family?'

Edgar shook his head. 'It would have all happened so quickly, before they had a chance to get a message out. The townsfolk are meant to be travelling to Tower Town. Maybe I can find them there,' he said, his gaze growing even more distant. 'It's a pity. The honeyblossoms would be in full bloom about now. I remember at school we would all pick the flowers in the yard. The only thing sweeter than a honeyblossom's perfume is its nectar. We'd sip it from the flowers like straws. I keep imagining the blossoms and my schoolyard and my home all burning. Same as Round Shield Ranch.'

Edgar shuddered, his voice breaking. It took him a moment to find it again. 'So, throwing a party seemed like a much better use of my time,' he said, shaking himself off. 'Shall we go back in?'

Joss wanted to ask him how he found it in him to keep going, much as he'd asked Hero all the way back in Illustra. He wanted to know how his friend could hold onto his rational mind in such irrational circumstances. What trick did he have? But what trick did any of them have? Deciding it was better not to push him, Joss kept his questions to himself.

As they walked back into the warmth of the parlour, they found that the noise of the party had lured a score of additional guests. The dance floor had become a battlefield of warring exhibitionists. Zeke had evolved his bartender volunteering into a vocation, taking orders and dispensing drinks with flair. Drake and Hero were throwing themselves into the dancing with unbridled enthusiasm, while Qorza and Lieutenant Tyne attempted to have a quiet game of *regiments* at the edge of all the revelry.

'Look who's arrived,' Edgar said with a subtle gesture. Eliza was hovering by the door. Joss was hit with a bomb blast of nerves, which frizzed as Edgar gave him a push in her direction.

'You should go talk to her.'

'What if she doesn't want to –? And what about you?'

'Just. Go. Talk to her.'

Wondering when the young steward had become so bold, Joss took his advice and crossed the room one hesitant step at a time. 'Hi,' he said as he came within distance of Eliza.

She greeted him with a look that gave nothing away.

'Pretty impressive, isn't it?' Joss said, looking around at the room. 'I swear, Edgar could conjure up his very own Tournament if given the time.'

A tiny smile glimmered on Eliza's face. 'You're right – he's pretty extraordinary.'

Deciding there was nothing else to do but do it, Joss screwed up his nerve and addressed the mammoth in the main hall.

'About today …' he croaked through a dry throat.

'I don't know if there's much else to say.'

'I know. I already said a lot. Much of which I regretted even while I was saying it. But if you'll let me explain?'

Eliza crossed her arms. 'So explain.'

Joss dipped his head, trying to pull words out that would rather stay where they were. 'I was young when I started at Round Shield Ranch,' he told her. 'Two years younger than the minimum age for a prentice. Everyone seemed to think I'd had strings pulled for me. Which, it turns out, is exactly what happened ...'

He thought of how Lord Malkus had told him that he'd carried Joss from the raft that had borne him and his mother from the Destruction of Daheed, how that experience had given Malkus a sense of responsibility for Joss, and how Malkus had ultimately betrayed that responsibility.

'But that's a story for another time,' he said. 'The point is, I always felt like I had to fight for my place. To prove myself. It was something that Sur Verity ... well, she never discouraged it. In fact, she often fanned the flame. I don't say that to speak ill of her. Everything I know, she taught me. And I'm forever grateful. But it's always played on my mind. Whether she wanted me as her prentice. Whether she felt I was worthy. I was left to guess at her every thought. Which is why it was so hard for me to see how proud she was of you. I ... didn't handle it well. At all. And I'm sorry. Not just for today, but for ever feeling I had any reason to resent you in the first place.'

He was amazed that he'd managed to say all of that. But Eliza didn't appear to share the feeling.

'You know it wasn't easy for me either,' she said. 'Sur Verity may have told you she was proud of me, but I was in the dark most of the time – just the same as you. I admired her, I respected her, I even idolised her. But that didn't mean she was an easy person to have as a mentor.'

'No. She wasn't,' Joss admitted. 'But she was still my hero.'

Eliza's shoulders dropped. 'Mine too.'

Together they sighed, and shared a guarded smile.

'Can I get you something to drink?' he asked her.

Eliza thought for a moment, then shrugged. 'Do they have any elderberry cordial?'

'Elderberry cordial?' Joss raised an eyebrow. 'Really?'

'We just patched things up and you want to try picking at the stitches?'

'Elderberry cordial it is.'

'Make mine a double!' Edgar exclaimed as he popped up behind them.

'Were you lurking there the entire time?' asked Joss, startled.

'I wasn't lurking,' replied Edgar with a pout. 'It was more of a friendly loiter.'

Joss and Eliza couldn't help but laugh, and dragged Edgar with them to fetch a drink from Zeke. For the first time since his arrival on the *Zenith* – for the first time in a long time – Joss felt like he could finally relax. Sipping his overly sweet elderberry cordial, he looked around at the unfolding celebration. The music was loud and the lights were low. Edgar and Eliza were huddled in close to each other to talk over the noise, while Crimson and Cloud showed off their dance moves, prompting others to jump in and join them.

'Looking to cut a rug?' Zeke asked Joss from over his shoulder while polishing a glass.

'I don't dance,' Joss replied.

'You've been tapping your toe for a good five minutes now.'

'My toe dances. I stay put.'

'If you say so,' Zeke told him, before adding a devilish smile. 'But I'm sure we can fix that.'

Joss laughed. 'There's that confidence I remember.'

'Just more bluster. Maybe when I've summoned the nerve to stand up against the old man we'll say different.'

Zeke's grin wilted while Joss searched for something supportive to say.

Sirens screamed. The rainbow of lights died, replaced by flashing amber emergency beacons.

'Tell me that's just some alarm that's wired to go off when it detects any criticism of your father ...' Joss said to Zeke as the prentices all stared at each other in fright.

'*All hands to battle stations! All hands to battle stations!*' the ship's address system blared. '*Dragons sighted off the starboard bow!*'

CHAPTER TWENTY-THREE

—

A GREATER DUTY

'I WANT all weapons targeting the enemy combatants!' Lord Xavier shouted at the crew members on the bridge. 'Throw everything we've got at them – is that understood?'

'*Yes, my lord!*' the crew responded.

Joss and the others panted as they rushed into the room. Every window they'd passed had given them a view of the two dragons curling around each other in the air, effortlessly evading the ship's cannon blasts.

'Lord Xavier!' Joss called. 'What do you want us to do?'

His lordship rounded on the new arrivals with an impatience that bordered on the homicidal. 'What do I want you to do? I want you to clear the bridge!' he thundered at them. 'This is no place for prentices.'

'But we can help!' said Eliza.

'Or don't you remember Nobleseat?' Joss added.

Grinding his jaw, Xavier scrutinised them. 'You have skyborne training?' he said.

'We do,' Hero replied.

'Then saddle up and see if you can draw those cursed creatures towards the cannons,' he told them. 'And keep out of the line of fire!'

As Joss and his brethren left, his lordship called out again, stopping them in their tracks. '*Ezekiel!* Where are you going?'

Zeke jerked his thumb in the direction of the hangar. 'I'm going to fire up the *Fat Lot of Good*, make it live up to its name.'

'That bucket of rotten gizzards will only prove a slow-moving target for those beasts,' Lord Xavier shouted. 'I want you aboard the *Zenith* on standby should I need to delegate any duties to you.'

'But Father –'

'That's an order!' Lord Xavier turned back to his station.

'Come on,' Joss said, clapping Zeke on the back. 'Let's go get those pterosaurs saddled.'

By the time they reached the hangar the service meks had already received the order to prepare the prentice's mounts. When Joss saw the pterosaurs bridled and waiting, a realisation dawned on him. 'I … I don't have a mount to fly.'

The words fell out of him the way Tempest had tumbled out of the sky. How could he have forgotten? He'd been so focused on the troubles at hand that everything else had lapsed into the background. Again he mourned the loss of his headstrong and heroic pterosaur, and wondered what use he could be in the lizard-bird's absence.

'Don't worry,' Drake said as he and Hero buttoned up their flight jackets. 'Hero and I can handle this. But if it takes a bad turn we'll need all of you to serve as reinforcements. Can you do that?'

Joss fumed at the prospect of being left on the sidelines, but what choice did he have? The *Zenith* had no spare winged mounts, other than those that he and his brethren had brought with them on their exodus from Round Shield Ranch. If Tempest had survived then Joss would have been saddling up with his brethren right now. All he could do instead was answer Drake with a single nod and then step back to watch as his brethren steered their pterosaurs to the bay doors.

'Ride well!' he called out. The doors opened with a whisper that was shouted down by the wind rushing inside. The pterosaurs didn't flinch; nor did their riders. Hero was the first through the hatch, dropping clear of the ship and taking wing with acrobatic elegance, followed just as gracefully by Drake. They were out of sight within seconds.

'We should be able to see them from the observation deck,' Zeke suggested once the bay doors had closed.

'You don't want to stay here in case your father changes his mind?' Joss asked, a sprout of hope coming with his next idea. 'Maybe we could pilot the *Fat Lot* together.'

'We'll both die of old age before the great and honourable Lord Xavier Zadkille will ever change his mind. Better that we go see what's happening than stay down here in the dark.'

Joss agreed, and with Edgar and Eliza stuck to their spurs they raced back up to the observation deck. The remaining partygoers – those who hadn't been called back to their posts – all had their faces pressed against the window, watching the silhouettes of their winged attackers against the dazzling bursts of fire from the ship's cannons. Joss, Zeke, Edgar and Eliza squeezed in among everyone to get a better view. The dragons were little more than a blur out in the darkness, but Joss could see them well enough to spot a critical difference.

'They don't look like any of the other dragons,' he said.

'No,' Qorza replied without looking away from the window. 'They don't.'

Where the other dragons they'd encountered had been behemoths with black hides veined in red, these beasts were smaller and sleeker, with glassy pale green scales that shimmered in the moonlight.

'Perhaps it's a different regiment,' Qorza said in the scholarly tone she used whenever she was presented with a new curiosity.

'You think these animals are regimented?' asked

Lieutenant Tyne with astonishment. 'Could they be that organised?'

'Possibly. The fact is we're dealing with creatures that were thought extinct for eons. What little we know of the species came from their kindred bloodline, the weredragons. And they were never a very forthcoming bunch.'

'We can't just stand here taking notes,' Joss said. He yanked the hatch open and stepped outside. The wind was a wild animal, howling in his ears and tearing at his hair. He steadied himself and drew his training blade; Edgar rushed out to join him, along with Eliza and Zeke. The dragons were circling overhead, too close for the *Zenith*'s cannons to target them, refusing to be drawn out by Drake and Hero's swooping attacks.

'Joss, what are you doing?! Those monsters will eat you alive!' Edgar exclaimed over the cannon fire.

Zeke was close behind him. 'Listen to him, Joss – this is madness!'

'Then go back inside,' Joss told them.

'Joss, what would Sur Verity tell you to do?' Eliza asked.

'She'd tell me,' he muttered, staring upward, 'that we're being watched.'

The others looked up and saw he wasn't lying. The dragons were swirling in the air directly above them, their eyes as bright as falling stars. They dropped down and landed at the far end of the deck with a tremor that shuddered violently through the steel plating. For the first time, Joss noticed they were wearing some form of cloak or scarf around their necks, much as a pet would wear a leash. But if these were the pets, where was their master?

He didn't have time to think about it. The dragons were staring straight at him.

'What do we do?' Edgar asked.

Joss knew only one answer. With his right hand he held tight to his training sword. With his left he drew the Champion's Blade, then started his advance. The dragons didn't rear up at his approach – didn't even expel a whiff of smoke or flame. Instead they doubled over, as if bowing. Joss stopped, his grip on his weapons slackening as he watched the dragons' bones shift beneath their skin, their scales recede, their claws retract and their fangs soften. He gasped as both dragons stood tall again, revealing their true forms.

———

Sur Verity was only just clinging to consciousness when she heard footsteps in the darkness. Struggling to open her eyes, she looked up to see Malkus looming over her.

'Wake up,' he said, his face shrouded in shadow. 'We have to go.'

'What? Where?' she croaked.

'Questions later. Action now,' was all he said, and pulled her up.

Stumbling out of her cell, her vision took a moment to adjust, and when it did she found herself standing on the edge of a circular chamber littered with engraved stones. Iron braziers and chandeliers sputtered with crimson flames, casting harsh shadows against the walls.

'What is this place?' she asked, tripping over one of the many deep channels in the granite floor.

'We call it the Shadow Chamber,' Malkus explained, crossing to a crude doorway that was half-hidden in the darkness. 'A place for us to convene and conduct our rituals.'

'You had this hidden beneath Round Shield Ranch all this time?'

'It was already here,' he said, leaning through the doorway long enough to ensure that nobody was on the other side, then gesturing for her to follow him. 'Early in his reign, Lord Kenneth Kye discovered what he believed to be ancient weredragon caves beneath the foundations of the fortress. He excavated them to incorporate secret passageways leading to and from his chambers, as well as vaults where he could hide his vast wealth. They were forgotten over time, but I rediscovered them not long after being named lord.'

'And you used them to house your collaborators and plan your betrayal,' Sur Verity noted as they exited the crimson-lit chamber and entered a winding tunnel spiked with an arsenal of stalactites and stalagmites. She scanned every dark corner as they went, refusing to trust that this wasn't some elaborate and sadistic ploy. 'While the rest of us remained oblivious.'

'Our court has a talent for masking its presence,' he said, leaving Sur Verity to gaze upon her old mentor with muted horror.

'I never really knew you at all – did I?' she asked. The feathers on his cloak bristled as he turned away from her.

'Nobody knows anybody.'

He pushed on through the treacherous path of sharp rocks and protruding boulders, coming to a narrow staircase hewn from the cavern wall. A black stream ran alongside it, rushing headlong into the yawning gullet of a rocky tunnel. Stopping at the foot of the stairs, Malkus turned to Sur Verity and pointed upwards.

'My chambers are at the top. You may be shocked at what you find there. Round Shield Ranch is a husk of what it once was. You'll need to ignore that and focus on getting through the outer gates. There's only a handful of guards stationed throughout the grounds; if you're quick and quiet and keep your wits about you, you should be able to reach the outside undetected. You'll find this stream connects with the river. More than a league downstream there's a raptor waiting for you. You'll need this.' Reaching into his cloak, he removed a sheathed weapon.

'My song sword,' Sur Verity gasped, the scabbard clinking in her grip as she readily accepted it.

Malkus took hold of her shoulder and pulled her in close. 'If you see Sarif,' he said, his silver teeth gleaming, 'you need to tell him –'

'Tell him what, brother?' a voice boomed from the top

of the stairs. Malkus and Sur Verity jumped at the sight of another Thrall staring down at them. He had three followers in lacquered masks and iron chestplates by his side, all wielding blades of black metal.

'You've removed your mask, I see,' the Thrall noted when Malkus didn't immediately answer him.

'Have I?' Malkus asked, touching his face with a faraway look in his eyes. 'So I have. I can never tell the difference anymore. It's felt like a second face for so long – my true face. Ever since the week I spent carving it from a slab of dark, wet stone from the shore of Crescent Cove ...'

Malkus paused to set his gaze on the masked man at the head of the staircase. 'But then you joined our ranks. And when I presented you with a stone of your own, you finished your mask within the night. It was then I knew just how much your devotion eclipsed my own.'

'Indeed,' replied the Thrall, taking a single step down. 'If only it had been me standing on that shore in your place. His Highness may have had a lieutenant worthier of his name, without a single splinter of doubt in his heart.'

'You presume too much, Blaek,' said Malkus, stunning Sur Verity with the identity of the man looming over them. 'None of this would have happened without me. Not the formation of the Court of Thralls, nor the fall of Round Shield Ranch, nor the horror that's soon to follow. I can only hope I find some way to make amends for all the suffering and destruction I've caused.'

Thrall – *Sur Blaek*, Verity had to remind herself – took

another step down. 'If you think that somehow involves setting this heretic free,' he said, 'you're gravely mistaken.'

'And you're a fool if you think I'm so easily intimidated, Blaek. Let alone by someone as wretched as you,' Malkus replied, drawing his sword.

'You'd do right not to talk with such disrespect, traitor,' one of Blaek's masked offsiders snarled while slashing at the air with feral-minded fervour. 'Lest I cut that curly tongue clear out of your skull.'

'There's no need for such threats, Lynch. I can dispense with Malkus myself. I wouldn't want you making the same calamity of it as you did the raid on Dragon's Toe.'

'Next time I see Sarif and his little accomplices, I swear retribution will be swift,' the underling muttered, earning Sur Verity's guarded curiosity.

'Until then, if you wish to atone for your failings and earn back the right to wear this crest …' Blaek tapped the inverted crown sigil on his underling's chest before turning his stony gaze on Sur Verity. 'Then bring me the woman's eye.'

The feral little offsider sniggered through his mask. His cohorts chuckled alongside him. 'Very well, m'lord.'

As the three thugs and their master made their advance, Malkus pulled Sur Verity aside. The stream rushed by her feet as he forced her to the water's edge.

'Remember, the water joins the river. You just have to hold your breath long enough to make it to the other side,' he hissed at her. 'Now go.'

'I'm not so weak that I can't stand and fight,' she told him, even as the fever that gripped her made her sway on the spot.

'You have a greater duty,' he said. 'Find Sarif. Lend your voice to his. Warn the world of what's to come. And when you do, tell them this –'

Leaning in close, he whispered dark portents that made her heart quicken and her soul shrink, and she knew she couldn't remain in the shadows.

'Go!' he told her, and raised his sword to fight. He met the four attackers at the foot of the stairs, steel blades shrieking sharply as they clashed against each other. Sur Verity took one last look at the man who had trained her, mentored her, raised her to the rank of paladero. She turned to look at the black stream rushing into the mouth of the tunnel. And then she took a breath, stepped forward, and leapt.

CHAPTER TWENTY-FOUR

A WARNING
OF ALL TO COME

LORD Xavier and his officers burst through the hatch and onto the exterior platform, then joined Joss and the other onlookers as they stared in amazement at the two figures standing in the middle of the deck.

'Where – where are they?' asked Lord Xavier. 'The dragons? Where did they go?'

'I don't know how to tell you this, my lord,' Joss said. 'But you're looking at them.'

He gestured to the pair of women gazing back at them. The taller of the two was lantern-jawed, with cropped auburn hair and three jagged scars across her sombre face. She wore a humble linen cloak and stood with the rigid composure of a soldier, somehow managing to keep a close watch on both her companion and everyone else on the deck at the same time.

The other woman was shorter, slighter, with molten scarlet hair and a fine patina of jade scales bordering her eyes like a bandit's mask. Her pupils were slitted like a sabretooth's and were the same shade of laurel green as her elegant silk cloak, which Joss realised was the sash he'd seen around the dragon's neck. Even after all the shapeshifters he'd encountered while preparing to become a paladero, he found it hard to think of these women as the same beings that had flown through the air only moments ago.

'It's not possible …' Lord Xavier whispered to himself.

The shorter woman either didn't hear him or chose to ignore his remark as she took a decisive step toward them. Everyone else took a half-step back.

'Greetings,' she declared in a highborn voice, her words as clear as a mountain spring. 'I am Lady Razeel of the House of Raza, daughter of the departed Lord Raza the Blacktooth and sister to our ruler, King Raza the Flamehearted.'

'*King?*' Joss heard Lord Xavier exclaim, as if the heresy of anyone but the Sleeping King laying claim to such a title was the most striking point from this turn of events.

Hero and Drake swooped in on their pterosaurs, their sudden arrival enough to make everyone jump – everyone but the two visitors.

'We lost them! I don't know how but we lost them, and – and –' Drake trailed off as he stared at the strangers, quickly piecing things together. 'That's not … surely they aren't …?'

'Weredragons!' Edgar exclaimed, barely able to contain himself as Drake and Hero dismounted. 'Lady Razeel and her companion – a pair of real live weredragons, Mister Drake! Can you believe it?'

'Your name is Drake?' said the Lady Razeel, exchanging a curious glance with her offsider. Drake sized up the strangers as he addressed them. 'Ganymede Drake. Of Starlight Fields in the Northern Tundra.'

'Drake – that's an old *draa'kin* name,' the taller of the two weredragons said.

'*Draa'kin?*' Hero repeated with confusion.

'The name of our people. And what we prefer to be called over "weredragons". Given your friend's family name, it's likely he had an ancestor of our bloodline,' Lady Razeel replied.

Qorza edged forward. 'But you were all meant to be gone. Exiled or extinct – we were never sure which.'

'Merely hiding,' the lady replied. 'Centuries ago we sought to escape the overwhelming spread of our mortal cousins, much as the fae had done shortly before us. Though rather than leave this realm altogether we withdrew to our best concealed strongholds, abandoning the other sites in the process.'

'You're talking about the hidden city of Dragon's Tooth,' Qorza said with wonder. 'I thought it was just a myth.'

Lady Razeel offered the barest of nods. 'We know it by another name. It's unpronounceable in your King's tongue but can be roughly translated as *Sanctum*. I come from there now to parley on behalf of my people.'

'If you wish to speak with anybody then you would be best served by the Ivory Palace and our regent, Augustus Greel,' Lord Xavier told her, striking an officious tone.

But Lady Razeel still looked undeterred. 'I have it on good authority that I would be well served in dealing with you, my lord.'

'And whose authority would that be?' Lord Xavier lingered on a heavy pause. 'My lady?'

The woman towering beside Lady Razeel implored her with a cautionary glance. 'My lady,' she said. 'I would strongly suggest the utmost discretion in what we reveal. A blazing house cannot go unburned.'

'Your concern is noted, though dark times demand desperate deeds.' Turning from her companion, Lady Razeel again addressed the crowd. 'You'll have to forgive Chamberlain Füm's reticence. She serves now as my aide-de-camp and personal protector, but before that she was a highly decorated officer in our royal wingforce – not to mention our clandestine services.'

'A spy,' Lord Xavier spat.

Lady Razeel let the insult slide by. 'If you wish to use that term. We see them as scouts. The truth is that despite having retreated from the world, we have maintained a watch on the surface through the covert operations of such officers. And one of their number –'

'My lady,' Chamberlain Füm interrupted, more sternly this time.

'One of their number,' Lady Razeel went on, determined not to be silenced. 'Was among those taken by the Court of Thralls at the place you call "Dragon's Toe".'

Joss thought back to the prisoners he'd unshackled, and the redheaded boy with the vivid green eyes who'd been among them. 'Ormar,' he said, the name popping out almost of its own volition. 'The Chief Warden's steward.'

Lady Razeel cocked her head in a manner that neither confirmed nor denied the charge, which in itself spoke volumes. 'Our scout attested to your courage and communicated your mission to our palace,' she said. 'We've come here in the hope of allying our forces to ensure the safety of our world.'

'And your people are all in agreement on this? Despite the profound efforts you've made to shroud your presence for all this time?' Lord Xavier asked.

A small but noticeable tic flickered across Lady Razeel's otherwise impassive face. 'I have to confess that my brother did not warm to the idea. In fact, he rejected the notion.'

Joss, his brethren and the rest of the *Zenith* crew regarded each other with a shared look of incredulity.

'But I am certain that he can be convinced, particularly if you were to petition him in person,' Lady Razeel went on. 'And if our scout's reports are as accurate as we believe them to be, you will need all the help you can muster in the battles to come.'

The uncertainty engulfing the group deepened.

'You would wage war on your own kind?' asked Lieutenant Tyne with an air of curiosity.

'The beasts unleashed on our ancient city are not of our own kind. But even if they were, do mortals not fight among themselves for survival?' Lady Razeel countered.

'Well – she's got us there,' said Zeke.

'True,' Joss admitted. Lord Xavier shot them both a look of admonishment, driving them back into silence.

'We'll need some time to deliberate on this,' his lordship said. 'If you could tell us when and where you wish to meet, we will endeavour to join you there – conditions permitting.'

The *draa'kin* women engaged in an entirely silent conversation of questioning glances and reproachful stares. With some reluctance, Lady Razeel drew breath to answer. 'That should be satisfactory,' she said, going on to explain how to find the city of Sanctum, from its position in the Backbone Ranges to the cave that served as its hidden entrance. 'Once there, you should see a marker bearing this symbol.'

She pointed to the insignia embroidered over her heart. It was no larger than a lapel pin, but nevertheless discernible as an eye with a fang for an iris, stitched in golden thread.

'We hope most sincerely to receive you there,' her ladyship concluded as her skin prickled with scales and a pair of wings sprouted from her back. With a swift flick she unfurled her cloak, obscuring everyone's vision of her final moments of transformation. When the cloak settled back around her shoulders, she was in her full and magnificent bestial state, her scales gleaming like freshly polished armour. Unleashing an almighty roar, she splayed her wings and leapt into the air with a similarly transformed Chamberlain Füm at her side.

'Aren't they *grand!*' Edgar wheezed as he watched the two dragons disappearing into the distance.

'I don't believe it! Weredragons ... real live weredragons!' Drake said, just as dumbstruck. 'Or real live *draa'kin*, as I should say.'

'And they said you might be part of the family,' noted Hero. 'I always knew you had fire in your belly.'

'We should file a report at once. Regent Greel will no doubt wish to handle this matter personally,' Lord Xavier declared.

The group stared at his lordship in stunned silence.

'But –' Joss said, voicing the thought he could see etched on his brethren's faces. 'The invitation was for us. Not the regent or his people.'

'We don't have the authority to make such treaties on our own.'

'Our mission is to marshal the kingdom's forces and secure as many alliances as we can. And time is running out,' Qorza said. 'If we wait for Regent Greel and the Ivory Palace, this chance could vanish right before our eyes. We need to act quickly if we're going to have any success.'

Lord Xavier cracked his jaw as he contemplated the situation. 'And what says our Blade Keeper?' he asked, turning his eye on Joss.

'Me?' Joss blinked in confusion.

'This whole enterprise came about from your beseeching His Excellency. Are you comfortable excluding him, to venture forth on what could prove to be a quagmire of our own pouring? No doubt he'll expect an explanation should that turn out to be the case, and I wouldn't be surprised if he demanded it of you.'

Joss couldn't believe what he was hearing. Was Lord Xavier threatening to pin everything on him if their mission failed? Or was this a test to see if Joss would rise to the occasion? With all eyes turned on him, he knew he couldn't afford to hesitate.

'I agree with Qorza,' he answered with all the confidence he could muster, steadfastly ignoring the feeling of lizards in his gizzards. 'We should go to Sanctum. We should meet with their king and convince him that we need to fight together. It may be the only way we can win.'

Lord Xavier's scowl cracked just enough to raise a single leery eyebrow. 'Very well – we'll set a course for the weredragons' secret city. Let's just hope this heretic king is as susceptible to persuasion as his sister would have us believe, and as you all seem to so fervently hope,' his lordship said as he marched from the deck. 'And somebody clean off all these cursed ethereon scratchings – if today doesn't disprove their worth, I don't know what will.'

———

The raptor scraped its clawed foot against the earth as it waited by the riverbank. The bitter odour of ash still clung to the air from the fires that had so recently ravaged the land. Monsters sailed overhead on wings as black and expansive as the night itself, screaming their war cries into the darkness. But for all the surrounding danger, the raptor remained calm. Not once did it pull at its reins, which had been left tied around the stump of a felled tree.

A solid mass of shadow drifted downstream. It sent ripples ringing as it drew closer to the shore, the currents parting to reveal a woman rising weakly to her feet.

'Levina?' the woman called out, and the raptor snorted and bounced at the sight of her master. Fighting her way free of the rushing water, Sur Verity held her left arm against her body. It hung loose in her grip, lifeless.

'It's more than I could have hoped for to see you here,' she told her loyal mount as she trudged up onto the riverbank. Approaching the raptor, she let go of her stricken arm long enough to give the animal a pat with her good hand. The effort nearly made her collapse. Levina whickered with concern.

'Don't fuss,' Sur Verity told her mount as she winced through the pain of pulling herself up into the saddle. 'We have bigger challenges ahead of us. And precious little time to face them.'

With a snap of the reins and a shout of '*Hyah!*', Sur Verity spurred her raptor into a gallop, riding with all her remaining strength to warn everyone of all that was to come.

—

CHAPTER TWENTY-FIVE

A Chance at Claiming Destiny

THE *Fat Lot of Good* pushed against the pounding winds, fighting hard to make landfall. The *Zenith* had flown in wide and low, tracing a long arc from the eastern face of the Backbone Ranges on its way to Dragon's Tooth. But Zadkille Station's flagship was far too large to make a safe mooring on such treacherous terrain, so the handpicked landing party had once again crowded onto the *Fat Lot of Good*. Zeke was at the control panel while Lord Xavier supervised from the corner of the wheelhouse, making his son sweat under his watchful eye.

The *Fat Lot* swung wildly as it made its final approach for landing. A quick ratcheting of the stabilisers pulled it back under Zeke's control, and he landed the ship with a thump in a cradle of rock at the mountain's peak.

'Last stop, *Dragon's Tooth!*' he called out, clearly elated at having pulled off such a challenging feat. 'Please ensure you have all your luggage and weapons with you as you exit the airship.'

'No need for the attempts at wit, boy. This is serious business we're on,' his father told him on his way out of the wheelhouse. The others followed, leading their saddled mounts from the hull. Unlike at Dragon's Toe, Zeke was permitted to accompany them this time, and quickly powered up his jet-cycle before his father could change his mind.

'Let's get this jester's quest underway,' Lord Xavier said, frowning as he led the group up the tight mountain path towards the cave opening that Lady Razeel had described.

As they made the trek, Joss glanced around at his companions. Drake, Hero, Edgar and Eliza were to act as witnesses of the Shadow God's power, just the same as him. Even Zeke could testify to that, if his father permitted him. Each of them looked as overwhelmed as Joss felt, struggling with the prospect of entering a forbidden city to meet with a royal court of mythical beings.

Not Qorza, though. She was beaming with excitement as she took everything in, all too happy to have been brought along should her arcane knowledge prove useful. Beside her, Lieutenant Tyne was executing his duty as acting field deputy of the *Zenith*'s armed forces – all of whom were marching along behind him – by scanning the terrain for any signs of hostility.

It demonstrated just how much he'd ingratiated himself

with Lord Xavier that Tyne had been entrusted with such an important responsibility. Joss was reminded of Lord Rayner back at Blade's Edge Acres and the understanding he'd shared with his master-of-arms, Captain Kardos. Joss had been suspicious of the pair at the time, and rightly so given their conspiratorial efforts to seize control of their order. Those efforts hadn't ended up involving the Court of Thralls, however, despite how convinced of it Joss had been; their aims had been far pettier than that. And Joss had been too blind to see it until it was too late. But that was the problem in dealing with black magic sorcerers and their dark overlords, he determined. It left you jumping at every shadow.

For all of Joss's scrutiny, Tyne showed no signs of noticing. He continued to search out looming threats while everyone else quietly hoped that the *draa'kin* ruler would prove to be more hospitable than one would assume. That is, if he were anywhere to be found.

The surroundings were devoid of any signs of life. There were no road markers, no tracks on the path, nothing except the cave. It was smaller than Joss had expected, but still large enough for Lord Xavier to plough his way inside without having to duck. The others followed close behind. Joss was surprised to find that the cave immediately opened up into a vaulted chamber big enough to accommodate them all.

They journeyed deeper and deeper into the cave until they came to a chasm spewing sulphuric smoke and steam.

The gas rolled upward in such thick waves it obscured everything, and Joss was sure the ferocity of its odour would drive away any unwitting interlopers.

'Everyone, look for the marker,' said Lord Xavier, coughing from the smoke. Inching his way through the blinding gas, Joss couldn't believe his luck as he tripped over a humble black rock adorned with the insignia from Lady Razeel's cloak.

'Over here!' Joss called out, and everyone ventured over to inspect his find. The rune seemed to shift in the light as Lord Xavier placed both feet upon the marker and spoke the words Lady Razeel had told them.

'*Here we seek sanctum.*'

Everyone's jaws dropped open as a deep rumbling coincided with the dispersal of the smoke, revealing a staircase of stone that was assembling itself within the chasm. The staircase led down into a stretch of blackness, lit at the distant bottom by what appeared to be glass lanterns. Lord Xavier examined the thin, slippery steps and grunted, 'We'll have to proceed on foot.'

The party broke to gather what they needed and pack away what they didn't. Joss sidled over to Edgar, who was busily stuffing provisions into a knapsack while humming merrily. It made what would come next all the more challenging.

'Edgar – will you do me a favour, please?' he asked. 'We need someone to stay here and keep an eye on the animals.'

A range of emotions played across Edgar's face, from

surprise to disappointment to resignation. 'I'd hoped I could see the dragon folk's city. It's not often an opportunity like this comes up – never, in fact.'

'True. But it's going to be dangerous down there and –'

'I can handle myself. You know I can.'

'Of course I do. There's nothing I'd like more than to have you with us,' Joss said, thinking not only of all the skill that Edgar had demonstrated over time, but the bravery too. And then he thought of Sur Verity, and of Tempest, and of the peril that Edgar had already found himself in once before when Joss had failed to protect him back at Crescent Cove, and he knew that sometimes skill and bravery simply weren't enough. 'But we may have to make a swift retreat. If that happens we'll need our mounts safe and ready to go. So that means we need someone we can rely on to look after them. And you'll also be guarding our only way in or out. Can you do that for me – for all of us?'

With relief, Joss watched as the mix of emotion that had flooded through Edgar a moment ago solidified into resolute certainty. 'I can.'

'Best of stewards and best of friends,' Joss told him with a gentle slap on the back.

'You're not joining us?' asked Eliza. She had hitched her borrowed mount to a nearby stalagmite and joined them, her disappointment palpable at overhearing Edgar's plans.

'Sitting this one out,' he sighed with resignation. 'But I'd appreciate it if you could bring me back a souvenir.'

'Of course. Maybe they'll have some special honeyblossom tea for you.'

Edgar and Eliza chuckled in a way that had more than the warmth of friendship to it, making Joss realise just how much time the pair had been spending together lately. He was still picking through the implications of it all as the group began their march into the abyss of the secret staircase.

'Good luck!' Edgar called out to them, watching as they went.

Joss had expected to find something waiting for them at the bottom of the staircase – a guide, perhaps, or even the city itself. Instead, it was just another cave. There wasn't even so much as a brazier to light their way, so the group had to rely on their torches.

'Fool's errand,' Lord Xavier groused as they marched through the all-encompassing shadows. 'We'll be lucky not to find ourselves entombed in a cave-in.'

'I wouldn't be so sure of that,' replied Qorza as the group entered the largest cavern yet, and found something more ornate and orderly than anything they'd seen so far. Floors of earth and mud and gravel gave way to a tiled corridor walled with fluted onyx, its vaulted ceilings arranged in strict geometric patterns. The next chamber was enclosed with walls of jade, the next with quartz – each section more opulent than the last.

Despite being so far underground, Joss was surprised at how clearly he could see. Every chamber was lit in gentle shades of orange and purple thanks to the discreet skylights that had been drilled into the overhead rock, the light shining off mirrored chandeliers. Shrines containing pillars lit with billowing flames had been erected all along the pathway, while dozens of elliptical stone wells ran the length of every chamber. The wells peered down on streams of golden magma boiling away leagues below. When Joss stole a glance over the side, the blast of heat sent him stumbling backwards.

Wherever their path was leading them, they were on the right track.

'Edgar would love this,' Eliza said as she studied the soft halos of light warming the lavish surrounds.

'Edgar loves most things,' Joss replied, smiling despite the pang of guilt he was feeling. 'But you're right. I can practically hear him marvelling at the craftsmanship.'

Eliza's smile was tinged with a shadow of unease. 'I hope he's safe where we left him.'

'The steward's fine. It's the rest of us who should be on guard rather than chatting away like schoolchildren,' Lieutenant Tyne grumbled as he rode past. Joss and the others swapped a look of grievance at the rebuke.

'For a leaf-eating county-dweller he sure has a lot of bite to him,' muttered Hero while Joss eyeballed the ranjer from behind his back.

'Maybe a spell from that bag of tricks there might knock some manners into him,' Zeke said, gesturing to the satchel slung over Qorza's shoulder.

'This? No magic spells here, I'm afraid. Just my usual supplies with the addition of what Dafne gave me.'

'You can fit that whole heavy grimoire in there?' asked Joss.

'Ha, no. That's back on the ship. I've only brought the essentials: mostly herbs for burning, a few wooden stakes, some silver blades, a charm or two, and a couple of bags of Sacred Sand.'

'Sacred Sand?' Eliza asked, just as perplexed as Joss. Qorza nodded.

'You'd be surprised at all its uses. It's listed in just about every arcane text.'

'Does it rate a mention in your mother's notes, Joss?' asked Zeke. Joss blanched at being asked such a direct question about something he'd been keeping so private. But if he couldn't open up to his friends about it, who else could he trust with this knowledge?

'Not that I've run across. Though I've mostly been concentrating on the Rakashi Revelations,' he replied.

'And what do those say?' asked Drake. 'It occurs to me that we've never actually heard this prophecy.'

Again Joss hesitated, though only for a moment. If he was going to have any chance at fulfilling his destiny and claiming the mantle of the *galamor* then he was going to have to be open about striving for it. So he reached into the inside pocket of his jacket – the only safe place he had for keeping his mother's journal and his father's nightscope – and passed the small leather-bound book to Drake.

'*From beyond silver seas,*' Drake read aloud after flipping to the page that Joss had folded over, reciting the words that had become engraved in Joss's mind like the runes on a paladero's song sword. '*From out of blue skies, from the ruins of a lost life, there will come a* galamor, *with right hand marked by fate and carrying a* vaartan rhazh. *Only the* galamor *will stand when all else fall, and rise when all else kneel. Only the* galamor *can bring light to the oncoming darkness, and draw hope from a dying dream. Only the* galamor, *and the* galamor *alone.*'

'Interesting …' Hero murmured as Drake handed the book back.

'Reminds me of what some of the older sailors would say back in Snowbridge. *Out of blue skies and silver seas,*' said Drake. 'Usually when they were describing a squall that had rolled up on them. Or a surprise attack from a leviathan.'

'So nothing ominous then?' Zeke chimed in.

The conversation was cut short as they found the first of what turned out to be a cluster of encampments set up in the largest caverns. They were like subterranean villages, with homes and taverns and municipal buildings built from stone in orderly grids. But every single one of these outposts sat empty, the residents having seemingly picked up and left not long before the *Zenith* crew's arrival.

'Strange,' said Drake. 'You don't think …?'

'What?' Joss asked him.

'That we're too late,' said Hero. 'That the Court of

Thralls has already been here.'

The thought sent a shiver through Joss, which he tried to shake off as they continued on their way. Finally, after hours of hiking, the group arrived at a pair of open iron doors, beyond which lay a cavern so large it could have housed the Ivory Palace's audience hall countless times over and still had room to spare.

'I don't believe it; we're here!' Qorza breathed as she gazed with the others at the subterranean metropolis. '*Dragon's Tooth* – the hidden city of the *draa'kin*!'

CHAPTER TWENTY-SIX

A SHARED THREAT

JOSS and his friends gazed in awe at their surroundings. Colossal stone dragons crouched at the highest reaches of the cavern, perched upon the top floors of hundreds, if not thousands, of apartments. The domiciles were built into the rocky walls, with black waterfalls pouring down between them from the mouths of the statues overhead. The water gushed into the gulf between the cave walls and flowed beneath the bridge upon which Joss and the others were standing, where it evaporated into billowing clouds of steam thanks to the river of lava glowing far below.

How was it possible that such a place could exist in secret for centuries, Joss wondered. And how could a city of such size be so utterly empty?

'We mustn't linger,' said Lord Xavier, and together the party continued along the central bridge which operated like a highway, with catwalks and bridges stemming from it like elevated streets – all of them empty. The apartments looked as vacant as the tiny townships had been, despite the occasional shifting shadow or distant clink. Joss wondered if it was just his mind playing tricks on him or if they were really being watched. He gripped the handle of the Champion's Blade tighter.

The group came to a juncture in the bridge that featured a large lantern forged from gold and bejewelled with rubies. Scenes from *draa'kin* history were etched into its glass surface, depicting past rulers, the founding of cities and the flight from the surface world.

'This is ridiculous,' Lord Xavier complained with little appreciation for the beauty before him. 'Are we to wander down here aimlessly for an eternity, or will someone eventually deign to receive us?'

'Maybe we'll have more luck up ahead,' said Lieutenant Tyne. 'I think I see some sort of platform.'

Venturing forward, they came to a public square and filed in. The moment the last of them stepped off the bridge, the nearest section dropped away with a rumble.

'Nothing ominous about that,' Zeke said.

'Public squares are where executions usually happen …' Hero mused.

'You're not helping,' Zeke told her.

'Weapons,' Lord Xavier commanded, and everyone drew their swords as they searched the shadows. Still there was nobody to be seen. The group's attention turned to the pair of soaring silver doors that dominated the far end of the square, reaching up to the same heights as the now distant apartment buildings. Joss expected them to swing open and a mob of Thralls and acolytes to come spilling out. But the doors remained shut.

Instead, a smaller door opened on the inconspicuous balcony perched high above, which observed the city below with detached authority. A regiment of guards in golden armour filed out in rigid formation, the stomping of their boots resounding throughout the cavern. A group of courtiers followed, each of them teetering beneath elaborate piles of hair and dressed in pale floating robes with frilled collars that reached to their chins. Joss saw neither Lady Razeel nor Chamberlain Füm in their number.

The guards took their positions around the balcony with their swords and spears drawn. Their chief, a solid man with a spiny helmet, stepped forward and declared, 'All hail King Raza the Flamehearted, crowned monarch of the *draa'kin* people, protector and rightful ruler of the trinity of sacred cities!'

A final figure emerged from the doorway. His robes seemed to have been stitched together from a thousand strings of rubies, cut low enough to expose his skeletal shoulders and his long, slender neck. His coppery hair ran all the way to his calves and was pulled back with thick gold bands. He stalked the balcony with an agile gait, scrutinising Joss and the others from behind a mask of green scales that wreathed a pair of slitted eyes.

'We will keep this brief – you have already taken up far too much of the crown's time with your unsolicited presence,' King Raza said as he took his place at the centre of the balcony. 'You are trespassers and political agitators, and you are not welcome here.'

'And you are a proud and profane man to take such a holy title as king!' Lord Xavier spat in response, eliciting shocked gasps from the courtiers and making Joss wince at his tactlessness.

'What did the mammal dare say?' King Raza demanded, his wild eyes growing all the more crazed.

'Apologies, your grace!' Qorza said, stepping forward. 'We came here on the invitation of your sister, the Lady Razeel. It was her feeling that the dark forces overrunning the surface world represent a shared threat, and that if we were to come here we would find steadfast allies in the war for our mutual survival. We only ask for an audience with you, to discuss how we can help each other in this effort.'

King Raza sneered. 'If my sister had asked we would have told her we have no interest whatsoever in allying with the barbarians who plundered our sacred cities and made slums of our hallowed burial sites. She would have been reminded that the *draa'kin* are a wise and strong people; that we are best at keeping our own counsel and have done so for millennia. And she would have been directed to keep her faith with her king, who has already secured a pact to ensure our safety in a war we never invited in the first place.'

Joss's eyes narrowed at Raza's last point. Any doubt about its meaning was dispelled as the great silver doors slammed open, turning Joss's earlier vision into a horrendous reality.

'*Malkus!*' Joss growled.

'No, boy,' the Thrall said as two more of his ilk emerged by his side. 'But you're not far wrong.'

'Sur Blaek,' Joss said, wielding both his swords. 'I've been wondering when we'd make our reunion. Let me show you how I've been putting your training into practice.'

The Thrall expelled a small chuckle, the tone striking Joss as entirely unfamiliar. 'Wrong again, boy. In fact, we've not met before,' the masked man told him. 'But I've heard much about you.'

'And we've heard much about you!' Qorza exclaimed, startling Joss as she lobbed something right at the Thrall's head. It landed like a fireball thrown from a catapult, making the masked man shriek and stagger backwards.

'How did you know to do that?' Joss asked her.

'I told you Sacred Sand had many uses,' she shrugged. 'But we can review tomes later. Look!'

She pointed to the two other Thralls. One was dizzyingly tall and cloaked in a wolf's pelt, while the other was squat and wearing a leather breastplate the shade of congealed blood. Both of them were running with their black swords drawn, spoiling for a fight.

Drake was quick to answer them. He leapt into the fray brandishing his Icefire spear, swinging for the two Thralls with all his might. The Thralls blocked his attack with their blades, slashing back with strikes of their own. Their combined strength was enough to send him stumbling. Hero took advantage of the distraction to launch a series of zamaraq strikes. The Thralls parried them like they were dropping dragonflies.

'You can confidently ward off the attacks of prentices,' Lord Xavier stepped forth to point his song sword at the masked pair. 'But how do you fare against a man more of your making?'

The Thralls regarded each other, silently conferring. Then, with a snap of their fingers, a wave of acolytes came pouring out from behind the silver doors to engage all of the *Zenith* crew in battle, brandishing axes and broadswords and bolt rifles with deadly intent.

As fast as they were, Zeke was even faster. He drew aim and fired his shock rifle, splitting their numbers and driving many of them back. Hero and Lieutenant Tyne lent their efforts to his, loosing a wave of zamaraqs and arrows at the foot soldiers who fell outside Zeke's range. Qorza did the same, lobbing whatever arcane objects she could pull from her satchel that might suffice. Yet a handful of acolytes still made their way through, where they were joined in combat by Eliza, Drake and the *Zenith* crewmembers, while Lord Xavier fended off the strikes of the two commanders.

That left only the first Thrall. Half his mask was burnt from Qorza's attack, but he had regained enough composure to sidestep the unfolding fracas.

'Prentice Sarif!' he said as he made his measured

advance. 'No bag of tricks to save you this time.'

'No ...' Joss replied. Standing tall, he set aside his lingering doubt, replacing it instead with steely determination. Years of training had finally culminated in this moment, he told himself. And he had the very weapon to meet it and claim his destiny. 'Just a *vaartan rhazh*.'

Joss swung the Champion's Blade with righteous fury, ready to fulfil the promise of his mother's work, ready to prove himself the *galamor* he truly was, ready to bring light and hope to a world too quickly edging toward darkness. Ready to seize his fate.

But with one gauntleted hand, Thrall seized the blade of Joss's sword.

'A *vaartan rhazh*?' the masked man scoffed. 'I think not.'

Spectral green lightning sparked from his fist. It coiled around his arm and ran the length of the Champion's Blade. Joss held on for as long as he could, but the sparks were too overwhelming. He hissed in pain as he let go, and could only watch with rising horror as the lightning intensified.

The blade began to bubble. The blade began to weep. The blade began to melt. Then, in one last burst of blinding green light, it was gone – with nothing left but a scorched handle that landed at Joss's feet with a thud.

He stared down in stunned disbelief.

The Champion's Blade had been destroyed.

CHAPTER TWENTY-SEVEN

A WORLDLY CONCERN

JOSS reeled, staring at the burnt hilt of the Champion's Blade as if he were staring at the blasted skull of his best friend. The sword that had belonged to him, to Sur Verity, and to every Blade Keeper before them had been destroyed with such terrible ease. And with it went his belief in the Rakashi Revelations, in his destiny, and in himself. How could he have been such a fool?

'Take heart, boy,' the Thrall towering over him said. 'I may have relieved you of your weapon, but you won't have to mourn its loss for long. I'll relieve you of all worldly concerns next.'

The Thrall's blade was long and black and sharp and pointed straight at Joss's face. He gazed at it with an eerie calm. There was no fight left in him. No move he could make, no trick he could pull. He was done.

'Do it if you're going to do it,' he muttered, preparing himself for the looming strike.

A blast rang out over Joss's shoulder. It hit the Thrall square in the chest and flung him backwards, hard and fast. He landed on the opposite side of the battlefield and lay where he fell.

'How's that for a worldly concern, you sucking void where a man should stand?' Zeke called out to him before offering Joss his outstretched hand. 'You alright?'

Joss stared up at Zeke, feeling a rush of relief: yet again, his friend had saved his life. Then he gazed back down at the burning hunk of sword handle.

'That's not –?' Zeke asked. 'Joss … I'm so sorry.'

'It's just a sword,' he replied. 'Better to lose that than anything truly valuable.' He wanted to believe what he was saying. He really did. But the words rang hollow even as he said them. He had lost the Champion's Blade. He had lost his *vaartan rhazh*. What was he going to do now?

But there was no time to dwell on such things. A large floor tile at the edge of the battle slid away and a head popped up from the opening. Joss squinted to see that it was Lady Razeel, gesturing to him.

'*You!*' he exclaimed as he and Zeke rushed over to her. 'It's your fault we're up past our mouths in this pile of muck!'

'Follow me and I can lead you all to safety,' she told them with such earnestness that Joss decided to set aside his distrust. For now.

'How do we get everyone clear from the battle?' he asked. 'Wherever we go, the Thralls and their acolytes will follow.'

'Leave that to Chamberlain Füm and her lieutenants,' she replied, and nodded to the winged figures gliding in from the furthest reaches of the cavern. They fell upon the battlefield within seconds, and Joss was stunned to see that they appeared to be neither mortal nor dragon, but some formidable hybrid. He recognised Chamberlain Füm just as she expelled a jet of fire from her open mouth, strafing the combatants with such accuracy that she was able to separate the Thralls and their acolytes from the *Zenith* crew as if she were merely splitting a log of wood.

'You can breathe fire?' Zeke said with astonishment.

'A talent exclusive to Chamberlain Füm's bloodline,' Lady Razeel revealed. 'Though this may be a better time for escape than explanations.'

Joss pressed his fingers to his lips and emitted a piercing whistle that was instantly recognisable to all thunderfolk. Every member of the *Zenith* crew swung their heads around to stare at him.

'*This way!*' he called, and waved them towards the trapdoor. Everyone ran for the escape hatch while Chamberlain Füm circled overhead, laying down walls of fire to keep the Court of Thralls away.

'*Fools!*' King Raza's voice echoed over the explosions. 'Get down there and stop them!'

Joss stole one last look at the Thrall who had taken

the Champion's Blade, his stone mask floating like an apparition behind the flickering flames. Then he grabbed his sword's charred handle and leapt into the escape hatch. Lady Razeel quickly jumped down after him and slid the tile back into place, then sealed it shut with the turn of an unwieldy lock.

'That should keep them at bay for now, though we have little time to waste,' she said, turning to Joss and the others. They were assembled along a suffocating stairwell, each of them glaring up at her ladyship as she pushed through to the head of the line.

'Indeed,' Lord Xavier grunted as she passed him. 'But first we'll know the meaning of this treachery.'

'I can only offer my most profound apologies. I had no idea of my brother's plans, nor of the presence of the Court of Thralls within our walls.'

'And how do we know this isn't still part of the trap?' asked Drake.

'I would hardly rescue you all from this killing field to simply turn around and throw you back into another. But if your concern lies with the expanse of my brother's reach then be assured – this is but one of many hidden passageways riddled throughout the under-city. I spent most of my youth exploring them and mapping them in my mind. Raza has never shown the same interest. We should be able to navigate our way to safety from here, if fortune favours us. And if we keep a quick pace.' She motioned for them to follow her, and they fell into line.

The stairs emptied out into a passageway with a low, curved roof and a series of barred windows. Peering past the bars, Joss looked down at what appeared to be a storage cellar, judging by the crates stacked along its walls. Joss looked closer, and saw that each crate was stamped with a Sunforge Industries insignia. One of them was open, and contained masses of glass orbs – all filled with swirling flames and capped at either end with a metal disc.

'Lord Xavier – was there something I heard about a raid in Hammerton?' Joss said, pointing to the crates.

Lord Xavier glanced through the barred windows, then turned to Lady Razeel. 'Care to offer any explanations, my lady?'

'I caught wind of the raid at the same time that I learned of my brother's plans for you all,' she said. 'This cache was part of their bargain. The Court of Thralls stole the materials from Hammerton and smuggled them here for priming.'

'And what are they, other than being both the prettiest and deadliest-looking baubles I've ever seen?' asked Zeke.

'*Inferno orbs*,' Lady Razeel replied, eschewing Zeke's attempts at humour to point out a stack of heavily embellished brass pipes sitting in the corner of the cellar, each with a handle and trigger attached to its midsection. 'In concert with those launchers, they would serve as a miracle weapon that could easily overpower any enemy force.'

The *Zenith* crew shared a look.

'We have to warn General Swift and the Royal Army,' Lord Xavier said.

'And we'll never do that if we don't get out of here,' replied Lieutenant Tyne. Joss paused to steal another glimpse at what sounded like a nightmare made of glass and metal and fiery death. He shuddered as he hastened along with the rest of the group, following Lady Razeel through an increasingly complex hive of passageways for what felt like an eternity until they emerged from behind a concealed door into the cavern where they'd left Edgar and their mounts.

The fair-haired prentice was staring in the opposite direction, and jumped when everyone rushed up from behind him. 'Sleeping King favour me!' he exclaimed with a small laugh of relief. 'You scared me muckless!' The smile fell from his face as he noticed everyone's grave demeanour. 'What's going on?'

'Remember how I wanted you to stay here in case we needed to make a fast escape?' Joss said as he clambered onto Azof's back.

'Take that speed and double it,' Eliza concluded for him.

'Right,' replied Edgar, jumping into his saddle. 'Then let's ride.'

A war horn resounded from deep within the cavern, followed by a chorus of roars.

'They're coming,' Hero noted as Callie's fur bristled.

'You need to go now,' Lady Razeel told them. 'I can stay and fend them off.'

'There are far too many of them,' Lord Xavier said, just as a winged figure came swooping out from between the iron doors, followed quickly by another. Azof hissed at the new arrivals while Joss instinctively reached for the Champion's Blade, only to grab at thin air. Clutching his fist, he steeled himself for the attack. Instead he saw Chamberlain Füm landing at Lady Razeel's side, along with a young offsider Joss recognised immediately.

'You!' he exclaimed. 'You're Ormar – the Chief Warden's steward.'

The young man raked a clawed hand through his flame-red hair and tucked his wings behind his back. 'Thank you again for your help at Dragon's Toe,' he said. 'I only wish I could have been as much help to the Chief Warden and the rest of the citizenry.'

With little patience for the reunion unfolding before her, Chamberlain Füm said, 'My lady, we must hasten. Your brother's forces approach.'

'Indeed,' said Lady Razeel as she looked at Lord Xavier. 'I have all the reinforcements I need. Take your people and go while you can. And leave with my sincerest regret and apologies.'

Joss shared one last look with the boy he'd freed back at Dragon's Toe, then turned his mount around and urged it into a run, racing out of the cave with the others as fast as they could go. Lord Xavier was at the head of the pack with his jet-cycle humming loudly, navigating the tight pathways through the cavern and finally out into daylight.

The *Fat Lot of Good* was sitting exactly where they'd left it.

'Get the mounts loaded,' Lord Xavier said. 'We need to maintain guard until we're in the air.'

Edgar was quick to lead the mounts inside while Joss and his brethren formed a watch around the ship, safeguarding themselves against a surprise attack.

Their efforts were in vain.

'We've got company,' Zeke exclaimed as shadows emerged from behind every rock and boulder that surrounded the *Fat Lot of Good*. Lacquered masks stared impassively at the *Zenith* crew, while the Thrall who had destroyed the Champion's Blade ascended a large stone directly above them.

'How helpful of you to rush here to meet us,' he said. 'Now, what say we finish what we started?'

CHAPTER TWENTY-EIGHT

A BLINDING SORROW

'EVERYONE onto the ship! *Now!*' Lord Xavier roared, startling the *Zenith* crew into action. Zeke lay down cover fire as an acolyte rushed to Thrall's side, offering him a crossbow the size of an executioner's axe. Handling the heavy weapon with casual ease, Thrall brought the stock of the crossbow up to his shoulder and took aim.

'*Josiah Sarif!*' he called out, and Joss froze like a frightened hatchling. 'Let this be your reunion with the dead of Daheed!'

The crossbow loosed, the bolt aiming for his heart.

And Edgar rose up to meet it. 'Joss, look out!' the young steward cried, leaping in front of his friend.

'*No!*' Joss screamed as the crossbow bolt hit Edgar hard in the chest, punching a small whimper out of him. His body fell slack, with Joss catching him just before he hit the ground. Struggling to hold him, Joss could feel the boy's body twitching from shock. His face was already pale, his mouth twisted in pain.

'Somebody – *somebody help!*' Joss cried out. Eliza added her strength to his as everyone rushed in behind them, and between the two of them they carried Edgar into the hull and onto one of the benches bolted to the cabin wall.

'*Get us in the air! Now!*' Lord Xavier roared. Zeke grunted with exertion as he clambered up into the wheelhouse, jammed on the control rods and gunned the *Fat Lot of Good*'s vertical thrusters.

The whole ship trembled from the bolt gun blasts buffeting its bow, the rat-a-tat tapping of arrows glancing off the hull while Thrall watched on from his place atop the rocky outcrop. Joss could hear Lord Xavier issuing orders over his comm-link to the *Zenith*, bellowing at them to open fire on the mountainside while the *Fat Lot* made its escape.

The commotion was mere white noise to the sound of Edgar's shallow breaths, his every small gasp and twitch of pain. Joss and Eliza were by his side as Qorza hovered over him, moving as fast as she could in an attempt to treat his wound. He was losing blood fast.

'Why would you do something so foolish, Edgar?' Joss asked, tears blurring his vision and seeping into the corners of his mouth, the taste of his own grief as salted as the sea. 'Why would you do something so damned stupid?'

'… My choice …' Edgar said as firmly as he could muster.

Through all the sorrow that was blinding him, Joss managed to say, 'A heroic choice.'

'… Not … not in vain?' Edgar asked. Joss gripped his hand.

'I swear.'

Edgar nodded, satisfied, before his gaze drifted. 'I think I … I think I smell honeyblossoms.'

'Stay here, Edgar. Stay with us,' Eliza begged him, but Edgar shook his head in the smallest and gentlest of ways.

'I'm going home, Eliza,' he whispered. 'Joss – can I … can I go home, Joss?'

'You go home, Edgar,' Joss said, trying to keep his voice from breaking as he squeezed his friend's hand. 'I'll see you there.'

The light in Edgar's watery eyes sparkled as he smiled one last time, then went dark. His hand shrivelled in Joss's grip. All the sunshine and warmth that had radiated from him so freely was extinguished.

He was gone.

CHAPTER TWENTY-NINE

A PALADERO'S FINAL RIDE

EDGAR was given an aeronaut's funeral.

After they had returned to the *Zenith*, his body was rushed to the ship's infirmary. It had felt more like a formality than anything else. All the physician did was confirm that there was nothing that could be done. The lad was dead.

Lord Xavier had taken to the bridge to navigate the *Zenith* away from Dragon's Tooth, with the crew bracing for the aerial battle to come. But it never did. Raza's forces let them go without pursuit, as did the Court of Thralls. The guarded wait for an attack that never arrived only added to the eerie, mournful quiet.

'We have to delay it,' Joss had said when Zeke mentioned Edgar's service had been set for the next morning. They were the first words Joss had spoken since their escape. 'We have to find his family. It's not right that his parents not be there.'

But with Resilient having fallen along with Round Shield Ranch, he knew tracking down Edgar's family in time would be impossible. So with deep reluctance and even deeper heartbreak, he had gone to the infirmary to oversee the wrapping of Edgar's remains in the aeronauts' black death shroud. It helped to focus on the completion of a task, step by step. It helped to have a distraction. Otherwise Joss would regard the loss that sat at the centre of his being like a sinkhole and allow himself to tumble down into it.

The service was held at sunrise on the observation deck, with every member of the crew in attendance. It was a testament to Edgar's character that he'd made so many friends in such a short span of time.

'A dream does not end,' said the ship's High Attendant, reciting from the Holy Somnium. 'A dream lingers in the mind. It lives on in the heart. A dream is shared and carried on. Everything that has ever been or will be was dreamt of first, and everything that ever was lives on in our dreams, our minds, our hearts, our souls.'

The High Attendant led the group in a prayer to the Sleeping King to keep the dream of Edgar alive. Then it was Joss's turn to speak.

With leaden feet he walked to the head of the circle they'd assembled around Edgar's shrouded body, which was harnessed to a stretcher that had a small black balloon attached to it. He couldn't believe this was where he was and this was what he was doing. Nothing seemed real anymore. Nothing seemed right. The world had been kicked violently off its axis and sent spinning into the unknown, dragging him with it. He wanted to escape to somewhere that made sense again.

Instead, he took his position at the focus of everyone's attention. He saw the tear stains on Qorza's glasses, Lieutenant Tyne's martial solemnity, Crimson and Cloud's confused sorrow, the upright stiffness of Lord Xavier. He saw Hero hiding behind her goggles, Drake's thin lips quivering, Zeke's pained grimace, Eliza's bloodshot eyes and trembling hands.

He didn't see Edgar.

He would never see Edgar again.

Clearing his throat, he began to speak. 'The best of stewards and the best of friends,' he said. 'That's what I told Edgar he was, just before he died. I doubt anyone who knew him would disagree. Simply to meet him was to know him as diligent, dedicated, loyal to a fault, generous in spirit and noble in deed. The only reason I'm standing here before you now is because –'

Joss choked, his voice cracking.

Squeezing his eyes shut, he fought to regain his composure and continued, 'Because of the sacrifice he made. He said to me recently that it falls to us to honour those who have made such sacrifices, to ensure their actions weren't in vain. I intend to do just that. Anything less would be to let down the stalwart prentice who greeted every challenge with wide-eyed awe and a spirited smile. Anything less would be a disservice to the best friend any of us could have ever hoped to have.'

Again he paused, lost in the roiling pain that welled up from deep within him to flood his every fibre. *Breathe,* he told himself. *Just breathe.* He could do this. He could find a way to keep going, to push through, to hold himself together. *Nothing is impossible.*

'May he ride well,' Joss concluded.

'May he ride well,' the crowd echoed.

As the ship's piper began to play the mournful dirge of 'A Paladero's Final Ride', Joss stepped forward and, along with the others who had been selected for the task, set about releasing Edgar's body from its earthly bonds.

Joss, Hero and Drake all untied the weights beneath the stretcher as Eliza pressed the button to ignite the rig's burner. The black balloon hovering above Edgar's stretcher rose into the air, floating up and away and taking Edgar with it.

Joss watched as the balloon and its cargo were taken up by the wind to be pulled higher and higher. Once it had reached a soaring altitude off in the distance, the igniter on the harness was triggered and set the flammable shroud ablaze.

From there the fire spread slowly, creeping up along the rigging to lick at the black balloon, which now began a slow descent. Somehow it managed to stay afloat even as it burned all the way down to the carpet of clouds below, sinking down into the thick grey coverage to become little more than a fiery glow, which eventually vanished.

With nothing left to see, everyone headed inside to drink to Edgar's memory. The lights that he'd set up for Cloud's party were all still in place, though they remained resolutely dark.

'Those were fine words, Joss,' Eliza told him through the tears sparkling in her eyes. 'Fine and true.'

'Thank you,' he replied, unsure of what else to say. It felt strange to be accepting such praise as if he deserved it, as if he had actually accomplished something, when all he'd done was get his best friend killed.

Breathe, he told himself again. *Just breathe.*

Lord Xavier added his compliments to Eliza's before returning to the bridge. His departure signalled the end of the formalities, with the crewmembers all drifting away until it was just those closest to Edgar who remained.

'Remember when we found him clinging above that vortex in Daheed?' said Drake as they sat around on the observation deck's gilded furniture while nursing their half-drunk tankards of sarsaparilla. 'He looked like a wet bear cub gripped to its mother's back in the middle of a raging river.'

'Well then, I must have encountered him as a full-grown tundra bear,' said Zeke. 'Remember? We were in Rowan's gardens at Blade's Edge Acres. He excused his language, then called me a duplicitous and dastardly scoundrel who wasn't worth two squirts of – well, I don't know what exactly because Joss interrupted him before he could finish. I may have been more offended if he weren't so spot on.'

Everyone laughed, then sighed. Everyone but Joss. He felt as if he were standing on the other side of a looking glass, staring in at everything happening around him. All he could think of was how he wanted to find somewhere to hide.

His opportunity came long after night had fallen. Excusing himself, he made a move for the door and kept going. He could feel himself breaking apart as he negotiated the stairwell, traversed the winding corridors and made it all the way back to his quarters.

He was alone. He was finally, mercifully, bitterly alone.

He collapsed onto the floor and wept.

CHAPTER THIRTY

——

A TOUCH OF PAIN

JOSS lay in his quarters, crumpled up like a broken kite. The shades were drawn and the only sound came from the drone of the ship's engines. Other than that, the world was silent. Empty. As devoid of life or movement as Joss was of hope.

Until there came a gentle rapping at his door.

'Joss? It's Zeke.'

The door cracked open. A beam of light shone along the carpet and across Joss's face.

'There you are,' Zeke said. 'How are you holding up?'

Joss answered honestly. 'I'm not.'

'Want to talk about it?' asked Zeke. He sat on the edge of the bed, where Joss was curled up in a tight ball with his arms wrapped around his knees.

Joss didn't move. If Zeke was so eager to catalogue the

contents of his head, why not let him have it in full?

'I was counting everyone who sacrificed themselves to keep me alive,' he said without looking up. 'Edgar. Sur Verity. Tempest. My parents. All of them died so that I could live. And for what? I thought it was because I was destined for something great. Something heroic. That they all made that sacrifice so I could go on to save the world. But what did that belief get me in the end? Just death and a bladeless hilt.'

He brandished the burnt handle of the Champion's Blade in Zeke's face, squeezing it so hard it made his whole fist shake. Zeke stared first at Joss's trembling hand, and then deep into Joss's eyes.

'I remember someone very wise saying it was up to us to honour their sacrifice and make sure it wasn't in vain. I remember it because it was just a few hours ago, and it was said by someone in this very room who may or may not be sitting right in front of me.'

Joss collapsed back onto the bed and curled himself up again. 'It was Edgar who said that. Not me.'

'But you committed yourself to doing it. Unless I was drinking something much stronger than I thought and hallucinated the whole thing. Wouldn't be the first time, I suppose …' Zeke trailed off, letting the half-joke hang. When Joss didn't reply, Zeke continued, sounding more serious and sober than Joss could recall him ever being before. 'You asked what your belief got you in the end. But this isn't the end. Not yet. Not by a long shot. And even if it were, those people who protected you didn't do it because they thought they were safeguarding the champion of the world. They did it because they loved you. And you're worthy of that love, Joss. Remember that.'

Joss didn't answer. He just hugged himself harder, pressing his face into his knees. But the more he thought about Zeke's words, the more he softened. 'When did you get so smart?' he asked, rubbing his face as he gradually sat up.

'I didn't. I'm just incredibly good at bluffing,' Zeke replied, and Joss found that he couldn't help but laugh. Zeke smiled, then clapped Joss on the back. 'Come on. Father's requested that we all join him on the bridge; he has something he wants to say.'

'He says a lot of things,' Joss muttered.

'True,' nodded Zeke.

Joss took the opportunity to tell his friend something that he'd been meaning to say for weeks. 'You don't deserve it, you know. The way he treats you.'

Zeke stiffened. 'I know,' he said, and paused. 'At least, I think I know. But it's the only way I've ever been treated, by him and my brothers and all the rest of my family, so it just feels normal. But the older I get the more I realise it's not normal – is it?'

'I don't know much about how families work,' Joss answered honestly. 'But I don't think so.'

Zeke's eyes were focused on the corner of the room, but his mind was clearly much further away. 'You should have seen his face when I came back from the Way empty-handed. And when I explained the reason? I'm amazed he didn't disown me then and there. I don't know if he was relieved or ashamed when I left to work as a fieldserv at Blade's Edge Acres. At least he didn't have to deal with me anymore after that. Until we showed up in Illustra, of course. The only way he could explain my position to the rest of our order and all his lordly friends at the Ivory Palace was by making up a story that I was sent to uncover the conspiracy that had taken root.'

'You can't be serious,' Joss said.

'It was the only way he could save face,' Zeke said. 'And the only reason he let me back in.'

'I suppose he's not far wrong, though. You did work to uncover whatever was happening there.'

'You and Hero and Drake and Edgar were the ones doing all the real work on that front.'

'Doesn't change everything you've done since then to stop the Court of Thralls. And it's more than he deserves to show your father such loyalty.' Joss placed his hand on his friend's. 'You're a good son, Zeke.'

Zeke sniffed, then offered Joss a pained smile. 'I'd rather be a good person.'

'We can work on that,' Joss smiled in return. Removing his hand from Zeke's, he gave his friend a playful tap on the arm.

The pain lifted from Zeke's face, if only a touch, before he cleared his throat and rose to his feet. 'Come on. Let's go see what the old man has to say. And if we don't like the sound of it then we can go.'

As they rounded the corridors leading towards the bridge, a question floated up in Joss's mind. 'Your father – you weren't tempted to challenge him back at the Ivory Palace, when he was making up stories to save face? To tell him what you really think?'

'Of course I was,' Zeke admitted. 'But I'm not as brave as you are, Joss. You can stand in front of a lord or a count or a grandmaster and tell 'em exactly what their problem is, right to their face. The best I can muster is to question an order or make a mocking remark. And even then I get a feeling like cogs are grinding up my guts.'

'You think I'm brave?' Joss said. He hoped his surprise wasn't too obvious.

'You're the bravest person I know,' Zeke told him. 'And I have no doubt Edgar would agree with me.'

Unsure of how to respond, Joss was relieved to arrive at the stairs to the bridge. Everyone else was already gathered and waiting for them, with Lord Xavier gazing down imperiously from his command platform.

'We started without you,' his lordship said. 'I just explained that I've made my report to the palace.'

'Did you tell them what we found?' asked Zeke.

'I told them there are miracle weapons being developed in the northern Backbones and that they need to either call down an airstrike on the location or prepare themselves for annihilation,' Lord Xavier replied.

'You didn't mention the *draa'kin*? Or Lady Razeel?' asked Qorza.

'I have no desire to be dismissed as a fool or a madman. I'm quite aware of how it would sound, this misadventure in a mythical city with creatures of legend. Regent Greel's advisers would all be in unanimous agreement that I be stripped of my commission on the spot.'

'You were perfectly comfortable with making a report when Lady Razeel first appeared,' Joss pointed out, Zeke's words echoing in his ears. 'What's changed?'

His lordship frowned, his mouth curling as if he were chewing on a thick wad of gristle. With his hands folded behind his back he began a slow march down the stairs, eyeing each member of the group in turn.

'The truth? Our mission has gone from bad to worse. Rather than impart the whole calamity in an illumivox transmission I intend instead to make a full report when we convene with the rest of the forces at Tower Town – in person, where I can make the strongest case. And in the meantime, I will put my house in order. Because I believe we have a traitor in our midst, and I intend to find out who.'

CHAPTER THIRTY-ONE

—

A Secret Name

'A TRAITOR?' Qorza said, struggling with Lord Xavier's declaration. 'Why would you suspect such a thing?'

Lord Xavier marched along the line of faces, eyeballing each of them. 'It only makes sense: someone on the inside informing Raza and the weredragons of our actions. Someone who orchestrated the attack on Nobleseat. The Court of Thralls has proven it operates through treachery and subterfuge. Why would it be any different here?'

'Indeed,' replied Lieutenant Tyne as he stepped forward. 'And I know exactly who it is.' He rounded on Crimson and Cloud, who both looked astonished at being singled out.

'Who? Us?' Crimson asked. 'You'd have to be foaming at the mouth to believe that! We're not in league with the

Shadow God and his cronies – we were attacked by them, remember?'

Lieutenant Tyne advanced on the two deckhands, drawing a few of the *Zenith* crewmembers with him. Crimson's defiance curdled into something more panicked, while Cloud looked stricken.

'Yes. You were,' said Tyne. 'And from all reports the Shadow God's influence acts like a contagion, affecting susceptible minds and bending them to his will. As deckhands you were perfectly positioned to monitor our activities without drawing undue attention to yourselves.'

'How'd you know that, lieutenant?' Joss asked, taking a step forward to place himself between Tyne and the two boys. 'About the Shadow God's influence? How do you know that? We discussed it at the summit but we haven't raised it since.'

Lieutenant Tyne shifted his footing. 'I must have read it somewhere. Or heard someone discussing it. What difference does it make?'

Joss looked away. Qorza was standing to his right, her satchel unclasped. Without hesitating, Joss grabbed a bag of Sacred Sand from the inside pocket and hurled it at Lieutenant Tyne. The whole crew gasped as the bag struck Tyne's face, making him clutch his head and shriek in pain, the sand scalding him like acid.

'*His Majesty's mercy!*' Lord Xavier exclaimed.

When Tyne dropped his hands again, his eyes were as wide and black as an endless abyss.

'You!' Joss said. 'You called down the dragon on Nobleseat to worm your way into our mission! You reported our whereabouts to the Court of Thralls, including our meeting with Lady Razeel and the *draa'kin*! You sold your soul just the same as Malkus and Blaek and all the other cowards who make up your master's forces! And your treachery cost Edgar his life.'

Tyne sneered around his burns. 'You call it selling my soul. I call it knowing which way the boughs are branching. In my time aboard this ship all I've witnessed is dysfunction and acrimony. If the Kingdom of Ai's forces are as pitifully ill-disciplined as all of you, this world stands no chance against the maelstrom to come.'

A tremor of dread undulated through the *Zenith* crew, Tyne's words reverberating with the power of prophecy.

But Joss knew how foolish it was to place too much faith in soothsaying. 'That's a real boast from someone so outnumbered,' he told Tyne. 'We'll see how confident you are under interrogation. Whatever your master has planned, you're going to tell us. Now.'

The *Zenith* crewmembers whom Tyne had turned against Crimson and Cloud now turned on him, their numbers boosted by Joss and the others. Backing away, Tyne drew his sword. 'Darkness take you all!' he growled as he flung his weapon at the nearest window, shattering the glass. Tyne was wrenched straight out, his cloak ripping on the frame as he went.

'*Blast shields!*' Lord Xavier shouted over the howl of air

being sucked from the bridge. One hand over the other, Zeke reached the control panel where a button was flashing red. With one punch a steel shutter slammed down, sealing the broken window.

'I ... I don't believe it,' Qorza puffed.

'I do,' Crimson muttered as he eyeballed the crewmembers who'd been so quick to turn on him.

Picking himself up, Joss staggered to the bank of windows and looked out. The clouds below looked completely undisturbed. Tyne had disappeared into them without a trace, as if he'd never been anything more than a ghost to begin with.

———

The observation deck had been cleared of all Edgar's blessingday decorations, save for a single string of lights the crew had overlooked. They blinked on as night fell, surprising Joss with their radiance. His vision was still bleary as he walked outside and discovered a mop-headed figure waiting there.

'Here you are,' Joss said, drawing Cloud's attention as he joined him by the railing. The boy looked just as shaken from his encounter with Tyne as he'd been when it had first happened. 'How are you?'

'Alright,' Cloud replied quietly. Joss stared at him a moment, confirming what he'd pieced together back on the bridge.

'I don't know why it's taken me this long, but I finally

worked out why you look so familiar,' he said. 'You're Wilem, aren't you? The stable boy from Freecloud. That's what Sur Blaek called you when we came through there. Though that was a while ago now. Before Sure Blaek turned against us. Much like Lieutenant Tyne.'

'Sur Blaek never turned against anyone. He was always that way. He just hid it until the time he didn't have to pretend anymore.'

Joss felt the bite of betrayal again. Drawing a breath, he let the hurt wash over him and then swept it away. 'You had family in Freecloud, didn't you?' he asked Cloud. 'Why aren't you with them?'

Cloud just shook his head. 'Anyone close to me is gone. Except Crimson. He's the one who dubbed me Cloud.'

'Certainly did,' Crimson called out from the doorway, before venturing over to wrap a hand around his friend's shoulder. 'I told him: you gotta keep your guard up. You have to know how to protect yourself. Starting with your name. They don't know nothing about you if they don't know your name. Keeping that a secret is key.'

'Well – your secret's safe with me,' Joss said.

The two deckhands offered him a guarded smile. 'We should go,' said Crimson. 'We may have survived being vilified and eviscerated but we still got jobs to do.' He paused. 'And if we didn't say it before? Thank you. For bringing us along, for standing up for us, for saving our hides. You're a good man, Sarif. Even if you're still just a kid like us.'

The pair vanished back inside before Joss could respond. He contented himself with turning back to his view of the infant moon and bathing himself in the twilight.

Of everything Crimson and Cloud had said, what struck him most was the importance of names. Sur Blaek and Lord Malkus had both kept their real name a secret. The name they shared. And Joss had thought he'd had a secret name of his own to rival theirs; a name that it was his destiny to claim for himself.

Galamor.

But that was gone now. Gone like the Champion's Blade. Gone like the brave young man whose body had been taken by the sky and swept into cinders.

There was no such thing as fate, he concluded. No such thing as destiny; no prophecies to be believed. The world was a cruel and chaotic place, as unforgiving to the innocent as it was the wicked. And yet somehow, deep down, he still believed it was worth fighting for. It was worth honouring Edgar's sacrifice, even if he no longer had fate on his side. Even if he was no longer the *galamor*.

He reached into his coat and removed the charred handle of the Champion's Blade. *A True Champion, A True Paladero* read the inscription. A bitter half-laugh escaped from Joss's tightened mouth as he ran his thumb over the words, smearing the soot that marred them.

Then, without thinking, he flung the hilt into the void, watching as it spiralled down and away until it disappeared from sight.

CHAPTER THIRTY-TWO

A PROFOUND LACK OF HONOUR

A S the *Zenith* made its final approach towards Tower Town, Joss heard the transmission from the control station.

'*You're all cleared for docking,* Zenith. *May the Sleeping King show you his mercy.'*

Somehow the crew pushed through the crosswinds pummelling the ship and docked at the enclosed skybridge that extended from the top of the tower. As the connection was secured, the *Zenith* crew made its plans for their audience with the Grandmaster Council.

Lord Xavier didn't want to crowd the Grandmasters' chambers, so Eliza, Crimson and Cloud were all to be left aboard the ship. Eliza seemed relieved at not having to leave her quarters, where she'd retreated following Edgar's funeral and Lieutenant Tyne's subsequent unmasking.

'Good luck,' she told Joss, Drake and Hero when they checked in on her. 'Maybe you can find some way to make all this actually count for something.'

From there they met up with Qorza and Zeke at the docking hatch in the hangar, where Lord Xavier arrived in his full set of armour with a purple cloak drawn around his shoulders. As they crossed the bridge, Joss glanced through the line of portholes. The camp city erected in the shadow of Tower Town on the surrounding salt flats looked desolate in comparison to his first visit, save for the handful of soldiers who had taken up residence.

Even from this height he could distinguish Count Barus's Ranjer Corps, with each of the hooded figures carrying a longbow and quiver. They were accompanied by the archers from Rok's Nest, plus a modest collection of paladeros from the handful of orders who'd confirmed their support in advance of Regent Greel's summit. There were no other forces present – not even those of the Royal Army.

'They say our way of life is dying,' Lord Xavier said as he tracked Joss's gaze. 'I'd say our profound lack of honour is outright killing it.'

While the camps outside were empty, the tower itself was anything but; people were packed into every spare inch of room, with bedrolls lined up along the hallways and whole families crammed into corners.

'They've taken in the surrounding populace, just like the other fortresses we visited,' Qorza observed. 'Thank goodness for small mercies.'

The only uncrowded places were the very top floors – the domain of the Grandmasters. A chirping little mek floated through the antechamber to scan everyone's faces before a side door opened, inviting them inside.

The Grandmaster's council room was much as Joss remembered it: the map of the Kingdom of Ai staked out on the ground, the iron pillars holding the roof aloft, the panoramic view of the tent city outside and the parched landscape of the Searing Sands beyond that.

The three Grandmasters were seated at a triangular table alongside a cluster of newcomers. Secretary Lovegood was next to the wizened Grandmaster Eno, while Count Barus was squeezed between Grandmasters Warburn and Gilmyn. That left one chair empty – an unspoken invitation for Lord Xavier to join them.

'Lord Xavier, welcome. Now that you're here we can strategise for the battle to come,' said Secretary Lovegood.

'I thought His Excellency would be here,' his lordship replied as he took his seat. 'Not to mention the Royal Army and the paladero lords who've brought the orders gathered below.'

'Those lords will be informed of the resolutions we draw here today when the time is right,' Grandmaster Warburn said.

'And General Swift?' Lord Xavier asked.

'A vortex opened just outside Illustra. Swift was lost in the resulting melee,' said Grandmaster Eno, eliciting shocked murmurs from the *Zenith* crew. Why had they not heard this news before now, Joss wondered – and what was the kingdom to do without its chief military leader? 'In the face of such harrowing circumstances, Regent Greel has understandably sent his regrets in lieu of attending in person,' Lovegood said with a wave of his white-gloved hand. 'Though he's been keeping abreast of your reports. Beyond your warnings of so-called *miracle weapons*, I must confess that it's been a challenge determining what progress has been made. Could you illuminate for us exactly what Operation Herald has achieved?'

Lord Xavier gestured to the window. 'See for yourself. Those gathered at the foot of the tower are all the reinforcements we expect to arrive. These are the few who could be convinced to heed their regent's call.'

'You mean the archers I brought,' Count Barus said, puffing out his chest. 'I accompanied them here in a show of goodwill. To see this spirit of camaraderie has not been returned by our fellow countrymen is truly astounding. But worse than that, Lord Xavier, I've had disturbing reports that you had Lieutenant Tyne executed for treason.'

Lord Xavier cracked his jaw.

'Lieutenant Tyne wasn't executed,' said Joss, leaping into the fray. 'He threw himself from our ship when he was exposed as a double agent for the Court of Thralls.'

Joss expected to be reprimanded for interrupting, but Lord Xavier turned his anger elsewhere. 'A fact you failed to uncover during his time in your service, Count Barus, before pawning him off on me to undermine our mission.'

Count Barus slammed his fist on the table, just once. It was enough to command everyone's attention. 'I would have you remember, Lord Xavier, whom it is you are addressing. My archers can always be marched straight back home.'

Lord Xavier bared his teeth to reply but was stopped short by Grandmaster Eno clearing his throat. 'Your Excellency, your lordship – let's all sheathe our claws, shall we, and remember that we're on the same side? So if the rest of your party would excuse us, we can get to the matter at hand.'

Joss was outraged. After the hard path they'd taken to get here, the sacrifices they'd made, the knowledge they'd fought to gain, they weren't to have any say in the meeting. He wanted to shout, to jump up and down and demand that they be allowed to stay. And he would have done just that if it weren't for a shudder on the horizon that made him stop and ask, 'What's that?'

He pointed to the caravan spilling across the furthest edge of the salt flats. As distant as they were, their number could still be seen to be comprised of all manner of wagons, saddled thunder lizards and circling pterosaurs. They carried no banners, they bore no standards, yet that just made them all the more recognisable.

'I don't believe it,' Drake breathed. 'It's the Nameless.'

'Nameless? Here?' Grandmaster Eno exclaimed. 'Why?'

Lord Xavier grimaced ever so slightly as he made his admission. 'We entreated them for their aid.'

The other officials muttered in discontent. 'You did what?' Eno demanded.

When Lord Xavier failed to speak, Joss did it for him. 'Dark times demand desperate deeds. Or so I've heard.'

Grandmaster Gilmyn sputtered with indignation. 'A handful of those brigands may be permitted at the occasional ceremony – but to ally ourselves with them? The very notion is outrageous! These are mercenaries without code or honour.'

'Calm yourself, Grandmaster Gilmyn,' said Grandmaster Eno. 'Lord Xavier, turn them away at once, before they come too close to the tower. These proceedings cannot continue while such a threat marches to our door.'

Lord Xavier's face was impossible to read as he stared at the grandmaster. 'Very well,' he said. 'Ezekiel – take the others with you and inform the Nameless that their presence is no longer required.'

Zeke looked to his friends in confusion, then back to his father. 'But we need their help. You know we do.'

'Ezekiel, the Grandmaster Council has made its wishes known. End of discussion. Now do as you've been told.'

'You're not listening! You never listen. Whether they're Nameless or not doesn't matter. We need all the help we can get and they've come to offer theirs. Is your ego really so fragile that, rather than sacrifice a scrap of pride, you'd let the whole world die? Why can't you all see that –'

Lord Xavier rose to his feet and slapped his son across the face.

Half the room gasped while Zeke clutched his cheek. The Grandmaster Council watched on dispassionately.

'I am beyond weary of your constant disobedience and endless disrespect,' Lord Xavier hissed through gritted teeth. 'Every opportunity you've been given, every blunder you've had expunged, every privilege you've taken for granted, all that I have provided for you and yet you still defy me. For once, obey an order without question. And when we've returned home we can talk about your future. Because if you're so eager to count yourself as Nameless, believe me, it can be very easily arranged.'

Zeke stared at his father with bloodshot eyes. He swelled with anger, with heartache, with a torrent of words dammed up inside him. 'Assuming there'll be any home still standing after all this,' he muttered, and walked from the room.

Joss remained where he was, glaring at his lordship.

'Something you wish to say, Sarif?' Lord Xavier asked.

'Just trying to understand, my lord, how someone can have so much and yet be so determined to throw it all away,' Joss said, choosing his words with sharpened precision.

'As someone might throw away their future?' Lord Xavier fired back. 'As someone might throw away a precious artefact with which they were entrusted?'

The jab silenced Joss. Lord Xavier smiled with petty satisfaction. 'That's what I thought. Now go.'

Joss and the others stalked out of the room. Zeke was waiting for them in the antechamber, pacing like a raptor in a pen. Everyone looked to Joss to see how best to offer Zeke some support. And Joss knew that the best way was with humour.

'I hate to say it,' Joss told Zeke once the hatch had sealed shut behind them, 'but your old man is a real refried muck nugget.'

Zeke burst out in a laugh. It was coarse and clipped and came with little comfort, but it was a laugh all the same. 'Yeah, he's a prize alright,' Zeke admitted, shaking his head.

'At least my parents had the excuse of being hardened criminals for acting the way they did,' Hero noted.

'And mine live in the Northern Tundra,' said Drake, earning himself a gamut of confused stares. 'What? It gets very cold up there. It messes with your head.'

'Temperature notwithstanding,' Qorza said. 'We have orders to carry out.'

Joss frowned, an ember of an idea flaring in his mind. 'What if we don't, though?'

'What do you mean?' Drake asked.

'What if we ride out there, meet the Nameless and explain the situation to them? That the Grandmaster Council is unsure of accepting their help, but maybe if Silas came up and met with them they could work out some sort of agreement?'

'Lord Xavier will be furious,' Qorza noted.

'Lord Xavier is furious when his toast isn't buttered thoroughly,' said Zeke. 'I say we do it.'

'You're assuming they're here to lend their help,' Drake replied. 'For all we know they've thrown their lot in with the Court of Thralls, just like the *draa'kin*. Or they've sensed an opportunity and they're here to declare their own war on Thunder Realm when the kingdom is already fractured and under siege.'

'Do you really believe that?' asked Hero.

'No,' Drake admitted after a moment's pause. 'But it never pays to assume.'

Tilting her head, Hero considered her options. 'I'm with Joss,' she concluded. 'There's too much at stake not to take the chance. Though let's keep our wits about us. I could do without falling into any more traps.'

Drake, Qorza and Zeke added their agreement, and together they set off towards the skybridge. They were just approaching the *Zenith*'s entry hatch when Drake drew in close to Joss. 'So … Lord Xavier noticed the Champion's Blade was missing,' he said.

Joss's back stiffened. 'You did, too?'

'Hard to miss,' Drake shrugged. 'Between that and Edgar – are you OK?'

'I'm still standing. Though if you have another spear handy, I wouldn't say no.'

'Sorry – family heirloom, remember?' said Drake, pointing at his Icefire spear.

They found Eliza in the hangar when they arrived back aboard, having emerged from her room to tend her mount in the pens. She wasn't alone.

'Dafne – you came!' Qorza exclaimed upon seeing the elderly wraithslayer. Dafne was standing beside one of the pantheras that had been pulling her wagon back in Lucium, the large black feline now saddled up and cleaning its paws after a long journey.

'There was a whisper in my bones that I should take up your offer to join you. The lass here was kind enough to let me on board.'

'You came to the ship? Not Tower Town or the Grandmaster Council?' asked Joss.

'I go where I'm guided,' Dafne said. Her quaverstaff flicked from left to right as she shrugged.

'In which case, will you go with us to meet with the Nameless?' Joss told her. 'You too, Eliza. We'll need your help in talking everything through with your uncle. If you'd be willing, that is.'

'Why do you think I was here saddling up in the first place?' Eliza replied, and set to helping Crimson and Cloud prepare everyone's mounts before loading them onto the *Fat Lot of Good*. Dafne's panthera hissed at Callie and the sabretooth responded in kind, but the pair soon settled into their pens alongside the other animals.

Zeke checked the jet-cycles, then took a moment to confer with the two young deckhands. 'We'll be on comms-channel 21-M if you need us.'

Crimson rolled his eyes. 'I'm sure the bridge crew would love to have us pawing all over their communications array. But sure, we'll bear that in mind.'

Zeke threw a look of exasperation at Joss.

'Remind me again why we brought them along?' he muttered as he drew shut the *Fat Lot*'s bay doors and ignited the engines. Within moments they were touching down on the salt flats, far enough away from the Nameless caravan to keep from startling their animals.

As the group rode out together, Joss contemplated the chances of his strategy actually working. The Nameless had already set aside their pride once in making the journey here, assuming they had come to help. Would they do it again when they learned the Grandmaster Council had ordered them to leave? And would the Grandmaster Council be willing to show the same humility?

'Tell me,' he said to Dafne. 'Every step of the way you've known more than you should. Does that mean you know if all this works out?'

Dafne's face was a blank mask as she looked across at him from her panthera's saddle.

'I know that I should be here with you now. The rest is a mystery.'

Joss bowed his head, nodding to himself.

'For you and me both.'

As he and the others drew closer to the Nameless caravan, he allowed himself to hope that he had found a way to honour Edgar's sacrifice – even as iron black clouds rolled in from the west, flashing with silvery veins of lightning.

CHAPTER THIRTY-THREE

A BEAST OF BURDEN

DRUMS pounded out a marching rhythm as the Nameless advanced on Tower Town. Silas Wildsmith led the caravan, perched on his armour-clad tyrannosaur, Balthasar. The beast offered a low growl as Joss and the others rode towards it, stopping at a safe distance.

Silas dismounted with enough force to kick up a cloud of salt, drawing the rest of the caravan to a standstill. He was dressed for war in an iron breastplate, boiled leather jodhpurs and plated boots, his face painted with a mess of black streaks that made his eyes appear to glint from beneath his oppressive brow. His scowl lightened a shade as he caught sight of Eliza.

'Uncle!' she called from her mount. 'What are you doing here?'

Silas slung his unwieldy song sword into its sheath and stretched his arms out wide. 'You mean what are *we* doing here?' he replied with a growl of a laugh. The Nameless behind him chortled. Joss and the others looked at each other with uncertainty. Now would be a cuss of a time to discover that one of Drake's theories about the Nameless's presence were correct.

'We took another vote,' Silas said. 'After you left. There was much argument and deliberation. More than a few blows thrown. But we reached a conclusion. You weren't wrong, you and your prentice friends. This is our land. Our people. And it's up to us to fight for it. So that's what we're here to do.'

Eliza broke out in a relieved smile as she and the others cantered to a stop before the assembled mass of Nameless riders. 'That's brilliant!' she exclaimed. 'I can't tell you how much this means.'

'Seems we're spoiled for help now with all these new arrivals,' said Drake, nodding to Dafne.

'If those bloody-minded, bone-skulled old beggars can be convinced of accepting it,' Zeke snorted.

'They have to,' said Joss, casting a glance over his shoulder at Tower Town. 'Which is why we need Silas to –' He stopped short as he caught sight of a lone figure on a raptor, riding in from the south. Although they were too far away to make out clearly, Joss could tell from the way the rider was slumped in the saddle that they were badly injured.

'Who is that?' Drake asked.

'Not one of ours,' Silas replied.

'Hang on,' Joss said as he rummaged in his pocket for his father's nightscope. Ordinarily it wouldn't be all that effective in the daytime, but the dark clouds that had rolled in had cast an eerie twilight. The nightscope's vision was acutely clear as he trained the device on the approaching figure.

A sensation like lightning ran through him. It sparked at his fingertips and fizzed through his every fibre, hitting him in the gut and stinging him in the eyes. His knees buckled. His heart somersaulted. His tongue lassoed itself.

'It – it's …' he stammered, unable to believe what he was about to say. 'It's Sur Verity!'

'What?!' exclaimed Eliza. She surged forward to claim the nightscope. Joss watched in shock as Eliza registered her mentor's presence. Sur Verity was crumpled atop her raptor Levina, pale and weak but very much alive.

Eliza spurred her mount on and rode hard to meet Sur Verity.

'Eliza, wait!' Joss called, urging Azof into a full-speed sprint. As he struggled to keep pace with Eliza, his mind stampeded with thoughts. How could Sur Verity be alive? He'd seen her final moments with his own eyes, just as he'd seen Edgar's. For a second he gave way to hope that his fallen friend would emerge from the distance to ride alongside Sur Verity, whole and happy – but he knew that, realistically, this must be some kind of trick. It wouldn't be the first time someone close to him had returned from the dead, only to be revealed as an impostor. Could Malkus and the Court of Thralls be using Joss's experience in Daheed as a ploy against him? Was it foolish of him to believe that this really was Sur Verity, ready to lend her sword to the coming battle?

The closer he and Eliza got to her, the more they could see her grave state. Her left arm hung limp, in ominous shades of enflamed red and gangrenous black. Swollen veins ran up her neck to an ashen face that was drenched with sweat. Her head was swinging in lazy circles, her one good eye blinking in a concerted effort to focus. She may have returned from the dead, but it looked like she'd only just managed to claw her way free.

'Sur Verity!' Joss called, and when she didn't acknowledge him he called again. 'Sur Verity! It's Josiah! Joss! And Eliza!'

The two prentices reached their master and dropped from their mounts. Grabbing hold of Levina's reins, they steadied the raptor as her rider tumbled loose, landing in a heap in Joss's arms.

———

Lord Xavier sat before the Grandmaster Council with his hands laid out on the table as if he were claiming it for himself. He spared no further attention to the Nameless gathered outside, confident that his orders would be carried out and the interlopers would be seen away. His attention belonged only to the men seated around him.

'I suggest we cut to the heart of the matter,' he said. 'We face an unprecedented threat. If you've read my reports to Regent Greel and his cabinet, I'm sure you'll agree that Lieutenant Tyne's betrayal proves how far this enemy's influence stretches. Attacks can come at any time and from any quarter. If we're to have any chance of survival, we need to strike quickly and with all our might.'

'And while this council respects your opinion, Lord Xavier, I can't help but notice how alarmist you sound,' Grandmaster Eno said. 'I think it best that we don't panic. I think it best that we remember who we are. We are paladeros. We do not bolt at the first hiss of a forked tongue. We stand strong. We stand together. And we make that stand here at Tower Town.'

'I don't understand,' said Lord Xavier, looking around him. 'Regent Greel charged us with leading the strike on the invading forces. The Royal Army is counting on us – now more than ever with General Swift missing.'

Grandmaster Warburn pinned him with an unflinching stare. 'Neither Regent Greel nor the Royal Army are thunderfolk.'

Lord Xavier blinked, dumbfounded. 'Secretary Lovegood,' he said, addressing the gentleman who'd been strangely silent all this time. 'What say you? Surely you don't condone this kind of talk?'

The secretary ran a hand along his lapel. 'Regent Greel isn't here. And far be it from me to interfere in council matters.'

Lord Xavier's head swayed as he struggled to comprehend what he was hearing. 'Secetary Lovegood is right,' said Grandmaster Gilmyn. 'For centuries we've safeguarded not only our herds but our traditions and our ideals. We are the custodians of all that is sacred in Thunder Realm. We will ensure it is preserved above all else.'

'Surely the Grandmaster Council agrees that most sacred to the paladero way of life are the oaths we swore to protect the kingdom?' Xavier said. 'Now is the time. And if we don't heed the call, it's not just the outrealmers who may perish. It's all the paladero orders beyond Tower Town's line of defence.'

Grandmaster Eno folded his hands on the tabletop. 'We will marshal our forces and fend off any attack the enemy is foolish enough to mount. We cannot bear responsibility for those who are unable or unwilling to avail themselves of our protection.'

Lord Xavier rounded on the man to his right. 'Count Barus,' he said, while His Grace wobbled in his chair at the unexpected attention. 'You claim being the Guardian of the Green as one of your many titles. You've seen for yourself the damage that can be wrought by even a single one of the beasts at our enemy's command. Would you leave your people to fend for themselves?'

Barus puffed out his chest and lifted his chin, though he kept his eyes averted. 'The countyfolk will understand that their leadership must be protected.'

'But – but this isn't protection,' Xavier sputtered. 'This

is retreat! This is saving our own skins at the cost of every vow we've ever made!'

'*Enough*, Lord Xavier!' Grandmaster Eno bellowed. 'We have indulged your insolent tongue long enough, just as we've indulged Regent Greel in his clumsy attempts to rule. Hard times call for hard choices. You can either abide by those choices or you can take your leave. All you need do is renounce your vows, relinquish your rank and title, set aside whatever aspirations you have of one day being considered as a Grandmaster and instead be marked from this day to your last day as Nameless. So, your ship and your crew await you, my lord – if they choose to follow a man who would forsake them all, that is. What say you?'

The chamber grew as quiet as a tomb. Lord Xavier rose from his seat. He stared into the faces of all those gathered around him. Turned his gaze on Grandmaster Eno. The Grandmaster did not flinch as he returned the defiant stare with his own. Then, unsteady on his feet, Lord Zavier sank back down. Turned his eyes from everyone. Bit his lip. Bowed his head.

And then a voice rang out from the corner of the room.

'I would say his lordship has made his choice,' the shadows at the far end of the chamber coalesced into a feather-cloaked form. 'Wouldn't you, Father?'

Thrall emerged to gasps from across the table. He carried a long iron chain that stretched into the darkness from which he'd appeared, and his mask was raised to reveal the pale face that lay beneath.

'Blaek!' Grandmaster Eno exclaimed, his eyes quivering at the sight of his son garbed in the enemy's dark livery. 'Then what I've heard is true. You really have surrendered to this madness. But how did you get in here?'

'Your defences leave a lot to be desired,' the man once known as Sur Blaek said in a voice as sharp as razor wire. 'I hope you don't mind that I've brought a friend. I understand you're already acquainted.'

He yanked on the chain and a second figure emerged. He was dressed similarly and was also unmasked, but with all the blood and bruises on his face it took a moment for everyone to recognise him.

'Lord Malkus,' Grandmaster Eno said, before turning on his son. 'What have you done to him?'

'I have broken him. Just as one breaks any beast of burden,' said Thrall. 'Just as I'll break you.'

—

CHAPTER THIRTY-FOUR

A MASTER'S FURY

'RUN ...' Lord Malkus wheezed through his bloodied lips and broken metal teeth, his voice too weak for anyone to hear him.

'What did he say?' asked Count Barus, shifting in his chair.

'You needn't concern yourself with that. He's not here for his insights. He's only here to serve as a sacrifice,' Sur Blaek said as he tightened the chain that kept Lord Malkus in place. He turned his gaze on Grandmaster Eno. 'A notion that surely eludes you, Father. After all, it's been decades since you or any of your ilk have been called on to make a sacrifice of your own. And the memory of youthful hardships has no doubt long faded. Now you sit up here in the highest reaches of your tower, lording over all those below and kicking down any ladders that may give them the chance to ascend alongside you. You've climbed so high that the rarefied air has clotted your minds. Time, I think, for a prevailing wind to clear all of that away.'

'… *Run!*' Malkus croaked, louder and more fervently this time. Everyone at the table stared at him. 'You have to run! *Now!*'

Lord Xavier leapt up. Count Barus wobbled nervously as Eno climbed unsteadily to his feet, while his fellow grandmasters rose beside him. The Thrall once known as Sur Blaek merely laughed.

'But Malkus – why would our brothers have cause to run?' he said, pressing his stone mask to his face. It settled into position with a malevolent whisper. 'Especially when they've set such a well-laid trap.'

'What –?!' exclaimed Lord Xavier, wheeling around to be confronted by the sight of Grandmaster Gilmyn and Grandmaster Warburn holding rune-studded masks.

'What disloyalty is this?!' Eno demanded, pulling away from his fellow grandmasters with horror.

'On the contrary; their loyalty is absolute,' said Lovegood as he revealed a stone mask of his own, his eyes as dead as Gilmyn and Waburn's. 'It just doesn't lie with you.'

Slipping on their masks, the three men were engulfed in a squall of black feathers. Shadows knitted together and fell from their shoulders as cloaks, revealing each of them in their full Thrall guise. Warburn stood out in his wolfskin cloak, while Gilmyn's leather breastplate was a distinct shade of muted red. Lovegood and Sur Blaek were indistinguishable from one another as they both reached into their cloaks and removed a pair of frighteningly familiar weapons.

'The inferno orbs,' Lord Xavier said flatly. 'You procured them from the weredragons.'

'Indeed,' Lovegood replied, his voice having taken on Thrall's grim resonance. 'You would be astonished at how many we were able to conceal in this very tower, on this very floor, long before you and your crew ever arrived.'

'… *run* …!' Malkus gasped one last time.

'Blaek …' said Grandmaster Eno, marshalling the last of whatever authority he'd once had over the masked man before him. 'What do you intend to do?'

'Simple, Father. I intend the darkness to take us,' the Thrall replied, raising his inferno orb.

'Darkness take us all,' responded his court.

'Blaek, wait –!' the Grandmaster said and reached out to his son, his words cut short as the Thralls smashed their miracle weapons and unleashed their master's fury.

———

Moments before the explosion, Sur Verity blinked awake.

'Jos– Josiah?' she said through a rolling fog of uncertainty.

'I'm here, Sur Verity. It's me,' Joss replied, cupping her hand in both of his. He watched closely as she struggled to retrieve something from her pocket.

'This ... this belongs to you,' she said, raising a golden necklace.

At first he was perplexed as to how Sur Verity could think he'd ever owned such a piece of jewellery. And then realisation flooded in on him like a tidal wave. 'This is my mother's betrothal necklace,' he said. 'Where did you get this?'

'Malkus,' Sur Verity replied. 'Your mother gave it to him for safekeeping, the same day she entrusted you to his care. The same day she ... she ...'

'The same day she died,' Joss concluded.

Sur Verity nodded and drew a breath. 'Witnessing the Destruction of Daheed – something got inside his head. His soul. Corrupted him and all those who stood on the shore watching. That corruption ... it's spread since then. But the one sliver of Malkus that remained held onto this like it was a talisman. It's why he watched over you, even as he did all that he did. His last act was to help me escape – an act he wouldn't have committed without – without the example of your mother and the promise he made to her. She passed this on to him. He passed it on to me. And I – I give it to you ...'

Her breathing growing more laboured by the moment, she dropped the golden necklace into Joss's hands. It shone there with purpose, glinting at him through the growing darkness.

'I –' he failed to find the right words, so he settled for the simplest ones that came to mind. 'Thank you.'

'There's more,' she said, struggling to pull herself up. 'Tower Town … it's a trap. He told me just before I fled – he – they –'

Veins curdled along Sur Verity's neck as she began coughing violently, then hacked up a glob of blood. Joss hunched forward, doing what little he could to comfort her as she fell to the ground and into unconsciousness.

'Sur Verity? Sur Verity!' he said, trying to shake her awake. He looked past Eliza's worried face to see the others riding towards them. '*Qorza!* Come quick!'

She was on a Zadkille cycle with Zeke, Drake and Hero by her side. Dafne was close behind, watching uneasily as the storm gathered around them. Dropping from her saddle, Qorza inspected Sur Verity's wound. 'It's badly infected,' she said, prying the chestplate open to get a better look at the mess beneath. 'And poisoned from the looks of it. Most likely a cursed blade. I need to debride the necrotic tissue and perform a blessing before it's too late.'

'We should get her back to Tower Town. They'll have facilities there,' said Drake.

Joss shook his head. 'She said Tower Town was a trap. She said –' He looked at the blood on his hands: it looked black under the dark clouds that smothered the sun. Joss looked up to face them and choked at the sight.

'Oh no,' he said, and spun around to see the clouds swirling above Tower Town. '*No!*'

The words had barely left his lips when the highest

reaches of the tower were torn apart in a blinding explosion. Torrents of fire arced across the sky, hurling shrapnel down on the masses below. Screams rose like smoke, curling towards the heavens. And then from high above came a cacophony of shrieks.

Joss watched, paralysed with horror, as a vortex ruptured the skies over the blazing ruin of Tower Town and the largest horde of dragons he'd ever seen spilled out. The beasts looked like they were sculpted from ashes and coal: their red eyes glowing like fresh embers, their fangs a serrated protrusion from their widening maws, their cries fuelled by hunger and hate.

'We're too late,' he gasped. 'It's here. The end of the world is here.'

CHAPTER THIRTY-FIVE

A STRONG AND RIGHTEOUS FORCE

BLACK clouds whirled around the flaming torch of Tower Town as the sky turned as red as blood. Lightning flashed in the distance, silent and eerily static. The vortex at the tower's peak was spewing dragons with increasing speed, the great winged beasts dropping down on the tent city below to snatch up anyone they could get their claws on. Paladero riders and Barus's archers all screamed as they were plucked up and guzzled down like field mice being hunted by birds of prey.

Joss and his brethren watched on from the distance of the Searing Sands, the horror rendering them mute. In one fell swoop their leaders had all been wiped out, from the Grandmaster Council to Lord Xavier, their fiery deaths ushering in this nightmare from which there was no awakening. Joss was still struggling to comprehend it all when he felt the earth rumbling beneath him and looked over to see Silas riding over on Balthasar's back with a cluster of Nameless at his side.

'His Majesty preserve me!' Silas exclaimed. 'It was all true! Every word of warning you gave!'

'Yes. It was,' Joss said, allowing himself to stare at the unfolding chaos for only one moment more. Then he slipped his mother's necklace over his head to sit alongside the betrothal necklace he'd inherited from his father, feeling the comforting touch of both the thunderbolt pendant and the sun medallion against his skin. 'We have to move. Qorza, can you get Sur Verity somewhere safe where you can tend to her?'

'We've got a physician's wagon with us,' Silas said.

Qorza nodded. 'I'll take care of her there.'

'What about skyborne riders?' Joss asked Silas. 'Did you bring them too?'

'Two dozen, including your friend Alabaster Jane and her cohorts.'

Joss looked at the dragons that continued to mass above them, already easily outnumbering the Nameless forces. 'We need them up there to keep those dragons at bay.'

Silas raised his hand and waved a sequence of gestures. Two dozen saddled pterosaurs took to the sky, flying for the vortex and the circling horde with Alabaster Jane leading the surge. Whatever quarrel he may have had with her before, Joss could only hope his resolve might prove as steely as hers.

'What do we do?' asked Eliza, helping Qorza load Sur Verity onto Levina's saddle.

'We don't have any chance of fighting off those dragons down here. We need to get back to the *Fat Lot of Good*,' Joss said. 'Zeke? Can you still be our pilot?'

Zeke was staring at the blazing peak of Tower Town, his face ashen and his arms limp. 'My father …' he muttered, unable to look away. 'He – he's gone.'

Taking Zeke by the shoulders, Joss turned him away from the burning building and stared into his eyes. 'Zeke? I am so, so sorry. He may have been many things, but he was still your father. To lose him like this is unimaginable. I know. My parents were taken the exact same way by this same monster. If we make our way out of this, then we can mourn for them and everyone else we've lost. But until then we have to fight. Can you fight, Zeke?'

Through the fog of his grief, Zeke focused enough to nod.

'I can fight,' he said, just as a single note rang out with the power of a Holy Messenger's horn. Joss wondered for one shining moment if it signalled the arrival of help. Then he looked at the horizon to see who it was, and all the hope drained from him.

A battalion of mounted acolytes stormed over the rise, dressed in spiked black-steel armour branded with the Crest of the Unhallowed, their lacquered masks serving as faceplates in their jagged helmets. They carried an array of swords, axes and halberds, augmented by thundersticks, bolt rifles and – most chillingly – the embellished brass pipe launchers that had been stockpiled back at Sanctum, all heavily loaded with blazing inferno orbs. Leading the charge with his black blade drawn was a Thrall that Joss would recognise anywhere, even among all his identically masked court. The Thrall who had killed Edgar.

He and his army were saddled atop a cavalry's worth of chimeras, the beasts' eyes all flashing hot and bright in the encroaching darkness. Each creature was encased in steel plates and chain mail, and the only noise greater than the rattling of their armour was their roars. The noise ripped through Joss's gut as the war horns sounded again, then were joined by the bellowing dragons above.

'Now we really have a fight on our hands,' Silas said with a mirthless laugh. 'Good thing I'm spoiling for one.'

'Do you have any holy folk in that company of yours?' Joss asked without looking away from the oncoming enemy.

Silas cocked an eyebrow at him. 'You think we're in need of prayers?'

'No. Sacred Sand,' said Joss as he shared a knowing look with Qorza and Dafne, then pointed to the Thrall charging for them. 'Gather up as much as you can and blast it all in that ghoul's stone-masked face.'

'Much obliged, lad. I think. And if I were to offer any advice in return, I'd say now's the time to get back to that ship of yours,' Silas said, then pressed thumb and finger to his lips to emit a piercing whistle. The Nameless riders fell into line behind their leader as he scaled Balthasar's armour, the tyrannosaur growling at the monsters charging across the horizon.

Joss looked back to see a mass of scared faces, some of them barely older than him. They watched as Silas pulled his immense song sword from the scabbard between his shoulders and raised it to the sky.

'*Brothers! Sisters! I see before me monsters of legend!*' he shouted above the cacophony of hooves stampeding toward them. 'Fearsome beasts spoken of only in whispers! A breed of enemy that would strike terror in the heart of any hardened warrior! This great and terrible legion knows no fear! Gives no ground! Has no name! *For we are the Nameless!*'

The uncertain faces among the Nameless started to solidify with resolve as they listened.

'*We are the strong and righteous force that the wicked most dread!*' Silas pressed on, sword slashing the air. 'And we will crush this rabid band of fiends the same as any other fools who seek to test our might! For honour! For valour! *For Thunder Realm!*'

'*FOR THUNDER REALM!*' the Nameless bellowed in unison, the tyrannosaur Balthasar lending his voice to theirs with a great and terrible roar. The power of it was enough to spur the riders into a gallop, hollering battle cries as they charged towards the Shadow God's army.

'We've got our cover,' Joss said, turning to his brethren. 'Now it's up to us to get to the ship.'

'And from there?' asked Drake.

'We'll work that out when we get there. One problem at a time, right?' he finished with a nod to Hero.

'One problem at a time,' she agreed.

Joss stole a glance at Qorza as she spirited Sur Verity away to the physician's wagon, then turned his steeliest gaze towards those gathered beside him. 'Let's ride,' he said. Spurring Azof on, he and his brethren galloped down the incline towards the surrounding desert flats and their awaiting airship.

'Next time I'm landing on the slope. I don't care what the onboard sensors say,' Zeke groused as they struggled to cover the distance, only to be cut short by a resounding screech and the beating of wings. A dragon was right above them, its jaws opening wide and its gullet glowing white hot.

'*Scatter!*' Joss shouted, and everyone swerved just in time to avoid the fireball that was coming straight for them. It hit with a rush of noise, scorching the earth and forcing them towards a crack in the ground that could barely be called a trench.

'Take cover!'

Their mounts leapt into the trench one after the other. Dafne landed nimbly beside Joss and Drake, her panthera casting a cool stare of judgement.

'Well,' said Zeke as he assessed the damage his cycle's levitators had taken from the drop. 'That could have gone better.'

'Now what?' Hero said, ducking down against Callie's back as another wave of flames rolled over their heads.

'Now we hunt around for salamanders or anything else that might barbeque up good,' Zeke replied.

'It's the end of the world, we're pinned in a trench by a fire-breathing dragon and you think it's a good time for jokes?' Hero asked.

'A little levity can help at moments of absolute panic and existential terror,' Zeke said, sitting up. 'And besides, who said I was joking?'

Joss blinked at him. 'What do you mean?'

Zeke snuck a look over the ridge. 'If I make a break for it now, maybe I can get to the ship and fly it over here.'

'Or get flash-fried in the attempt,' said Drake.

'Serve me up as a meal to the mounts if need be. I'm sure a bucket of crispy Zadkille would be a welcome treat at the end of a long doomsday,' Zeke shrugged, then yanked on the jet-cycle's vertical control pin. 'Keep your heads down and with his majesty's mercy I'll be back with the wagon. I might even do some good for the family name.'

'Zeke, wait!' Joss called out, but he was too late. With the control pin disabled, Zeke flew up into the air in a dizzying rush, arcing wide to land out of sight of the trench. There was a screech as the dragon caught sight of him and stomped off to give chase.

Joss cursed to himself and tugged on Azof's reins, guiding the raptor towards a dip in the trench that led to higher ground.

'Joss, you're not doing anything as crazy as that. Are you?' Drake asked.

'No crazier than usual,' he replied, urging Azof into a gallop. '*Hyah!*'

The raptor showed no fear as he burst out onto the battlefield. Dragons were still soaring overhead, pursuing the skyborne riders. But a few had dropped down among the ground forces to attack the Nameless – including the monster that was charging after Zeke with its maw wide open.

'Hey! *Hey!*' Joss shouted. 'Over here, you mucking monster! *Over here!*'

Unable to be heard over the clamour of battle, and with the dragon only a short distance from Zeke, Joss pried loose the bola on his belt. Swinging it at speed, he sent it flying and clipped the creature's hindquarters. The dragon stopped, turned around and roared.

'Uh oh,' said Joss.

Azof needed little prompting to turn and run faster than he ever had before. Now facing the opposite direction, Joss could see that his brethren had followed him from the trench. He waved his arms wildly. 'Run! *Run!*' he shouted as the dragon barrelled towards him, the air on the back of his neck already growing hot as he heard the monster swallow a breath. Drake and Hero and the others were shouting at him, all of them giving different directions.

A deafening blast rang out. The earth behind him exploded. Salt and sand rained down. Looking over his shoulder, Joss saw the dragon halted in its tracks, shaking its head. He looked up. The *Zenith* had broken free of its dock and was on the attack, its cannons smoking from the shot it had taken at the dragon. Joss cheered, but it was cut short by the sensation of air swirling around him, as if the dragon had taken flight to confront its attacker.

He couldn't have been more wrong. Its engines thundering, the *Fat Lot of Good* swung into view and Zeke's voice echoed over the ship's loudspeakers.

'Need a lift?'

CHAPTER THIRTY-SIX

A FIGURE AMONG SMOKING RUINS

JOSS rode fast, spurring Azof into the safety of the *Fat Lot of Good*'s hull. Stealing a glance over his shoulder, he could already see the dragon regaining its bearings. It wouldn't be long before it attacked again. Once Azof was secure in his pen, Joss scaled the ladder leading above deck to find Zeke in the wheelhouse, preparing the ship for an emergency take-off.

'Thanks,' Joss said as he approached. 'You saved our hides.'

'You should direct those thanks skywards,' Zeke replied, pointing to the *Zenith*. 'We've got some help on hand.'

'*Ahoy there, Captain Sarif! Or would it be lieutenant?*' a familiar voice chimed in over the communications array. '*This is Ensign Crimson and Cabin Boy Cloud reporting for duty!*'

'*Why am I the cabin boy?*'

'*Don't question the ranking officer!*'

'Crimson,' Joss said, stunned. 'What are you doing?'

'They've commandeered the gun deck and are laying down suppressing fire,' Zeke told him, and when he saw Joss's face he added, 'I know. I'm as shocked as you are.'

'*I heard that!*' Crimson chimed in. '*And by the way, that big nasty is back.*'

Joss and Zeke both saw the dragon stalking towards them, its wings folded close to its body and its tail whipping back and forth.

'Can you get this bucket moving any faster?' Joss asked, sweat running down his face as the dragon grew closer.

'I'm trying, I'm trying!' Zeke said, ratcheting the accelerator in a desperate fight to gain altitude. His efforts were quickly overshadowed by another blast from the *Zenith*'s gun deck, which sent the dragon tumbling to the ground.

'*Direct hit!*' Crimson crowed over the speakers.

Joss punched the broadcast button. 'Nice work, ensign,' he said. 'Think you can keep us and the skyborne covered?'

'*Does a pterosaur muck from above?*' came the crude reply. '*Though you may want to give it a moment before taking off. You've got company.*'

Joss and Zeke both jumped at the thought of another dragon, but it was only their brethren with Eliza and Dafne in tow. Within moments they were climbing into the wheelhouse.

'What are you waiting for?' Hero asked. 'Let's get this crate in the air already.'

'Aye-aye,' Zeke said as he worked the controls to pull the ship upward. Bursts of flame erupted all around as the dragon horde continued its pursuit of Alabaster Jane and the skyborne Nameless, the riders pulling all manner of death-defying rolls and dives to keep from getting caught.

'Looks like they could use an assist,' said Hero, stepping onto the foredeck. Firmly planting her feet, she fished a pair of zamaraqs from her bandolier, took aim, and let loose. One zamaraq flew in a wide circle, taking a chunk out of a dragon's wing before swinging back around to the *Fat Lot of Good*, where Hero snatched it out of the air. The other landed much more decisively, hitting one of the smaller dragons in the ridge of its brow and forcing it from the sky.

'What a shot!' Zeke whooped, prompting the others to join Hero in the attack. Dafne was quick to perform a balletic routine with her quaverstaff, the music she made striking the ear much like a song sword's defensive tune. It worked to keep the horde at bay while Hero kept launching her zamaraqs, relinquishing with grim satisfaction those that never came back.

The coal-and-crimson skies had become a cauldron swirling around Tower Town; the flames at the peak had died away to reveal the blackened ribcage of its scaffolding. And in the place where the Grandmaster Council had once sat, Joss could now see a figure among the smoking ruins.

'Who is that?' he whispered, then repeated it loud enough for the others to hear.

Drake squinted. 'Can't say.'

But Joss could. 'It's Thrall,' he exclaimed. 'It has to be.'

'Thrall?' Zeke repeated from the wheelhouse. 'Really?'

'One of them at least. He's probably leading the battle from up there, giving orders to the others. If we can stop him, we can stop this whole nightmare right here and now.'

'You really think so?' Drake asked with a crinkled brow.

'What else can we do?' Joss replied.

Drake nodded soberly, taking a firm hold of his Icefire spear.

'We've still got the abseiling cords from the mission at Blade's Edge Acres,' Hero said. She gestured to the ropes bundled together by the portside railing. 'We can use those to drop onto the roof.'

Joss immediately set to readying the ropes with Eliza's help. As they worked together, he kept a close eye on the tower. The flames had died down to a handful of spot fires, but the smoke was still thick enough to obscure the figure moving among them. From what Joss could see the figure was dressed in black, though he appeared to be without a cloak. If he was a Thrall, he was unlike the others. If he wasn't a Thrall, Joss didn't dare imagine what else he could be.

'We're ready,' he called out when the job was done, and Drake and Hero rushed over to prepare for their respective jumps. That left Dafne at the bow of the airship, still whirling her quaverstaff in the air.

'Are you able to ward off the incoming horde?' Joss called out to her.

'I believe I heard something about pterosaurs mucking from above as we came aboard. Serves to reason that dragons would do the same,' said Dafne, too occupied with her dance to spare him a look.

Taking that as a 'yes', Joss ducked his head into the wheelhouse to speak to Zeke. 'Bring us to the far side of the tower. We'll need some distance between us and the Thrall so we can all land together.'

'Understood,' Zeke replied with a small salute. When the ship was within jumping distance of the tower, Zeke called out, 'Eliza! Have you ever piloted an airship?'

The prentice stared at him with wide eyes. 'Uh –'

'Trust me, there's nothing to it,' he said, gesturing for her to join him by the control array. 'You pull this, you push that, and you swing this around to make the whole thing move.'

'OK, that seems easy enough, I suppose –'

'And you stabilise equilibrium by pumping that and you gain altitude by ratcheting this. And pushing down on this lever makes you tilt up and pushing up makes you go down. You open the cargo hatch with this button but don't press the button next to it or you'll dump everything in the hold, including the animals. And if this light starts flashing red, you need to abandon ship immediately. I mean *immediately*. Got it?'

Eliza stared at the controls as if they were a rabid carnivore she was being forced to handfeed, then turned back to Zeke. 'Where are you going?'

Stepping from the wheelhouse, Zeke joined Joss and the others on the foredeck. 'I'm going with my brethren to confront the cold-blooded cuss who killed my father,' he said, slinging the strap of his pulse rifle over his shoulder. 'And together we're going to end this madness. One way or the other.'

Zeke leaned over to whisper in Joss's ear. 'Did that sound confident? Because truth be told I'm mucking myself right about now.'

Joss couldn't help laughing. 'I've been mucking myself ever since those dragons showed up.'

'Glad I'm not the only one,' Zeke winked.

Struggling to keep his hands steady, Joss pulled the harness into place.

'Everyone ready?' he asked once the cord was tied off.

'As ever,' Hero noted, holding her cord tight.

Zeke forced a grin onto his face. 'May His Majesty favour the fools.'

'Then let's go do something foolish,' said Joss, and walked to the edge of the ship.

Eliza, who was proving remarkably adept behind the wheel of the *Fat Lot of Good*, brought them in close enough to reach the tower, and steadily enough that they might land without breaking any bones.

Joss double-checked his safety line, spared a thought

for his mother and father as he asked them to watch over him, then stole a breath and jumped. The cord shrieked in his grip as he plummeted faster than he'd expected. He hit the scorched steel of Tower Town with the velocity of a boulder flung from a trebuchet while his brethren landed in a row beside him, surefooted and precise.

'One of these days I'll be as agile as a raptor and it's going to be spectacular,' he groaned, his back teeth practically rattling.

Zeke laughed and helped him to his feet. 'Well – here we are again. All four of us. Bound to a blade, bound for life.'

'Sounded like an awful long time originally,' said Hero. 'Now I'm not so sure.'

'Whatever happens, I'm glad it's all of you I'm standing beside,' Joss told his brethren.

'The feeling's more than mutual,' said Drake, unslinging his spear from over his shoulder. 'Shall we?'

They all levelled their gaze at the other side of the tower. Together they drew their weapons and began a slow march across the blasted metal terrain. The dark figure was still stirring through the smoke, and it was only as they came within shouting distance that they were able to see him properly.

It wasn't Thrall.

His back was turned to them as he surveyed the battlefield below, his hands folded courteously behind him. He wore a military dress uniform of midnight black with ornate silver epaulettes cresting his shoulders and a long curved sabre strapped to his side. His coppery blond hair had been slicked back and left to set like resin, crowning a pallid face turned only slightly towards the prentices, offering the barest hint of a profile.

From what little Joss could see he looked like any other man in his middle years, his waxen flesh cobwebbed with fine lines. But he had a presence that set him apart somehow, that distinguished him as regal. Perhaps it was the statuesque posture. Perhaps it was the self-possessed calm with which he assessed all the chaos around him.

'I had been wondering when I might expect company,' he said, turning to meet them with an arched brow. He had eyes of cerulean blue and a miserly little stripe of a smile. 'It strikes me as only too appropriate that it would be the four of you.'

Zeke looked around at his fellow prentices, then back at the man in black. 'I'm sorry – have we met?'

The man expelled a single dry snigger. 'We have not had the pleasure until now. Though you have all become quite well-acquainted with my emissaries.'

Understanding washed over Joss like a crashing wave of ice water. 'You're him ... aren't you?' he asked, though he already knew the answer.

The man in black's expression confirmed it, as did the insignia emblazoned on his chest as he finally turned to face the prentices head on.

'You're the Shadow God.'

—

CHAPTER THIRTY-SEVEN

AN ARROW
SCRAPING A MIRAGE

'PLEASED to meet you, Josiah,' the Shadow God said, his laughter crackling like the flames that encircled them. Spikes of blinding light bounced off the Crest of the Unhallowed pinned to his coat, wrought in silver and catching the glow of the fire.

Joss grimaced. 'You know my name?'

'I know all of your names,' the man in black replied. 'I know your parents' names. I know the names of the lords and paladeros you serve, the orders to which you have all pledged your allegiance. I know your secret names. The names you dare not breathe a word of to anyone but those you trust the most.'

He fixed Drake and Hero in turn with his bitterly cold stare. The two prentices looked to each other for comfort.

'You would be astonished by how much I know. You would be devastated by my understanding,' the Shadow God continued, his smile growing sharper as he savoured the discomfort he'd caused. 'Though while we are on the subject, I must say I have never been overfond of that name. *The Shadow God.* So reductive.'

'What name would you prefer?' Hero asked through gritted teeth.

The Shadow God looked up and away in earnest contemplation. 'Hard to say. I have so many. "Shoda", for one, as dubbed by the Vaalish people countless eons ago. "The Pale Prince" was always one I had a liking for: simultaneously distinguished and malevolent. But for now let's keep things simple. Do me the requisite honour of referring to me as Your Highness, and pledge your fealty to me as your rightful ruler.'

Zeke scoffed. 'You're joking.'

'Do I strike you as a jester, Ezekiel? Do I seem to you a fool? No. In fact, only a fool would gaze upon the maelstrom unfolding around us and think it witty or wise to antagonise its orchestrator.'

'So you really are the mastermind behind all this destruction, then,' said Drake. 'But why? Why would you do this?'

The Shadow God's smile sharpened. 'I'm glad you asked, Ganymede. If I can call you Ganymede,' he said as he began to slowly pace the very edge of the building. 'The answer to your question is simple: survival. I do all this merely to survive. You may not believe me, but it's true. If I may explain …'

Though the prentices were all wary, none of them denied him.

The Shadow God continued, 'You are all no doubt versed in the lore of your land, of the Sleeping King and the Dream of Ai. But just as there can be no day without night, nor sun without the moon, there can be no dream without a nightmare. When the Sleeping King dreamt Ai into existence, the kingdom was created as a bright and radiant vision. But with that vision there came a shadow. A nightmare realm, twinned to this world but separate from it, a repository for every monster, wraith and demon; the place where I was born, to serve as a shadow to your so-called Sleeping King. Born into an abyss not of my own making, left to wander the starless skies and poison them with my very presence.'

'Poison?' Joss asked. 'What do you mean, *poison?*'

'The cruel irony of the shadow realm. Its own inhabitants corrode it, just as a cancer left unchecked will weaken and ultimately kill its host. Which explains why there have been countless attempts at escape. From the beginning of time itself we have clawed and scratched and ripped at the veil between the worlds. On occasion one of our number would break through, emerging into the blinding light of your pristine dream world. Just as often they would be sent back, exorcised by your sorcerers and ethereons and wraithslayers. Thrown back into the prison from which they had fought so hard to flee.

'There were exceptions, of course. The creatures who escaped detection, who claimed their place among the mortals. The centaurs and the weredragons, the vampire clans and the great beasts of the Eastern Wilds – they all draw their heritage from our realm. Once they come to realise this they will no doubt flock to our cause.'

'Not if you lay waste to their homes the same as you did to mine,' Joss told him.

The Shadow God stopped pacing long enough to fix Joss with a concocted look of innocence. 'You really must speak more plainly. What home could you possibly mean?'

'*Daheed!*' Joss spat. 'You tore the sky above it wide open and killed everyone living there. All my friends, my entire family. *Everyone!*'

'Ah, yes. Daheed. My first true attempt at breaking through. It is …' the Shadow God paused as he searched for the right word. '*Regrettable* – what happened there. Perhaps I was too hasty. Too eager for freedom. I had watched the smaller creatures for centuries by that point, seen them pierce the barrier with great effort but little consequence. I assumed it would be the same for me. I was wrong. The rift was overpowering and could not be sustained. I had no choice but to abandon it. Though the attempt was not without its benefits. The tear gave me my first proper foothold in the Sleeping King's realm. I drew emissaries to my side, to herald and safeguard my arrival. And as you can see, they have been extraordinarily successful.'

Raising his hands, he gestured to the dragon hordes plucking the skyborne from their saddles, then to the chimera forces overwhelming Silas's riders, and finally to the roiling skies and the rift at the heart of it all.

'For this my supporters will be handsomely rewarded in the new kingdom we build together. My adversaries? They will be eternally punished. So you see, the time has come for you all to make your final choice. You have fought valiantly, and for that you have my respect. But your fight is over and you have lost. Now I ask: do you stand with me, or do you suffer the consequences of standing against me?'

Joss looked to his brethren. Without a hint of hesitation they each raised their weapons.

The prince's face soured. 'I see. I truly do not know what I expected from such a rabble of malcontents. Look at you all. A band of juvenile misfits with no clue of their predicament. An orphan boy from an island so backward it could hardly act to save itself, so divorced from his place in the world that he would attempt to be a paladero of all things. Is it any wonder what a failure you have proven to be? The lord of your order revealed as your greatest enemy. The paladero you served deceived, defeated and at death's door. Your tenure as Blade Keeper an abject failure, your destiny unmet, your dreams for naught. What an utterly pitiful creature you are.'

The prince's words ripped through Joss like raptor claws. He struggled to stop himself from splitting apart as the Shadow God shifted his focus down the line.

'Speaking of pitiful – here we have the daughter of thieves, a woebegone urchin who fancies herself a hero. Did you ever truly believe you were worthy of being here, Henrietta? That you could possibly hope to overcome your disgraceful origins? That men as proud and honourable as those in Thunder Realm would stand for such a stain on their reputations? The notion would be laughable were it not so pathetic. You were born trash and you will die trash, dedicated to a community that never desired your service in the first place. And as for this one?'

Leaving Hero pale and shell-shocked, the prince pointed contemptuously at Drake.

'The less said about your birth the better. You disdain your family when you should be grateful that they did not stamp you out for being such an abomination.'

'What's he talking about?' asked Zeke, bewildered.

Drake took a moment to clear his throat. Purse his lips. Then spoke. 'The fact that I was attributed a name and gender when I was born that never reflected who I truly am,' he said to Zeke, holding his Icefire spear steady. 'He's trying to shame me. Silence me. But I know who I am. And I am not ashamed. And I will not be silenced.'

The man in black issued a small laugh, clipped and cruel. 'You can tell yourself that,' he said. 'But we both know the truth.'

'Yes,' said Hero, standing by Drake's side along with Joss. 'We do.'

The Pale Prince cocked his head. 'What tremendous and heartwarming loyalty. Do you not agree, Ezekiel?'

The prince fixed Zeke with his cold stare. Zeke faltered at its intensity.

'But you would have no sense of such a notion, would you?' the prince continued. 'You rage and mourn for a father who never truly loved you. And all that unkindness you suffered throughout your lonely childhood has only served to make you unkind in turn. You stand here with your so-called brethren as if you are worthy of doing so, when we all know the truth. You would turn on them all in a heartbeat if it satisfied your own vain self-interest.'

'That's not true,' Zeke said. 'The worst thing I ever did was betray them. I would never do that again.'

'Is that so? Or, like the serpent you truly are, are you simply waiting for the opportune moment to strike? If I were to offer you the chance right now to not only survive this crisis but to prosper from it, I have no doubt you would –'

The barrel of Zeke's pulse rifle exploded with a staccato burst of thunderbolts, blasting the prince where he stood.

But the man in black remained exactly where he'd been, unscathed and smiling darkly at all of them. Zeke frowned, first in confusion and then with wrath as he fired again at the figure. But every blast simply passed through the Shadow God with no hint of touching him, much as an arrow would have no hope of scraping a mirage.

The Pale Prince laughed, loud and booming. Thunder

resounded in the distance. 'You poor, foolish boy. You think this is my true form? This is merely a shadow of my full majesty. An image I placed in your heads so that I might gauge each of you in turn. And I have found you all … *lacking*. It's a shame you will not survive long enough to see my real face, impressive and dreadful as it is. But you do not deserve the honour. Value your world in its final moments, children. I come now to make it anew.'

Shadows formed across the prince's pale face. Everything went dark, as if he were sucking all light and sound and warmth into the very centre of his being. Joss stumbled forward as the force of it threatened to yank him off his feet. And then the prince exploded in a lightning storm of unearthly black energy, throwing Joss and the others so high into the air it felt as if they'd all been wrenched up into the heavens. Higher and higher they flew, leaving Joss to wonder if it were true. Was he dead? Had the explosion killed them all?

The earth and the sky and the tower all whirled around him in a harrowing blur, slowing down only for him and his brethren to hang suspended for a moment high above the battlefield, higher even than the dragons and pterosaurs warring below. The wind ripped at him, the cold rush of air chilled him, the realisation of his dire predicament struck him.

And then he began to fall.

CHAPTER THIRTY-EIGHT

AN UNHOLY THUNDER

JOSS struggled to remain calm as he plummeted to earth. Forcing himself to push through his terror he realised that, despite the force the Pale Prince had used to throw him and his brethren from the tower, he was still holding the practice blade he'd carried into battle. He tightened his hold on the leather grip, recited a short and silent prayer, and began to swipe the sword through the air.

He had to fight with all his strength against the crosswinds battering him, the act of wielding his sword more like paddling an oar through hardening mortar. Nevertheless he persisted, moving the blade over and over again in a desperate attempt to make it sing. The ground grew closer as the sword remained dormant, panic scratching at the edges of Joss's mind until something finally gave and the blade burst into glowing, harmonious life.

He kept going, performing a very specific summoning song, frantically hoping it would not go unheard.

Pleasepleasepleasepleasepleasepleaseplease!

Just as his terror was reaching an overwhelming crescendo, a shadow fell across him, then swept beneath him. A riderless pterosaur was flapping its wings below him with a look of expectation on its face, its saddle empty and waiting. Joss reached out with one hand and grabbed the lizard-bird's reins, using them to yank himself into place.

A single smoking boot wedged in the stirrups told Joss what had happened to the pterosaur's previous rider. Though he felt a twinge of guilt about it, he kicked the boot loose and stuck his foot in its place, taking full control of the mount. From the safety of his saddle he could see that Eliza had scooped up Zeke and Hero, who were now aboard the *Fat Lot of Good*. The pair were gesturing wildly, pointing towards Drake, who was still falling. Hunching forward, Joss spurred his new mount into a controlled dive.

The ground was coming at him even faster now, with only a few precious moments until the inevitable collision. Joss ignored it, despite the screeching of his pterosaur. His mind had been focused entirely on his own survival before. Now it was focused only on Drake's.

'*Ganymede!*' he shouted as he drew near. Looking terror-stricken, Drake held out his Icefire spear to bridge the gap between them. Joss nearly fell out of his saddle as he stretched to grab hold of the weapon, using it to haul Drake towards him.

'Hold on!' he called, fighting against the velocity of their fall to pull Drake into the saddle behind him. Joss gave a forceful tug of the reins, making the pterosaur shriek as it swooped down so low its belly scraped against the salt flats before zipping back up again. Joss burst out in a whooping cry of victory, but it was cut short as they climbed back up towards the full threat bearing down on them.

The dragon horde had eliminated almost all of the skyborne, save Alabaster Jane and two of her comrades. The chimera infantry had Silas's forces surrounded, with many of the riders falling to their knees in surrender. And the sky was swirling faster and darker and louder now, the vortex widening into an immense chasm.

'Thanks for the help,' Drake said from over Joss's shoulder. 'But now what do we do?'

Joss wished he had an answer. Instead, he guided the pterosaur back to the *Fat Lot of Good*, which was hovering directly below the vortex. Dafne was still working hard with her quaverstaff to keep the dragons away, her brow dripping with sweat. As Joss landed the pterosaur on the deck, Zeke and Hero rushed over to them.

'Sleeping King preserve me, you're both safe!' Hero exclaimed, rushing in to grab Drake from his saddle and pull him into a steel trap of a hug.

'Well … we survived the fall at least,' Joss said. 'But we're a long way from safe.'

'Maybe I should have held off on striking first,' said Zeke. 'I mean, he said it himself. I was just waiting for the chance. But if I don't get to apologise later, let me say sorry for that now.'

'At least you didn't sell us out,' Hero told him. 'Keep at it and I may end up genuinely liking you.'

Zeke offered a wry smile. 'I'll take that as the sterling commendation it no doubt is.'

'Are you serious?' said Joss. 'We're staring down the end of the world and you two are still wisecracking?'

'What would you have us do, Joss?' Zeke asked. 'If this is the end, I'd rather go with a smile than with tears.'

'We shouldn't be going at all!' Joss raged. 'I was meant to stop this! The Rakashi Revelations said a hero would come from across the Silver Sea with a right hand marked by fate, carrying a champion's blade. They said –'

'Joss. The Champion's Blade is gone,' said Hero. 'We've been giving you space to deal with it but that doesn't change the fact. Whatever you believed it represented …'

'I know it's gone. And I know it's a silly thing to believe. But deep down, somehow, I still thought … maybe …'

He struggled to explain what he'd come to believe. Probably because he didn't really know. His rational mind had given up on the Rakashi Revelations and all they represented. But his heart was another matter entirely. It throbbed painfully as he stared into the doubtful faces of his closest friends, his brethren, the people who mattered most to him in the world. Even Drake's well-noted scepticism seemed acutely pointed as he stared at Joss, the sharp tip of his spear gleaming with the light of the fires below and the lightning above.

'Wait,' Joss muttered, his words gaining strength as the realisation formed in his head. *'Wait!* Ganymede – your spear ...'

Drake stared at him quizzically. 'What about it?'

'Your grandfather received it when he won the Tundra Games, right? Just like what happens with the Champion's Blade?'

'That's right. Why?'

Joss's entire being felt as if it had suddenly flipped upside down. How could he have been so blind? *'From beyond silver seas,'* he began to recite as Drake and the others stared at him uncertainly. *'From out of blue skies, from the ruins of a lost life, there will come a* galamor, *with right hand marked by fate.'*

Joss grabbed Drake's wrist and lifted it up to reveal the scar running along the palm of his right hand. *'And carrying a* vaartan rhazh – a champion's blade! *Only the* galamor *will stand when all else fall, and rise when all else kneel. Only the* galamor *can bring light to the oncoming darkness, and draw hope from a dying dream. Only the* galamor, *and the* galamor *alone.'*

Drake stared at him as if Joss were a rabid direwolf howling at the moon. 'You cannot be serious.'

'It's you, Ganymede! You're the *galamor*! I should have seen it sooner – you're the *galamor* and the Icefire spear is your *vaartan rhazh.'*

Drake continued to gape at him incredulously, even as the others blinked at each other like they might actually believe what he was saying.

'And I'm supposed to, what? Throw my spear at a spectre? Zeke didn't have any luck in hitting it. It's crazy to think that I'd have any better chance.'

'Is it, though?' asked Hero.

'Don't tell me you're putting your faith in this hocus-pocus?' Drake said, then pivoted back to Joss. 'No offense, Joss. I know your heart's in the right place, but it's just not possible.'

'Look around, Ganymede!' Hero snapped at him. 'None of this should be happening. But it is. Who's to say what else is possible?'

Drake chewed his cheek, then shot Hero and Joss a critical look. 'Say you're right – how's a spear supposed to defeat that thing? Especially when the Shadow God – or the Pale Prince, or whatever he wants to call himself – has vanished into thin air?'

Unholy thunder sounded from on high, so loud and discordant it made the prentices grit their teeth and clamp their hands over their ears. Together they saw the sky crack like a thawing lake around the vortex, which tore open wider and wider to reveal the limitless void beyond. And from the shadows of that void there now snaked a nest of pale and prickled tentacles, hauling forth a dark mass larger than any creature Joss had ever seen or even imagined before.

'Call it whatever you want …' Joss said to Drake while staring up at the creature that had come to end their world. 'It's here. And you're the only one who can stop it.'

—

CHAPTER THIRTY-NINE

A BLACK WAVE CURLING TOWARDS OBLIVION

PALE white tentacles spilled from the vortex over Tower Town like gizzards from a disembowelled beast. The prentices stood in awestruck horror at the sight, numbed by all the madness and destruction. Pulling himself together, Joss rushed for the wheelhouse to find Eliza frozen behind the *Fat Lot of Good*'s control panel.

'*Zenith*, can you hear me? *Zenith*, are you there?' Joss said, jamming on the communications array. 'Crimson! Cloud! Answer me, damn it!'

A dull buzz filled the line, then a small voice replied, 'Uh – sorry. We're here. We're all just … we … well, we're trying not to melt into pools of congealed blubber right now. I mean, what *is* that thing?' said Cloud.

'Cloud, we don't have much time. We need all the cover fire you can muster. Do you understand?'

The buzz on the line intensified. Not for the first time, Joss wished Edgar was there to lend a hand. But Edgar was gone, and they'd all be following him if Joss didn't marshal some kind of defence while they still had the chance, however slim it may be.

'*Cloud!* Do you understand?'

'Yessir!' the reply shot back. 'Covering fire. We're on it.'

The buzz gave way to silence, which was quickly filled with the boom of the *Zenith*'s cannons firing indiscriminately at the circling dragon horde. But rather than scatter them, it only emboldened the beasts. Several broke away and flew for the airship, while the largest of the creatures set its sights on the *Fat Lot of Good*. Red eyes blazing, it beat its mighty wings and gave pursuit.

'*Eliza!*' Zeke shouted from the deck as he levelled his pulse rifle and fired at the dragon. The shots went wide, failing to slow down their target in the slightest. 'Get us out of here!'

'I'm trying!' Eliza shouted back, her hand clenched so tight around the accelerator that her knuckles were white. 'This heap is moving as fast as it can!'

'Use the booster rockets!' Zeke told her, repowering his rifle while Hero sent her zamaraqs flying.

'The what?'

'The booster rockets! Use the booster rockets!'

'You didn't tell me anything about any booster rockets!'

'Hit the red button beneath the wheel mount!'

'Which button?'

'*That button!*' Joss cried, looking away from the dragon

long enough to point out the boosters. When he turned back the dragon was so close that its obsidian scales and scarlet belly could be seen in harrowing detail.

'You mean this button –?' Eliza asked, and the ship burst forward in a dizzying surge. Joss and the others were thrown off their feet as the *Fat Lot of Good* rocketed up and away. By the time the boosters flared out, the dragon was a small spot in the distance. But that only left them even further from their true enemy.

All the dragons that hadn't pursued the *Zenith* had formed a defensive wall around the vortex, where the Shadow God was still spilling free. The tentacles were extended so far now that some were scraping the earth, while others coiled around Tower Town to help pull the creature from its chasm.

'How are we going to get near it now?' Joss asked. Everywhere he looked, he saw defeat. Alabaster Jane and her cohort were scattered, flying hard against the wind to evade the dragons hunting them down. The ground forces weren't faring any better. Joss recognised Parsefal kneeling over the prone body of Kade, showing the enemy he was unarmed as they advanced on him. Only Silas, Ichabod and Archibald and a fraction of the other riders remained fighting at the heart of the battlefield, with all others forced to surrender.

I AM ARRIVED.

The words erupted in Joss's head like a firestorm, just like when he'd been in the Northern Tundra and the Mighty Bhashvirak had communicated with him in a wordless voice only he could hear. But this was different. Now, wincing through the pain, he turned to see all his friends in similar distress, clutching their heads as the silent voice spoke again.

SUBMIT. OR PERISH.

'What in Shoda's Pits is that noise?' Eliza cursed.

'Funny you should ask,' Joss rasped. 'It's Shoda. The real Shoda. Or the Shadow God, or the Pale Prince, or whatever this ugly, forsaken thing wants to call itself. It speaks the same way Bhashvirak did.'

'Bash-who?' asked Eliza.

'My thoughts exactly,' Zeke said. 'My screaming, searing thoughts …'

'Doesn't matter,' said Joss. 'How are we going to get close enough for Ganymede to hit it with his spear?'

'Joss, I really don't think –' Drake started, his objection silenced by a rush of motion overhead.

'*Dragon!*' Joss shouted, scrambling to the deck along with the others while Eliza whirled the *Fat Lot of Good* around in a defensive manoeuvre. Weapons drawn, the prentices steeled themselves for the attack. Instead, a silver blur launched itself onto the prow of the ship, steam and smoke spilling from its shoulder to reveal a familiar form.

'Lady Razeel!' exclaimed Joss.

'*Draa'kin*, if I'm not mistaken,' Dafne said, watching closely while swinging her quaverstaff. 'How marvellous.'

'What are you doing here?' Joss asked the princess.

'Confessing my guilt at arriving at so late an hour,' she replied, her red hair waving like a battle flag as she balanced on the railing with sure-footed poise. 'I was waylaid in dealing with my brother. His recent actions have only fuelled the discontent that had been brewing against him. He had maintained loyalty among his closest courtiers with little grasp of the wider sentiment among his people. After you were forced to flee, I was able to rally the citizens of Sanctum and successfully depose him. He's being held now awaiting trial, along with his allies.'

'Does that mean –?' Hero said.

Her unasked question was met with a knowing smile from Lady Razeel. 'We're here to help.'

At their leader's word, the *draa'kin*'s entire royal wingforce descended from the clouds in their bestial forms, with Chamberlain Füm leading the assault and Ormar serving as her second. While the *draa'kin* were lacking in size compared to their burlier cousins, they made up for it in ferocity, immediately putting the Shadow God's forces on the defensive. But the Shadow God continued to pull itself clear of the vortex, the sky growing darker the closer it came to freeing itself.

'I take it our great adversary has finally revealed its true face,' said Lady Razeel, staring with contempt at the monster bearing down on them.

'Handsome sonovaserpent, isn't he?' replied Zeke.

'A face only a monster could love,' Lady Razeel sneered. 'I shall lead the wingforce in a direct strike.'

'About that,' Joss spoke up. 'I know this may sound crazy, but –'

'Joss,' Drake said, shaking his head at him.

Joss continued. 'But we believe Ganymede here may be the key to our victory. There's this prophecy –'

'A prophecy?' Lady Razeel interrupted. 'You would have our lives and the fate of the entire world hang on the musings of warlocks and soothsayers?'

'Like I said. Crazy. I know. But also possibly true. All we need is the chance to strike. Just one clear shot. If your wingforce can provide us with that, maybe we can finish this here and now.'

'And if not?'

'Then we all die anyway,' Joss said. 'Are you in?'

Lady Razeel considered the question. 'You said it was Master Drake who would be leading the attack?' she asked, casting a quizzical eye Drake's way. Joss nodded.

'If any young mortal might stand a chance at such a mad endeavour, I find it easiest to believe that it would be the one with dragon blood warming his veins,' Lady Razeel concluded. 'Very well. We shall keep the beasts from your backs. And if you falter we'll do what we can to fill the breach, even though it may prove too late. So don't falter.'

'Understood,' said Joss.

Wrapping her cloak around herself, Lady Razeel shut her eyes and shifted her form, scales bursting out across her skin as her bones snapped, spurted and strengthened. Within a microraptor's heartbeat she was back in the air, rallying the wingforce combatants to her side and pressing the attack against the Shadow God's dragons. Alabaster Jane and the remaining skyborne were quick to join her, fighting back the horde and clearing the way for the *Fat Lot of Good* to make its attack. Joss was just about to call out to Zeke and Eliza when he felt a hand around his elbow.

'Joss – wait,' Drake said. 'You have to listen to me. You keep talking about this prophecy like it's some kind of magical remedy rather than a vague notion concocted centuries ago in a distant desert somewhere. I'm not the *galamor* or whatever it is you think I am. I'm not.'

Joss looked at the faces gathered on the deck, huddled together on what felt like a lifeboat on a black wave curling towards oblivion. All it would take was one small nudge and they could tip in either direction. Frowning through his doubt, he resolved to give them all a heartfelt push.

'Ganymede – in all the time we've known each other, we've learned so much. We've learned to ride and we've learned to fight. We've learned how to muster and make spells of music and we've even learned to fly. I've learned who my true friends are. Who my real family is …'

His brethren stared at him, uncertain but listening intently. Hero lowered her goggles, revealing her keen grey eyes. Zeke gazed at him with a lifted chin, while Drake bowed his head in contemplation. Eliza and Dafne hovered in the background, and again Joss felt a pang as he thought of Edgar and felt the bite of his absence. He swallowed the bitter taste of it as he concluded, 'But the one thing I've learned above all else is this: the only time you're sure to fail is when you never even try. So let's try.'

Drake closed his eyes. Drew a small, controlled breath. When he opened his eyes, his gaze was set. 'Alright,' he said. 'Let's do it.'

'I knew you'd come around,' Joss grinned, grabbing his friend's wrist and giving it a hearty shake before turning to Zeke and Eliza. 'Let's get this bucket swinging, shall we?'

Everyone set to action, only to freeze as Hero called out, 'Wait!' Striding across the deck, she fixed her eyes on Drake's as she gathered him in her arms. Her intent was unmistakable. So was his. Their kiss looked almost magnetic, as if neither of them could have pulled themselves away even if they'd wanted to.

Joss was stunned, but not surprised. And as much as he didn't want to ruin anything for either of them, he knew the end of the world wouldn't wait. 'I hate to interrupt a moment …' he said. 'But time is short.'

'Exactly,' Hero replied as she and Drake parted. 'And I didn't want it to get away from me.'

Drake smiled. Caressed her arm. 'Away from *us*, you mean.'

A flutter of a smile floated across Hero's face, and was quickly swept away as she shot a look of stern resolve Joss's way. 'Continue.'

Joss nodded, then turned again to Zeke and Eliza. 'You heard her – let's go.'

'Yo ho, captain!' Zeke called out, settling in beside Eliza to co-pilot the *Fat Lot of Good*. They swung the ship around and accelerated toward the vortex. Lady Razeel had proven true to her word, leading the wingforce in a blockade manoeuvre that gave the *Fat Lot* a clear run towards the monster in the sky. Alabaster Jane and her fellow skyborne riders had joined in the effort, fighting back the Shadow

God's forces with all their might.

But even with all that help, the horde proved overwhelming. Breaking through the ranks, a pair of dragons flew straight for the *Fat Lot* with their maws smouldering.

'Look out!' Joss cried as the dragons strafed the deck. Flames erupted around the prentices as they ducked and scrambled for cover. The only one who remained standing was Hero, who rushed to the railing and loosed a volley of zamaraqs at the creatures, hitting one in the neck and sending it screeching away. Poking her head out from behind the crate where she'd hidden, Dafne leapt forward to starting weaving her quaverstaff's magic again. That left Joss and Drake clear for the task at hand.

'Ganymede, we need you at the prow!' said Joss, hurrying Drake to the front of the ship. 'Are you ready?'

'Ready,' Drake replied, brandishing the Icefire spear with an iron grip. The *Fat Lot* was getting closer by the moment, swiftly coming within striking distance of the Shadow God. The beast was almost entirely free of the vortex now, its tentacles swirling like a whirlpool.

YOU WOULD CHALLENGE MY DIVINE POWER? the Prince's voice blasted through everyone's heads, making them flinch and gasp.

PATHETIC! The monster's spiked tendrils lashed out at the ship, slashing its hull and shredding the engine. With the ease of a thunder lizard crushing a sparrow, the Shadow God ripped the airship from the sky to send Joss and his brethren crashing down.

CHAPTER FORTY

A GALAMOR ALONE

JOSS held tight as the *Fat Lot of Good* spiralled to the earth below. Klaxons wailed from the wheelhouse, and the emergency beacon flashed in Zeke and Eliza's faces as they fought to keep the ship in the air.

'I may be stating the obvious but we have a situation here!' Zeke shouted over the sirens. 'If we're going to stop old octochops we'll have to grow wings, jump ship or find some other mode of flight.'

Joss craned his neck around the wheelhouse to where the pterosaur he'd ridden earlier was hunkering down. He shared a look with Drake.

'Oh, no. No way,' Drake immediately said. 'I know you have this insane faith in me but there's no way I can fly a pterosaur with a practice blade, fend off those tentacles and harpoon an enormous interdimensional monster all at the same time. There's just no way.'

'Then you'll need someone to take the reins while you concentrate on the task at hand. Hero?'

Hero was braced against the railing, keeping a stream of dragons at bay with a rapid-fire salvo of zamaraqs. 'Got my hands full here,' she said as she snatched a returning zamaraq from the air and sent it soaring again. 'You'll have to do it.'

'But I –' Joss started to protest, then thought better of it. If Drake had to believe in himself, he had no choice but to do the same. 'Alright. Let's go.'

The pterosaur screeched as Joss and Drake saddled up, its grousing soon quelled by the song from Joss's practice blade. Taking firm hold of the reins, Joss spared a moment to ask Zeke, 'You'll all be OK?'

Zeke looked up from the controls, wiped the sweat from his forehead and shot Joss a carefree grin. 'Don't worry about us. We'll keep this hunk of metal moving. Won't we, Wildsmith?'

'I think I'm going to be sick.'

'That's the spirit. Now, you two go while the getting's good. And give that pile of tentacled tripe an extra jab for all of us.'

'Thanks, Zeke,' Joss said, then spurred the pterosaur on. '*Hyah!*'

The lizard-bird launched itself from the ailing ship and into the fiery void. Beneath them, Silas and his remaining Nameless were battling the Shadow God's acolytes, dodging the blasts of exploding inferno orbs and answering with the flash of their lightning rifles. The *draa'kin* wingforce was lending its aid to the Nameless's efforts, with Chamberlain Füm spitting fire to pick off as many acolytes as she could while they stopped to reload their launchers. That left Joss and Drake on their own to penetrate the Shadow God's aerial defences – until Lady Razeel and Ormar glided in alongside them.

'A pair of young men in need of an armed escort, I see,' her ladyship said, having shifted halfway back to her mortal form long enough to offer her support.

'Lucky for them we're both armed and dangerous!' Alabaster Jane called out as she fell into formation on the right. She offered a quick thumbs up then set to proving her word, savagely beating back the oncoming dragon horde while Lady Razeel and Ormar changed into their full bestial states to join the attack.

Their path cleared, Joss guided the mount towards their target. The Shadow God's tendrils were now as thick and overflowing as a bale of barbed wire.

As he struggled to keep their pterosaur calm through the mounting obstacles, Joss thought of Edgar. He thought of Tempest. He thought of the Mighty Bhashvirak, of Sur Verity, of the refugees in Illustra, of all the people in Dragon's Toe and Resilient and throughout the Kingdom of Ai. He thought of his parents. He thought of his childhood friends and closest family, of every living soul on Daheed that had been snuffed out at this creature's first attempt to conquer their world. He thought of every single person who'd been lost to this cause, and he used that as the motivation he needed to keep a tight hold of his reins and a firm grip on his heart.

'*Look!*' he gasped as they cleared the heaviest thicket of tentacles, pointing to the pulpy mass at their centre. Having only caught glimpses of it before, Joss and Drake now saw in horrific detail the immense and tumorous form of the Shadow God. A thousand eyes pockmarked its craggy flesh, which was marbled with black veins and throbbing with every onerous beat of its heart.

YOU WILL DIE SCREAMING! the creature boomed, its words ripping through their heads, its eyes boiling over with raw hatred towards the two prentices. *YOU WILL BE UNMADE AND UNMOURNED AND UNREMEMBERED!*

'Joss?' Drake asked, panic creeping in. 'All I see is eyes, tentacles and wrinkled skin. What do I aim for?'

Joss scrutinised the wretched topography before them, trying to work out where to strike. With surprise, he spotted a cluster of marks at the apex of the creature's body that looked almost like a birthmark.

'*There!*' Joss shouted. 'The Crest of the Unhallowed!'

It was stunning to see how clearly formed it was; a crown of silver turned upside down, adorning the spot where the creature's flesh pulsated the most. Joss hunkered down in his saddle and spurred the pterosaur upward. He swore he could see a spark of fear flaring in the thousand eyes of the Shadow God as it whipped its tentacles even more furiously around them.

'*Hold tight!*' Joss called out to Drake, and swung the pterosaur into a complex sequence of dives and barrel rolls, doing everything he could to avoid the thorny lash of the Shadow God's tendrils. But for all his fancy flying, the tentacles were coming too fast. One tore across his shoulder, ripping his jacket and drawing blood. He hissed in pain and kept going, even as another tentacle scoured Drake's back, making him cry out and almost lose his grip on the Icefire spear.

The tentacles massed around them. If there had been any daylight left in the world, they would have blocked out the sun. Joss wondered how he could possibly navigate through them when a blast rang out from on high, bursting apart the nearest clump of tentacles and making the Shadow God screech in agony.

Over his shoulder, Joss saw the *Zenith* hovering behind them, its cannons focused on the Shadow God. It wasn't alone. Alabaster Jane and the skyborne, Lady Razeel and Ormar and the *draa'kin* wingforce; they all swept in to lend their aid. Even the *Fat Lot of Good* bobbed into view, its engines throwing off sparks and belching black smoke. Zeke was at the wheel with Eliza while Hero unleashed the last of her zamaraqs, and Dafne continued to light up the night with her glowing quaverstaff.

Everyone was here, doing all they could to ensure Joss and Drake had their chance to finish this. Coiled tight in his saddle, Joss was determined not to fail them.

The Shadow God felt otherwise.

YOU CANNOT DEFEAT THE DIVINE! the monster raged. *YOU ARE NOTHING!*

A tentacle struck Drake in the chest, sending him hurtling.

'*Ganymede!*' Joss exclaimed, unable to do anything to keep his friend from falling. Drake landed with a painful crash on the rocky landscape of the Shadow God's flesh, grabbing hold of whatever crags and toeholds he could find to keep himself from slipping further. The Icefire spear had landed just a few feet away from him. Quickly he snagged it from another tentacle that had reared up in an attempt to steal it away.

Joss watched as Drake raised himself up, took firm hold of his weapon and, like an aeronaut taking the first tentative steps on an unknown land, began the slow march up the Shadow God's body towards the Crest of the Unhallowed. Tentacles whipped at him from every angle. Most of them were held back by cannon fire, by a precisely thrown zamaraq, by the snap of a *draa'kin* warrior's jaws or a burst of flame; even by Joss's own blade as he circled among the mass of tendrils. But the attacks came too quickly to block all of them. Drake winced and flinched as he was lashed across the legs, the hands, the face.

He kept walking.

And with every inch of progress he made, a shrill screech grew louder and louder. It was the Shadow God, boring into everyone's minds like a pneumatic drill. Joss gritted his teeth and kept flying, kept slashing back the tentacles as best he could.

DID YOU NOT HEAR? the creature demanded as Drake neared the Crest, its thousand bloodshot eyes glaring at him. *DO YOU NOT UNDERSTAND? TURN BACK NOW! SURRENDER! WHAT CHANCE DO YOU HAVE? I AM EVERYTHING! YOU ARE NOTHING!*

'You're wrong. I'm Ganymede Drake, Bladebound prentice of Starlight Fields,' he said, his breath coming in ragged gasps as he held his spear aloft. 'And I am ending you!'

He drove the weapon down and stabbed the Crest of the Unhallowed with all his strength. The screech in Joss's head became an explosive cry that almost knocked him from his saddle. Shaking his head, he saw Drake struggling to remain on his feet as the Shadow God's body began to teeter and shake.

'*Hyah!*' Joss cried, urging his pterosaur into a spiral dive. Tentacles whirled around him in a frenzied death throe. The Shadow God's already pale flesh was draining away to a transculent husk, his skin flaking off in a blizzard. Joss fought through the haze and made it to Drake's side, where he scooped his brethren up into the saddle.

'Fly!' Drake gasped as tentacles toppled around them like felled oaks. Looking up, Joss caught sight of the largest tendril teetering just above them, threatening to crush them under its colossal weight.

'*From beyond silver seas,*' he recited as the pterosaur

took a hard roll to the left. '*From out of blue skies, from the ruins of a lost life, there will come a* galamor, *with right hand marked by fate and carrying a* vaartan rhazh.'

The pterosaur screeched as the shadow of the tentacle grew darker. Joss urged it on to fly as hard as it could. They rocketed clear of the thorny mass with less than a second to spare, only to be caught in the severe crosswind from the tendril's collapse.

'*Only the* galamor *will stand when all else fall, and rise when all else kneel,*' Joss grunted as he held on for dear life, the wind threatening to pluck him from his saddle. With surprise he heard Drake lending his voice to the recitation, his hands holding tight to Joss's shoulders. '*Only the* galamor *can bring light to the oncoming darkness, and draw hope from a dying dream. Only the* galamor, *and the* galamor –'

The winds eased. The light shifted. Joss heaved a sigh of relief: they were free of the tentacles, free of the Shadow God's reach. Until the largest dragon he'd ever seen reared up before them, bellowing its full-throated rage.

'*Alone!*' he gasped.

CHAPTER FORTY-ONE

—

A LESSON LEARNED

THE dragon lunged forward, making Joss and Drake's pterosaur shriek in fright. There was no time to escape, nowhere to flee. All Joss could do was close his eyes and brace for what was to come. But the dragon wasn't hunting. It was spewing cinders from the back of its gullet while its wings crumbled to blackened ash.

All around them the dragon horde was dropping from the sky. The dark spell that had summoned the monsters to the mortal realm had been severed, leaving them to splinter and disintegrate. Even the chimeras had been affected, their bristly hides fading into thin shadows, their passing marked with an eerie whisper.

The Shadow God, however, was not leaving so quietly. Joss could still feel the creature's wordless scream boring into his brain. The sound of it, coupled with the blunted roaring of the dragon horde, made for a cacophonous symphony that underscored Joss's flight with Drake across the bloodshot sky.

The *Fat Lot of Good* added to the clamour as it bobbed back into view, its engines fighting a losing battle. Joss could only hope it might rally to win the fight as he guided the pterosaur to land on the main deck. Instantly the others were beside them, cheering their return.

'You did it!' Hero exclaimed as they both dropped from the saddle. Joss had never seen her so elated as she grabbed them both in a celebratory hug.

'We did – didn't we?' Drake said as if he couldn't quite believe it.

'See for yourself,' Dafne said, resting her weight on her quaverstaff while gesturing to the sky.

Joss and Drake turned back to see the Shadow God hanging lifelessly from the rapidly contracting vortex as the last of the dragon horde plummeted around it. The sight reminded Joss of the Mighty Bhashvirak's corpse hanging from the rafters of the Ivory Palace, though this time he didn't feel in any way sorry for the fate this beast had suffered.

Its multitude of eyes stared blankly in a dozen different directions as rivers of thick ichor wept down the length of its limp tentacles. The edge of the vortex swirled faster and faster around it and then, with an abrupt surge and a snap of thunder, the vortex tore through the creature's carcass. Half the Shadow God's corpse was sent tumbling down the side of Tower Town's scorched edifice, while the other half receded into the shrinking portal until, like a nightmare brought to an end by the arrival of sunrise, it vanished entirely.

Joss and the others watched in astonishment, not daring to believe that the battle was really won. They were still staring when the *Fat Lot of Good* lurched to the side and the alarm bells renewed their blaring.

'Hold onto your hindquarters, everyone!' Zeke shouted from the wheelhouse. 'We're taking an unscheduled dirt bath!'

The klaxons wailed all the way down as the airship dropped with sickening speed. The pterosaur launched into the air and left Joss to his fate.

The *Fat Lot* landed like an overstuffed sack, ricocheting across the salt flats and shedding scrap metal with every bump. Finally it skidded to a stop in the shadow of Tower Town, broken and billowing smoke. Silence fell upon the ship from the deck to the wheelhouse, a deathly quiet that was only interrupted by the crackle of the radio.

'Zenith *to* Fat Lot of Good, *are you receiving?* Fat Lot of Good, *come in!*' Cloud's voice floated in over the speakers, which wailed with feedback as Crimson burst onto the microphone.

'Oi! Are any of you alive down there?'

Coughing, Zeke reached up to the console and jabbed the transmission button.

'We hear you, *Zenith* – just give us a moment to

piece our skulls back together,' he croaked, brushing the shattered glass of the windshield off his shoulders. 'Roll call! Is everyone present and accounted for?'

'I'm here,' Eliza replied, sticking her hand up. 'Barely.'

'Same,' said Hero.

'Me too,' Drake called out.

'My hip aches and my neck hurts. But that's nothing new,' Dafne groaned.

'Joss?' asked Zeke. There was silence. 'Joss? Are you alright?'

Joss coughed and sputtered, struggling to clear his head. 'Here.'

Zeke slackened with relief. 'Don't scare me like that.'

'Then don't crash our airship.'

'Fair point. Though I want it noted that you didn't remind me to buckle my harness,' Zeke said, looking around at the sorry state of the *Fat Lot of Good*. 'Not that I'll be buckling anything anytime soon, judging by this mess ...'

Joss chuckled, which made Zeke laugh, which made Joss laugh that much harder, which made the others join in, the pressure they'd been under now bubbling over into hysterical relief.

'*I'll take that as an affirmative,*' Cloud chimed in over the speakers, only making everyone laugh all the harder. Joss couldn't believe it. Only minutes ago they had been staring down the end of everything. Now here they were, revelling in the fact that they had done it. They had stopped the

Shadow God. They had saved the world.

The sound of distant shouting cut the laughter short.

'Do you hear that?' asked Eliza, poking her head out through the broken wheelhouse window. Joss and the others clambered up and peered out alongside her. They could see a crowd not far away, could hear their violent cries.

'We're not done yet,' Joss grumbled, before hoisting himself over the *Fat Lot*'s railing to skim down its hull. He landed with both boots in the salt and started to run, the others fast on his heels.

They arrived at the edge of the crowd and pushed their way through to see the Thrall who'd led the charge against the Nameless now fending them off with his twisted blade. He had lost his chimera, and the handful of acolytes at his back looked as if all the fight had gone out of them. Half his stone mask was shattered, exposing the wretched and wrathful face that lay beneath.

'It's Lord Ivo!' gasped Eliza. 'Uncle Silas was right – he was a Thrall all along!'

'Fools! *Cowards!*' Ivo shouted, his flesh scalded from the Sacred Sand that was spilling from his shoulders as he swung his blade at anyone who dared approach him. 'I may be the last of my court standing, but we aren't defeated yet! The darkness can never be bested, as the night can never be denied! Our master will rise again, and you would be wise not to anger him with this heretical insolence!'

'You murder children and you have the nerve to call us

heretics?' Joss demanded, his voice ringing out over the crowd of Nameless all demanding Lord Ivo's surrender. 'If I were you I'd shut my mouth before someone decides to slam it shut permanently.'

'Strong words, boy! But your hands aren't so clean. You and your brethren have all drawn your share of blood.'

'We have,' Joss admitted. 'Starting with the Thrall we defeated all the way back in Daheed.'

Lord Ivo sneered through the remains of his mask. 'I heard of Lord Hammond's fate. A shame for you that the ocean is half a kingdom away and there's not a shark in sight to do your dirty deeds for you.'

'True,' said Joss. 'But we do have a tyrannosaur.'

'What –?' Ivo gulped as the earth rumbled around him. The crowd watched as Silas's tyrannosaur stomped into view, pausing to unleash a ravenous roar before it hunched forward, grabbed Lord Ivo in its jaws and chomped. His lordship didn't even have time to scream as the giant thunder lizard swallowed him whole.

'As satisfying as I always imagined it to be,' Silas crowed from high atop his saddle, patting Balthasar's head.

'How uncompromising,' said Lady Razeel as she landed in the centre of the circle with Chamberlain Füm, Ormar and Alabaster Jane by her side. 'Such services may be required following my brother's trial. Depending on the verdict, of course.'

Silas grinned and gave a wink as his tyrannosaur swallowed noisily.

'Always open to new job opportunities, my lady. Especially for someone who's proven such a surprising and stalwart ally. But first let's figure out what to do with the Shadow God's collaborators we have gathered here.' He turned to the acolytes below. 'Now, a show of hands; who here would like to surrender?'

Every acolyte's hand shot straight up.

'I thought as much.'

One acolyte pushed forward. 'Please, sir ... have mercy!' he cried. Joss knew exactly who it was even before he removed his mask, which he did with shaking hands to reveal a narrow little face filled with fear. 'We weren't in our right minds. We had no choice but to follow orders.'

'You seemed pretty confident with your choice back at Blade's Edge Acres,' Joss said, drawing the crowd's attention as he addressed the unmasked Lynch.

The prentice twitched as if he was sitting at a card table and his bluff had just been called. 'The Thralls had us under their control the whole time,' he said, his expression darkening. 'I swear.'

Joss fixed Lynch with a critical eye. 'That'll have to be determined at your trial – just as it'll be for Lady Razeel's brother and the rest of your masked brethren here.'

'And the Nameless will only be too happy to keep 'em all under lock and key back at Gravemarker while they await their day in court,' said Silas, which gave Joss a sense of grim satisfaction. There may have been no bringing Edgar back, but at least he had been avenged.

The Shadow God's desiccated shell of a corpse made a thunderous crashing sound as it collapsed into dust, blowing away in a whirlwind of ash along with the scattered remains of his dragon horde. Joss turned his face to the sky, where a few tentative rays of sunshine pierced the black and warmed the swirling red to a rosy pink.

'I must say,' Dafne piped up beside him, 'I wasn't sure if I was mistaken in coming here, despite what the fates were whispering to me. But all you westerly folk proved to be not as misguided as I first took you to be. Or ignorant. Or inept. In short, it was an honour to fight alongside you all.'

Joss shared an amused look with his brethren.

'The wraithslayer has it right,' Lady Razeel said. 'You proved true to your word, as did your prophecy. I shouldn't have doubted it. You may be young, but you are heroes nevertheless. And you deserve a hero's thanks. Chamberlain Füm?'

The chamberlain wheeled around. '*Draa'kin!*' she shouted. Ormar and all of Lady Razeel's forces snapped to attention. 'On my command: *Rôr!*'

The *draa'kin* soldiers erupted in a chorus of roars that was amplified with the stomping of their feet and the pounding of their fists against their chests. Silas, not to be outdone, held his arms out wide and addressed the Nameless riders.

'You heard the lady, you lot of lollygaggers! Let's show these valiant prentices our gratitude! They only saved the whole mucking world after all!'

The Nameless added their cheers to those of the *draa'kin*. Even Alabaster Jane joined in, clapping both Joss and Drake on the back as she leaned in to tell them, 'That was some fancy flying up there. Not to mention the steady hand you had with that spear.'

Joss and Drake looked at each other with hesitation, neither of them sure of how to respond. 'We only got as close as we did thanks to all the help we had,' said Drake, shrugging off the accolades.

'Yourself included,' Joss added.

'I'd give the tyrannosaur's take of the credit to the lady weredragon and her kin,' Jane replied. 'Not to mention your friend with her singing staff and that dark-haired lass with her zamaraqs. The less said about my being helpful, the better. I've got a reputation to maintain, after all.'

She winked as she receded into the crowd, where the cheers were swiftly turning into full-throated revelry. The marching drums that had announced the arrival of the Nameless's caravan had broken out into a celebratory rhythm, which Parsefal answered with the keen strumming of a chordophone that he'd retrieved from his saddle.

'We should get Crimson and Cloud back on the line,' said Zeke, watching the celebration breaking out around them as well as the acolytes being led to the armoured wagons at the scorched edge of the battlefield. 'There's about a dozen or so barrels aboard the *Zenith* that would come in handy about now.'

'You want to throw a party?' asked Drake, incredulous.

Zeke shrugged. 'A small token of thanks for everyone here who came to our aid. Not to mention a wake for all those we lost.'

Joss placed a consolatory hand on his shoulder. 'Your father was a lucky man to have a son as devoted as you. Even with all his flaws, I have no doubt he'd have been proud of everything you did today.'

Glassy-eyed, Zeke nodded.

'I hate to sour the celebrations, but we still have hard weather ahead of us,' Hero noted. 'The Grandmaster Council is gone. Thunder Realm is in ruins, as is half the kingdom. And you can't have anyone stand trial if you have nowhere to hold it.'

Joss looked again at Tower Town. The last sooty remnants of the Shadow God were being collected by the rising wind. The tower itself was burned and broken at its highest reaches but still strong and solid at its base. The darkness had come for it, but had been unable to claim it. It felt like a lesson Joss had learned a number of times over but that he only now truly understood.

'We'll take hope from tragedy,' he said, echoing words he'd carried across his life. 'And build something new from the wreckage of the old.'

CHAPTER FORTY-TWO

—

A NEW BEGINNING

THE golden disc of Joss's mother's betrothal necklace flashed as he rotated it between his fingers while watching canvassers circulate through the camp city. The tents and pavilions that had been set up at the foot of Tower Town had quadrupled in the season since the Shadow God's fall, housing not only those who'd been displaced by the attack but also an influx of new residents, most of whom comprised the workforce putting the building back together.

It wasn't just the structure itself undergoing restoration. All of Thunder Realm was in the midst of a political renewal, starting with the mayoral race here in Tower Town. Half a dozen candidates had stepped forward in a bid to replace Mayor Bovis, all of them promising a better tomorrow for thunderfolk across the realm.

'A vote for the Bluebell Party is a vote for change!' one canvasser shouted, before adding an increasingly popular refrain: 'I swear to the Sleeping King himself, you'll never catch any of 'em sporting a stone mask!'

'Think they've got a chance?' asked Zeke.

'Time will tell,' Joss replied with a shrug, wondering if such a victory could signal the start of a broader change. With the Grandmasters gone, the remaining paladero orders had taken inspiration from the Tower Town mayoral race by planning elections of their own. The idea was to form a new council that would be more broadly representative of Thunder Realm as a whole, replacing the old system of having the Grandmasters make their own appointments. For the first time in history, the thunderfolk would be responsible for governing themselves.

That sense of optimism had even extended to the Nameless, who had been invited to participate in the elections. A seat was all but guaranteed for Silas Wildsmith in recognition of the heroism he and his riders had shown against the Shadow God's forces. Joss wouldn't have been surprised if even Lady Razeel had been offered an honorary role, given how enthusiastically the kingdom had come to embrace her and the *draa'kin* since their dramatic reintroduction to the world, though she seemed far too occupied with matters of state back in Sanctum to spend her time on such mortal affairs.

'What are the chances that Crimson and Cloud are down there campaigning, seeing as they've been going on about fieldservs' rights so much lately?' said Zeke.

'They'd be there if they were old enough to work as canvassers,' Hero pointed out.

'And if they weren't already back at Round Shield Ranch as part of the clean-up crew,' added Drake.

'Are they? Really?' Zeke asked with surprise.

'They left last week,' Eliza replied.

'Huh. Well – my point still stands. They may be young but they're as eager for revolution as the rest of the kingdom.'

He wasn't wrong. The spirit of change had even reached as far as Illustra, where Regent Greel faced increasing criticism for his mishandling of the crisis – it didn't help that a member of his own cabinet had turned out to be a Thrall – and was likely to lose his office.

'Whatever the outcome, it's already clear the world has changed. We'll have to make sure Round Shield Ranch reflects that change once it's up and running again,' said Lord Verity.

Joss still hadn't gotten used to her new title. 'I thought lords were meant to remain impartial?' he asked.

Her lordship shrugged. 'We're allowed to have an opinion or two,' she said. 'Especially in this brave new world.'

They were gathered on a rise near where the Battle of Tower Town had begun, on the same road Joss and Sur Verity had ridden when he'd started his journey towards becoming a paladero almost a full year ago. The gravel made of pulverised bone crunched underfoot as Azof whickered from behind Joss, the raptor's saddle laden with baggage and camping equipment. The others kept chatting about the upcoming elections as Joss calmed his mount.

'Easy, boy. We'll be leaving soon. The others just want to say goodbye first.'

'Not to mention wish you a happy blessingday,' said Lord Verity.

'That too,' Joss admitted. He had to keep reminding himself that not only was it his blessingday, but he was supposed to be happy about it. Ever since the last celebration he'd attended, blessingdays had lost their air of festivity for him. The memory of Edgar lingered like smoke from an extinguished candle.

'Fine beast, this raptor of yours,' said Lord Verity, patting Azof. 'The same hatchling I gave you, isn't it?'

'For being named as a Prentice of First Merit,' Joss nodded.

'One of my better moments as a mentor, I would imagine.' Joss looked at her, confused. 'I had a lot of time to think as I regained my strength,' she went on. 'And I wanted you to know that I'm sorry.'

'For what?'

'I was tough on you,' Lord Verity said, stroking Azof's vibrant plumage. 'Too tough. I thought I was preparing you for the challenges you would face in becoming a paladero. I knew what it was like, after all. Being an outsider in an insular world. Having to fight for every scrap of recognition, every ounce of success. And yes, you needed a taskmaster to put you through your paces, to ensure you were ready for all the thunder you'd be forced to weather. But you also needed a friend. Or a sympathetic ear, at least. I could have been that for you, and I wasn't, and for that I'm sorry.'

Joss hesitated as he took in all she'd said, his mind churning. 'You're right. You were tough. Maybe too tough at times,' he said, surprising himself with his candour. 'Most of all on yourself.'

Lord Verity's good eye twinkled. 'Very gracious of you. You've matured into a wise and magnanimous young man. That's why I've decided –'

A loud bleeping trilled in the air. Drake started searching his pockets, embarrassed. He'd shed his customary coat – leaving him only in his boots, trousers and dress shirt – but it still took him a while to find the Scryer that Joss had given him.

'Sorry,' Drake said as he plucked it from his pocket, 'I'm not used to carrying this around yet. And I wanted to make sure I didn't miss this transmission.' He hit the receiver button and Qorza's face materialised before them.

'Hello! I hope I haven't missed anything,' she said, before noticing the surrounding figures. 'Oh, is that Lord Verity? How's my favourite patient?'

Lord Verity offered a tight smile, which for her was practically beaming. 'Alive, thanks to you.'

'And the arm?'

Lord Verity raised her left arm, the servos and pneumatic pistons of the artificial limb whirring as she flexed her titanium fingers. 'Still taking some getting used to – which is what I could also say about the new title.'

'I'm sure both will feel quite natural before too long,' Qorza said, then turned her attention to Joss. 'And here's the blessingday boy himself. I'm so glad I managed to catch you before you left.'

'So glad to be caught, Qorza. As always,' Joss replied as he returned her smile.

'I tried to get Dafne on the line too but she had to send her apologies,' said Drake. 'Too busy chasing up the chimeras that escaped the Shadow God's fall. And the only illumivox she has access to is the public one at the tavern a league from her hut. But really, it was Qorza I most wanted to get in touch with. You see, I've been thinking about your theory, Joss. About the Rakashi Revelations. And without wanting to be either self-indulgent or overly modest, I decided it might be worth asking Qorza to look into it some more, which she kindly agreed to do.'

'It was no trouble,' Qorza replied, her projection flickering around the edges. 'I'd already been making some enquiries from Joss's earlier request. As luck would have it, one of my academic contacts back in Mraba recently had a breakthrough on the subject, having discovered an ancient Kahrani text which helped in better translating the remaining words.'

'This is where it gets good,' Drake smiled. 'Ready?'

'This academic's theory is that *galamor* isn't just a singular noun. It can also be a collective. Meaning –'

The implication clicked in Joss's brain. 'Meaning that we're all the *galamor*,' he said, then immediately turned to Drake. 'Ganymede, you shouldn't –'

'I didn't. Or I haven't. Like I said, I'm not trying to be modest. The faith you had in me when I had so little in myself means more than I can say. And for all I know this academic friend of Qorza's is wrong, and the *galamor* is a single person, and that person may well be me. Or maybe the prophecy never meant anything, and defeating the Shadow God was just a stroke of luck.'

'Luck and determination,' Hero noted.

'And talent. Don't forget pure, raw talent,' added Zeke.

'The fact is,' Drake continued, 'we may never really be sure what was destiny and what was grit. The only thing I'm certain of is that I wouldn't have been there to land that blow without you and everyone else working as one to make it happen. Together we brought light to the darkness, together we drew hope from a dying dream. Together we won. I wanted you to know that, before you left.'

Overwhelmed by the limitlessness of Drake's generosity, Joss didn't know what to say. All he could do was wrap his friend in a heartfelt hug.

'One of us or all of us – we can let the historians argue about that,' Joss told him. 'But I can say this for sure, I know who *my* heroes are.'

He took a step back to look at them all. These were the people who had come to mean the most to him in all the world. His people. And now he was leaving them behind. He wondered, not for the first time, if he was making a horrible mistake.

'I was about to say,' Lord Verity interjected with a cough. 'That I've come to a decision. Josiah – *Joss* – the valour you showed on the battlefield and beyond has proven your worthiness of ascension. While your brethren will be named as Sur Hero and Sur Ganymede when they return with me to rebuild Round Shield Ranch, it struck me as unjust that you should go unrecognised for all the good you've done. And I don't see why we can't have a ceremony of our own right here and now. Eliza? Fetch my sword, if you would.'

Dutifully, Eliza hurried over to Levina, detached the sheathed song sword from Lord Verity's saddle, and offered it up on bended knee. The blade flared in the dawn light as Lord Verity drew it from its scabbard, the runes along its length appearing to pirouette. Dumbstruck, Joss looked from Drake to Hero to Zeke for reassurance that he wasn't imagining it all, and then back at Lord Verity.

'Wait,' he said, holding up a hand to stop her. 'You know I'm going. And I don't know when or even if I'll be coming back. All I've ever wanted to be was a paladero, but after everything that we've been through – the death, the destruction, the betrayal – I don't know if I want that life anymore. There's a whole world out there beyond the borders of Thunder Realm, a world I've yet to really see. I don't want to make any promises I can't keep. And I don't want to put you in the position of having to brand me Nameless when I turn around and leave.'

If Lord Verity was insulted by this refusal, she didn't show it. 'Joss – we find ourselves in strange times. Changing times. The lords and leaders who would have once demanded your loyalty have proven themselves unworthy of such devotion. Yes, to be a paladero means to honour the past. And yes, when you were Bladebound and sent on the Way, you swore to obey your lord and devote yourself to your order, and to heed the call of your ruler in times of crisis. To be named as a paladero, you would have been obligated to recommit to this oath. But I've come to believe that as the times change, so too must we, while still making sure we focus on what matters most. So I would ask that you kneel, and answer me this: Josiah Sarif, do you swear to ride with honour, and to raise your weapon only in defence of those who cannot defend themselves?'

Joss considered the question and all that it involved. He looked at his brethren's encouraging faces. Squeezing his mother's necklace tight, he knelt. 'I do.'

'Then as Lord of Round Shield Ranch, I raise you to the rank of paladero and name you Sur Josiah Sarif – a title to be carried with you wherever you may roam.' With the flat of her blade, Lord Verity touched him on each shoulder, then once more on the forehead. 'Rise, Sur Josiah.'

The circle of friends erupted into applause as Joss stood. Even Qorza was cheering and clapping, the sound coming through with a tinny echo via the Scryer transmission. Lord Verity nodded to Eliza, who retrieved a package wrapped in cloth from the cantle bag of Levina's saddle.

'A paladero needs a song sword,' Lord Verity said, presenting the bundle to Joss. 'And with today being your blessingday, I knew I had the perfect gift for you.'

Joss unwrapped it, his eyes growing as round as polished shields. 'I don't believe it,' he said. The scabbard was long and narrow, made of metal and encased in polished titanaboa leather with a bronze locket and chape, which matched the pommel and cross-guard on the sword itself. The blade whispered sweetly to Joss as he slid it free, revealing the dozens of fine pinholes that pricked its surface and runes that were brighter than jewels.

'This is really for me?' he asked.

Lord Verity smiled. 'You more than deserve it.'

He took a long moment to appreciate the sword in all its grandeur before slipping it back into its sheath and fixing it to his belt. 'I'll guard it with my life,' he said. 'Thank you.'

Drake coughed, nudging Hero. 'Our gift is going to look pretty dull in comparison,' he said, prompting her to present a package wrapped in brown paper.

'We all went in together and got you this,' she said. 'We figured you could use it after all the wear and tear the last one took.'

Joss ripped open the packaging. 'A new jacket!' he gasped.

'Like I said – dull by comparison,' Drake shrugged modestly.

'Are you mad? This isn't dull in the slightest,' he said, eagerly swapping his old jacket for the new one. It slid onto his shoulders as if it was always meant to be there.

'Look at the branding on the inside pocket,' Hero said.

'*Made from genuine Round Shield Ranch leather*,' he read aloud from the label, running his fingertips across his order's emblem.

'We thought this way you'd have a little piece of home with you wherever you go,' said Drake.

Joss's chin quivered. 'Thank you. All of you. So much.'

'It was Zeke's idea,' Drake explained.

Zeke smiled goofily in response. 'And all I had to trade for it was a beaten-up jet-cycle,' he said. 'There's just the question of what you're going to do with the old one.'

Joss didn't have to think for long. 'Eliza,' he said. 'Fancy a slightly-used and stitched-together leather coat?'

The young prentice stared at him as if he'd just offered her his song sword. 'Are you jesting?'

'It's all yours,' he replied, holding it out to her. She readily accepted, slipping her arms through the sleeves and wrapping the full length of it around her.

'I'll wear it with pride,' she told him, beaming. 'Though there was something I wanted to give you, too. It's less of a gift and more, well –' She retrieved a bouquet from her saddlebag. Joss was quick to recognise the type of flower.

'Honeyblossoms,' he said, taking them in hand.

'Edgar's favourite,' she nodded, then rubbed her palm at the corner of her eye. 'I was hoping you might lay them at the memorial on your way out of town.'

'It would be my honour,' he told her. There was a moment of silence as everybody thought of Edgar. Joss drew a deep breath. 'Well – I think it's time,' he said. 'Can't put it off for forever.'

Everybody shuffled around as Joss went down the line, shaking wrists and patting backs, wishing Eliza the best on her path to becoming a paladero and reminding Lord

Verity not to be too hard on her. He gave Qorza a wave across the illumivox line, and then he was down to the last pair of people to wish farewell. He tried to keep himself steady as he approached them.

'Don't get hurt out there,' Hero told him with a smirk. 'You won't have me there to watch your back, after all.'

'I'll try my best to survive. But you know me. Always getting into trouble,' Joss told her, and she grinned.

'And don't forget,' Drake was quick to add, 'we're here for you. Whenever and however you need us. Bound to a blade, bound for life.'

Joss felt a tug in his chest and a hook in his throat. 'I'll remember. I promise.'

The brethren embraced each other in a tight hug, and then Joss was up and in his saddle with Azof nattering away in the ear of another raptor. This other beast was temperamental enough to have earned himself the honour of being dubbed Tempest the Second.

When Zeke had shown up with his new mount, Joss had assumed he'd left his cycle aboard the *Zenith* along with the *Fat Lot of Good*, to be shipped off and stored back at Zadkille Station. Only later did he realise what was actually happening.

The idea of leaving had been growing in Joss's head for a while – ever since their time on the *Zenith,* and probably all the way back to Illustra – but it had taken him a long time to have the confidence to admit it to himself, let alone say it out loud. And when he had finally confessed it, the person he'd entrusted with that information was Zeke.

Rather than being shocked or scandalised, Zeke had made him an offer. 'I'll come with you,' he'd said. Joss could still remember how surprised he'd felt. Zeke had explained: 'Before I met you, my whole life was already written for me. Every choice already made. Now I get to write the story I want to tell. And it's because of you that I get to do that.' The words still made Joss glow. He couldn't possibly say how grateful he was as Zeke mounted up alongside him, settling into Tempest the Second's saddle with a confident ease.

'Shall we?' he asked, and Joss nodded.

'Ride well,' Lord Verity told them.

'Ride well,' Joss replied, looking at each of them in turn before he swung Azof around and guided him up the gravel road. He glanced back only once, committing to memory the sight of them all gathered together, smiling and waving to him. He didn't know when or even if he'd see them all again. But he knew he would carry them with him. Always.

———

Before long, Joss and Zeke came to a crystal effigy of the Sleeping King lying out in a sandy field. It had been blown here in the Tower Town explosion, landing perfectly on its back without a single fracture. Awed by this apparent miracle, the locals had taken to leaving tributes here for the fallen, the entire site having become an improvised memorial.

Joss slid from his saddle and picked his way through the vibrant tessellation of flowers. Zeke followed, and together they laid their respective tributes to the departed. Eliza's honeyblossom bouquet seemed to sigh as Joss placed it with care at the base of the Sleeping King's statue, while Zeke memorialised his father in his own way by placing the spare ignition rod for his old jet-cycle delicately on the veiled statue's dais, spooling its chain into a discreet pile on top of it.

'I still can't believe they're gone,' Zeke said after some time, staring at the monument. 'My mind keeps fooling itself that they've just gone somewhere else for a time and that they'll be back, and when that happens we'll pick up right where we left off aboard the *Zenith*. Edgar will be full of wide-eyed wonder. My father will be a stern and unstoppable force. Everything will be just as it was. But it's not going to be that way. And it never will be again.'

'Who knows?' Joss said. 'Maybe someday it will. In this dream or the next.'

'You really think so?'

'Nothing is impossible.'

The words came to him almost reflexively now, bequeathed to him by a man Joss had dismissed as a monster but who'd still had a heroic heart, even if it had been buried deep.

Their respects paid, the two riders returned to their mounts. 'I've been thinking ...' Joss said as he settled into his saddle.

'Always a worry,' Zeke teased, then sealed his mouth shut after the look he received.

Joss continued, 'I remember when I was young, on Daheed – what's called your blessingday here was called a birthday there. As a child you're given gifts, just the same as what happens in Ai. But when you come of age, the custom is that for everyone who gives you a gift, you give them one in return. It's how people would show they care for one another.'

'Sounds like a nice tradition,' Zeke replied. 'I may have turned out remarkably less selfish and juvenile if I'd grown up doing the same.'

Joss rolled his eyes while giving Zeke a quizzical smile. 'Seeing as you traded away your jet-cycle to get me this coat, I think it's only right that I offer something in return,' he said, and held out his mother's necklace. 'I want to give you this.'

The golden disc practically pulsated from the light of the rising sun, as if Joss were holding a small and delicate heart. Zeke eyed it hesitantly, clearly overwhelmed. 'Joss – that was your mother's. I … I couldn't possibly accept.'

'Then consider that you're holding onto it for me. For safekeeping.'

Zeke contemplated the notion. 'Safekeeping?' he said. 'I can do that.'

He smiled, warm and genuine, then slipped the necklace over his head. Joss's smile grew broader, matching Zeke's, just as they came to a fork in the road.

'So – where to from here, Sur Josiah?'

Joss tried not to be thrown by the surreal sound of his new title as he read down the list of towns on the signpost before them.

'Resilient,' he said, pointing to the last name on the post. If they were in luck, they might yet track down Edgar's family and let them know of their son's heroic sacrifice. Joss couldn't imagine how the conversation would go, but he knew it was one he had to have. He owed Edgar nothing less.

'And from there?' Zeke asked.

Joss took a moment to breathe in the morning air, to appreciate the promise of an open road before him and no master to serve but himself.

'The world,' he said. 'The whole wild and wonderful world.'

And so they rode for the sunrise, on toward tomorrow, and the promise of a new beginning.

The End

ACKNOWLEDGEMENTS

THIS story has been six years in the making and now it's at an end. As always, there are too many people to thank and not enough pages in which to do it.

So let me start with Hardie Grant Egmont – specifically Marisa Pintado, Luna Soo, Tess Cullity, Penelope White, Kate Brown, Tye Cattanach, Emily Wilson, Ella Meave, Sasha Beekman, Julia Kumschik, Pooja Desai, Mandy Wildsmith, Joanne Foster, Julie Lambert, Annabel Barker and all of the team for their hard work, expertise and encouragement. Thanks also to Hilary Rodgers, without whom this project may never have come together in the first place.

Jeremy Love is an illustrator of the highest calibre. Every one of his covers has been a work of art and this book has been no exception. A big thank you to him.

A big thank you also to my agent Clare Forster and her colleagues at Curtis Brown Australia for their ongoing support and advice, as well as to the Young Australia Workshop for all their efforts.

The line, 'Everything that has ever been or will be was dreamt of first' was paraphrased from a speech I saw Neil Gaiman give about the importance of stories. My deepest thanks to him, not only for those words in particular but for all his words of inspiration over the years.

'Best of stewards and best of friends' was inspired by a line from Lin Manuel-Miranda's *Hamilton*, which came from Ron Chernow's book about Hamilton, which came from the writings of Alexander Hamilton himself. Thanks to all three.

Thanks also to my brother-in-lore Luke Arnold, who's provided me with more drive and motivation through our talks about books and writing than I think he could ever realise.

To all my friends and family for their steadfast support, my deepest gratitude – most of all to Simone and Max. As wonderful as telling this story has been, the story we're telling together is the greatest I could ever hope to imagine.

Finally, thank you to all of the Readers of Thunder Realm out there. This book is for you.

About the Author

Steven Lochran spent his childhood writing stories and now he gets to do it for a living. He graduated from Queensland University of Technology with a Bachelor's degree in Creative Writing before going on to write the critically acclaimed *Paladero* and *Vanguard Prime* series. In addition to his career as an author, Steven has spent the past decade working in the publishing industry, first in the marketing department and then in sales. He lives in Melbourne with his wife and son.